WHEN THE PIRATE PRAYS

Borgo Press Books by JAMES B. JOHNSON

Counterclockwise: A Science Fiction Novel
Habu: A Science Fiction Novel
Trekmaster: A Science Fiction Novel
When the Pirate Prays: A Comic Crime Novel

WHEN THE PIRATE PRAYS

A COMIC CRIME NOVEL

JAMES B. JOHNSON

THE BORGO PRESS

MMXIII

WHEN THE PIRATE PRAYS

FIRST EDITION

Published by Wildside Press LLC

www.wildsidebooks.com

DEDICATION

For everybody I know and some I don't; but I
especially dedicate this book to good and
faithful readers across the land.

When the pirate prays, there is great danger.

—Dr. Thomas Fuller,

Gnomoloqia: Adages and Proverbs

    I did some illegal stuff at the time and now the statute of limitations must have kicked in. Wild things happened, not all of them my fault, but enough. Since then, people have moved on, they've died, or are otherwise long gone. I didn't use real names, not all of them anyway. So now, after all these years, the story can be told.

—Billy Birthday

CONTENTS

1: MONDAY, 6:30 A.M.

He wasn't a bad fellow—even if he was out jogging. We picked him up at the old Port Boca Grande Lighthouse on account of the storm squalls boiling off the Gulf of Mexico. I didn't recognize him then because of his four-day growth of beard and the fact he was wetter than a guppy on bath day.

"Another storm without a name," he said, not even breathing hard after running against the wind and rain. His black hair was pasted back in a cinematic over-done fashion.

The three of us in the cab of my green '66 Chevy pickup steamed the windows and, along with the now-lashing rain outside, made it difficult to see where I was driving.

I double-clutched down to second and left it there hoping it was only my imagination that the Gulf was looping over the dunes and onto the road already. Here at the southern tip of the island was where the pirate José Gaspar, in a fit of murderous rage a couple of hundred years ago, beheaded a princess. The mental image made me shiver, for I superimposed the vision of this intriguing good-looking woman with different color eyes back at the hotel. I love a pony tail anyway, and this intriguing woman, she had a pony tail I'd kill for. Not only that, but she smelled good and, something I didn't understand yet, she had a case of the hiccups you wouldn't believe. Her name was Mary Lynn.

Tapes sat in the middle, his long Texas legs jammed into his chest from straddling the hump. "This ain't the most fun I've had in a long time."

"Me, neither," I said. I'd just had to see the lighthouse one more time before we left. It is my intention to visit every lighthouse in America before I die—and Canada, too, if I should live that long. We have upward of 440 or 450, including Puerto Rico and the Virgin Islands. And there are a couple of lighthouses on St. Paul Island and the Main-à-Dieu Light on Scatari Island, Nova Scotia I've been looking forward to visiting. I couldn't figure out where Gaspar buried the headless woman. It's said her ghost at times wanders the beach looking for her head. Ugh. I looked, but never saw her—probably too windy.

I had the Chevy GT's wipers on max. Wind and rain buffeted the truck rudely. The green truck was long past truck social security age but performed like it was forty years younger. We were now driving north on Gulf Boulevard.

The jogger leaned forward. He wore running shoes and blue shorts and orange shirt which had THE SKY IS BLUE AND THE SUN IS ORANGE SO GOD MUST BE A GATOR written on it, referring to the University of Florida Gators and their colors. In addition to the scrubby face, he had thick dark eyebrows and a wide cutting jawline.

"There's something familiar about this guy," I told Tapes, straining to think.

A strong gust blew my GT onto the shoulder of the road, and likely sand-blasted the left side.

We'd been on the very southernmost tip of Gasparilla Island for one last look at the lighthouse, wanting to see it at sunrise. Unfortunately, the storm had generated overnight and squalls had blown in right after we got to the Old Port Boca Grande Lighthouse. Now we were heading back to the JG Inn to have breakfast, pack our stuff, and leave. I wanted to return to the mainland, head south and see the Sanibel Island Lighthouse. The jogger had made the same mistake we had and we offered him a ride back to the tiny town.

"There is something familiar about me," said the jogger with a disarming smile.

"I told you so," I said. "Is this twenty questions?" When I'm out of sorts, I tend to have a sharp tongue. Right now I didn't need to split my attention between driving in the storm and verbal sparring.

"Look, Shortcut, if he wants us to know who he is he'll tell us." Tapes took out his tin of Copenhagen, shook his head, and returned it to his pocket. He was trying to quit. He's got a great deal of willpower and likely would succeed. On the other hand, maybe Tapes was in fact human and having a difficult time weaning himself from nicotine.

We passed the Rear Range Lighthouse, a straight metal cylinder with a lattice-work of struts and supports. The Old Port Boca Grande Lighthouse is a wooden structure like an old Southern home, with wraparound porches on three sides of the first level. The next level up was like a crow's nest, a pudgy neck to the building before you get to the top level. Which is the light itself, a third order Fresnel lens, surrounded by a wooden catwalk. It was three-and-a-half power with a red flash every twenty seconds. I'd timed it. The whole thing rested on pilings so that wind and water could pass through. It was one of the thirty formal and official lighthouses in Florida. When we finished seeing them, we were going to return to Arizona where I needed a job, having just quit mine in disgust, and Tapes already had a job mothballing aircraft in Tucson, passing, of course, through God's Country, otherwise known as Texas, our birthplace and frequent home. My job had been in Tallahassee and when Becky and I broke up—

"Got it," I said.

"Windmills or lighthouses?" Tapes asked rhetorically.

We argued about damn near everything. This particular ongoing argument was whether windmills were more aesthetic than lighthouses. I liked lighthouses better than windmills. Tapes preferred windmills. 'Course, lighthouses always had the best locations and scenery.

"Neither," I said. "He is familiar." I hooked my thumb toward the jogger. His approximate age, forty-five, finally led me to it.

"Well?" Tapes demanded.

"Henry Beauchamps Gonzáles," I said smugly.

Tapes scratched his head which was brushing the roof of the cab. "Name's familiar."

"You're from Texas and Arizona and don't need to know Florida stuff," I said. "The beard and drowned hair disguised him. Besides, people don't look the same in person as they do on television on the news."

Gonzáles looked like he wanted to pull his hair out we were taking so long to acknowledge him. A little vanity never hurt nobody.

"The Democrat Governor of Florida," Tapes said.

Gonzáles nodded emphatically.

"How come you're out jogging alone?" I asked, keeping my voice neutral, for running wasn't anything I was near fond of. Neither was Tapes.

"This island is my home. I own the José Gaspar Inn. I live there, too. I jog every morning and my assigned Florida Highway Patrol trooper feels it's safe enough before dawn."

There it was again. Everything around here named for the nasty hombre himself. José Gaspar had kidnapped, imprisoned, raped women all along this coast, not to mention your basic pillaging and plundering. Say 1873, until he killed himself twenty-six years later.

Since then, Gaspar's become a local legend, time being kind to him as to other killers such as Billy the Kid. Just south of Gasparilla Island stretches Captiva Island, a key where Gaspar kept his kidnapped women. He had captured the Spanish princess and she spurned him, and spit in his face. That's why he whacked off her head.

The Gulf coast of the island was perhaps fifty yards to the west and I saw no ghosts, headless or not. The wind was now blowing with serious intent and pushing big rollers ahead of it over the dunes, through the brush, and onto the roadway. A dog-sized wad of Gulf froth slapped the windshield and slewed off like spit in the wind.

"Many years ago," the governor said, "maybe in the early eighties, in Sarasota just north of here—"

"I know geography, we drove through there," I said and immediately regretted my short-tempered interruption. I'm vain about geography.

"You have to forgive him," Tapes said, "he just broke up with—"

"You leave Rebecca out of this—"

"Becky," Tapes corrected, nodding earnestly, "and he ain't his real self nowadays. Jeez. You got to be especially sensitive around him—"

"The governor doesn't need to know about my nonexistent love life," I said testily.

Gonzáles was glancing between us, looking like he just swallowed a handful of chili powder.

I stared at him expectantly, one eye on the road disappearing in and out of the wipers. "Well?"

"Well what?"

"The Sarasota no-name storm," I prompted.

"Oh, yes. It caused more damage than any named storm or hurricane in a long time." He scratched his incipient beard. "It dissipated rapidly."

I grinned at Tapes. "'Dissipated rapidly'?"

"Now you done it," Tapes accused Gonzáles with a frown.

"Done what? I mean, did what?"

"Shortcut will use it to death. Everything now will dissipate rapidly. Dinner, clouds—"

"Beer," I added.

"You're Shortcut?" asked the governor.

"You've heard of me?" I asked.

"Not at all," said Gonzáles with a twinkle in his voice. Right then, I liked him; he was giving it back to me in kind and, hell, I deserved it. Damn Rebecca—Becky, rather—for putting me in such sour circumstance.

How was I to know Governor Henry Beauchamps Gonzáles would be dead in less than ten minutes? And right after I decided

I liked him, him being a politician and all.

"You drive very well," Gonzáles told me.

"Thanks." I avoided an ocean by driving on the shoulder of the road I couldn't see and through a flower bed. The salt water coming up from the Gulf would kill all the flowers anyway. "Like Alcibiades in a chariot race." It hadn't been my intention to bring that up, but it just slipped out, my mind being occupied with concentrating on driving and all.

"Who?" asked Gonzáles.

I'd never talked to anybody who knew how to pronounce Alcibiades' name, so I was guessing. Of course, I ain't in the classics social circles.

"Alcibiades," I said, and Tapes groaned. I pronounced it like "Al-kye-bye-aye-dees." I shrugged mentally. What the hell. I'd never been out to impress people anyway. On the other hand, I hated to make a jerk out of myself. "One of the guys Plutarch wrote about."

"Ah, the traitor," said Gonzáles. "He betrayed Athens in favor of the Spartans and ruined democracy."

"He got a bum rap," I said. "You ever read what Plutarch says about that?"

"Gimme a break," said Tapes.

Wrenching the steering wheel to the side to compensate for a strong gust, not to mention not being able to see, I thought about paybacks to Tapes. "Once, Alcibiades entered seven teams in the Olympics. One account has it that he won first, second, and fourth; Euripides disagreed, reporting Alcibiades came in third and that was it. Have I ever told you that, Tapes?" I was not needling him, just reminding him of my idiosyncrasies.

"A hundred times, Shortcut. And you never pronounce his name the same."

"Well, here's one I haven't told you. A. J. Foyt said, 'Every year I get older and go faster. It's a helluva deal.' A. J. must've been talking about me." I looked around Tapes to the governor. "A. J.'s from Texas, too."

"Who *are* you people?" asked the governor. "You talk like

cowboys, yet you quote Plutarch. You dress like cowboys and drive a forty-eleven-year-old truck."

"I'm Shortcut. He's Tapes."

"Nicknames," said the governor. "Do you have a real name you answer to?"

"I don't give that out freely."

"He doesn't tell strangers," Tapes said simultaneously, always protective of my fragile ego.

Gonzáles stiffened.

We'd abused our newly found friendship. I waved my hand in a disarming manner and suddenly the truck slewed and banged into something I couldn't see. I grabbed the wheel like an astronaut cut loose from the space shuttle. "I'm Billy Birthday and this is Wallace Francis Fidgle." Tapes was born with the bark on. He was wearing a pullover shirt upon which burgeoned a mushroom cloud over which appeared the words "MADE IN AMERICA," and under the A-bomb explosion were the words "JUST TRY US." Very tacky.

Gonzáles nodded approvingly. "What are Plutarch-quoting cowboys doing on Gasparilla Island, Florida?"

"Vacationing and checking out lighthouses," I said. Generally, Tapes lets me do the talking for both of us. He's usually very quiet: unlike me, if he doesn't have anything to say, he doesn't say it.

"It figgers," said Gonzáles like he knew he wasn't going to get a straight answer. "You have a way with words."

"He says he's as eloquent as Cicero," said Tapes, surprising me. We hadn't seen each other for a few months and he wasn't used to not talking yet.

"I got a GED," I said.

Have you ever seen a lighthouse lonely against dark seas and skies? Standing on a spit of sand or stone, lancing oceans and seas, gutting clouds, slicing fog? A majestic version of human engineering, a bastion against the absolute worst nature throws? Were lighthouses music, grown men would cry more frequently.

"Turn right," Gonzáles directed, indicating with his right

pointy finger.

Perceptively, the wind decreased. We drove down a lane lined with giant banyan trees along both sides. The resultant canopy made it even darker. The wind funneled through from behind us, west to east, and scooted my truck along faster.

"Where we going?" I asked.

"The Inn. Surely the bridge will be closed. Might even wash out."

"We haven't checked out yet." The way it looked, we'd be here a few more days.

The governor's face scrunched up as he stared at banyan limbs whipping about us. "I grew up on the island, and I've never seen a storm come on so quickly." He rubbed a misted spot off the side window. "If that high pressure system is stalled just to the north of us, this storm will sit here for a while."

"Meteorology comes naturally to some people," I said, making my smile disarming. "Too bad talking about the weather's become a cliché."

"Not at all," he said. "I listen to NOAA weather radio every morning."

A flying object shot into my line of sight, just for a second at the end of a wiper arc, and I braced against the seat.

The truck shook and we heard the metallic clang even over the storm sounds. I held the wheel hard, trying not to overcompensate and worrying about the new metallic green paint-job.

Tapes leaned forward. "Left front quarter-panel."

The GT was driving without malfunction. "Damn. I hate body work."

Tapes gave me that look.

"Okay, okay." I shook my head. Tapes usually fixed body damage and I worked on the engine and accessories.

Gonzáles directed us left and right and a couple turns I wasn't altogether sure about, and there was the José Gaspar Inn. I recalled that in addition to being a lawyer, he had family money. I guess the grand old hotel was part of that.

I drove through the turnaround under the flapping canopy

and we dropped him off.

"Thanks," he said without any sense of closure.

We went and parked the truck, selecting what I thought would be a safe location. Knowing Gonzáles owed us for the ride, I didn't mind driving over his lawn and parking on the lee side of the big, sprawling inn. The GT nestled alongside the east wing up against a giant gardenia bush which was whipping around like a gutted snake.

Something had hit the roof and ripped the CB antenna off. The CB was inop anyway, and I hadn't fixed it since modern cell phones came upon the scene.

With a minimum amount of guilt, I hoped that intriguing woman named Mary Lynn was stuck here, too. Tapes says I fall in love at the drop of a hat. But the fact is I'm seldom attracted at first sight. And once I was old enough to figure life out, I've tried not to let the fact that a woman is very attractive sway me to favor her. Sure. But this woman's high forehead and arched eyebrows spoke of quick intelligence. Her two-color piercing eyes got my attention like a red flag to El Toro Diablo and her legs made my gut contract like a tropical disease. Then the specter of Rebecca in Tallahassee cast a great shadow over the cold, desolate land that was my love life.

Henry Beauchamps Gonzáles was probably dead before we reached the side door.

Tapes retrieved his twenty-five-foot Lufkin Unilok tape measure from the glove compartment and, battling the increasing wind, I got our wet weather gear from the cross-body Trukbox in the pickup's bed. I believe in the Boy Scout motto or, more specifically, the Seven P Principle: Proper Prior Planning Prevents Piss Poor Performance.

It didn't help the governor a bit.

2: MONDAY, 7:00 A.M.

We came in the east wing door of the Inn, along the high-ceilinged hall, arguing as usual.

"I think John Wayne's Alamo movie was best," I said, picking up the conversation we were in the middle of when the governor joined us.

Tapes snorted. "With Frankie Avalon in it?"

I had nothing against Frankie, but he'd never won any Oscars, or Grammys for that matter. "The Walt Disney one had Buddy Ebsen in it," I pointed out.

"It also had Mike Fink and the other Davy Crockett stuff John Wayne conveniently left out." Tapes slung water off his brow.

I couldn't argue that, so I said, "I can't argue that. But how about this: Richard Boone was in the Duke's version."

We passed rooms on each side, the doors topped by old-fashioned transoms. Seemingly as an afterthought, somebody had installed fire-sprinklers and the assorted PVC and hardware right on the high ceiling of the passageway. The José Gaspar Inn was built sometime around the twenties and echoed that style. Old-timey carpeting in the corridors, high ceilings, big rooms with giant paddle fans. Bogart in Latin America, sitting there smoking and drinking, overhead fan moving slowly. Atmosphere. This hotel had four wings laid out on the cardinal points.

We'd checked in yesterday evening and had a ground floor room; since it wasn't tourist season or tarpon tournament time, the sallow-faced manager who'd assigned us the room had told me that all the guests were staying downstairs along this east wing hall. And the permanent residents, like himself—and, I guess, Governor Gonzáles—lived on the third and top floor.

"That's not fair," Tapes said, "nobody can top Richard Boone."

"See, I told you so," I said, and somebody screamed.

I just knew it was a female-in-terror scream like you hear in the movies.

Wrong.

We hustled down the corridor and in the middle where the wings adjoin and the grand staircase zigzags up to the third floor, we found the governor—make that the late governor—and a man standing over him.

The man had screamed. He was a dapper little man wearing a white short-sleeved shirt and a bow tie.

He whimpered lower this time, evoking the memory of his louder scream.

Tapes and I skidded to a stop.

"Uh oh," I said.

Tapes said nothing.

Henry Beauchamps Gonzáles had been a living, thriving human being not minutes ago sharing human concerns with us. Like "rapidly dissipated" and the weather.

Still dressed in his wet jogging outfit, he lay there at the foot of the stairwell very dead. His neck was askew.

"He told us he was no meteorologist," I said, the words and thought inane, but it was all I could think to say.

His slicked back hair was mussed and drying.

I knelt quickly and apprehensively, gulped a lot, and checked the pulse at his neck. None. Not with his neck bent and twisted like that.

"There," Tapes said and pointed.

Following his line of sight, I saw the railing at the top of the stairs on the third floor broken and splintered.

The guy standing next to us had been frozen to this time. He whimpered again.

"Look," I said. "Move to the left a bit."

Tapes did so. "Oh, shit."

So did the geek.

He started moaning in higher squeals, drowning out a motor.

There was a big red streak across Gonzáles' forehead, the skin stripped back on each side.

Again I pointed.

Off to the side, where it had obviously fallen, was a tennis racquet, a blue and orange tennis racquet, with an alligator ghost painted on the racquet's sweet spot, obviously the gator mascot/symbol of the University of Florida. One curve of the racquet was bloody.

"What do you call the top corner arc of a tennis racquet?" I asked. "On an ear, it's the helix,"

Tapes shrugged. He didn't share my penchant for oddball terms and expressions.

The manager slewed to a stop alongside the geek who was moaning. Silas Smith, the manager, wore plaid slacks and a white shirt. His sallow face was yellow. There were deep scars on his neck. He was so ugly he ought to wear a mask. I'd bet he'd had one hellacious childhood. His first concern was the squealing geek, but then Smith saw the governor.

Other people were coming down the halls and in from the wings.

An overly pregnant woman waddled toward us from the kitchen wing, eyes bulging, fist jammed into her mouth, and eyes fixated on the body.

A hefty guy who looked like an ex-NFL lineman in a T-shirt and brown slacks with a dark stripe down each side lurched from the opposite wing where the bar and lounge were located.

More people entered from the lobby and some came from the rooms behind us down the corridor we'd just walked.

"Ohmygod!" said Silas Smith, his hand against his mouth in a parody of a cliché. "Governor Gonzáles fell." His voice was octaves higher than it had been last night.

"Not necessarily," I said, still squatting there. I smelled the storm rain on the body and oddly it made the gorge rise in my throat. I stood and fought back the nausea. Gonzáles was dead and had just been alive talking and riding with me and Tapes. It was an odd juxtaposition to think about. We'd discussed Plutarch and the weather. Jeez.

The big bulky guy shoved his way through. "Let me in, I'm lawn forcement." He had a bottle of Yukon Jack liquor in his hand and his eyes were bloodshot and his breath foul, and he was unshaven. He staggered up to me. "Just exactly what the fuck's goin' on here?" He looked down at me suspiciously.

"You got a murder on your hands, officer," I said mildly.

"I'm 'Trooper,' and how the fuck do you know it's murder, Shorty?" His eyes focused on me then shifted to the body.

Now I greatly dislike anybody making fun of my inordinate lack of great height. I always like to think of myself as a younger Alan Ladd without the highwater pants; what with a similar height, my hair and a certain jut of jaw give that impression if you're real creative in your mind's eye.

"I saw it on a *Magnum* rerun," I shot back at Trooper while wondering if Tapes could take him. Tapes was skinny enough to bathe in a shotgun barrel, but he was deceptively strong. Also, he was about a foot taller than me. Not to mention he usually got us out of the trouble my mouth got us into. "You can check him, he's rapidly assuming room temperature," I said quoting the guy on the radio.

Trooper's face blanched and three guys who hadn't shaved more than the trooper and wore hunting camouflage gear edged up behind him. They were obviously curious and rude, because they pushed an old lady out of their way.

Turning to Silas Smith, I said, "You'd better call the law." I glanced at Trooper. "The real law."

Trooper snarled. "I'm the governor's fucking bodyguard, Shorty. I'll make the decisions here."

"You did a wonderful job," I said, regretting the dig immediately.

Trooper started to reach for me then something changed on his face. "Didjou say he's dead?"

"You could draw that conclusion."

Trooper's face fell, beef turning to bristly jowls, a tear actually eeking from his right eye. He sniffled. "Henry B. was my friend." Trooper's voice sounded strangled.

"Call the law," I told Smith again.

"Oh, God, I'll do it." He trotted down the hall toward the front desk.

The geek's teeth were chattering.

"What happened?" I asked.

He put four left fingers into his mouth and his eyes were still bulging, locked onto the body.

"Tell us," I said.

"I...I don't know. I was walking to breakfast and...there he was on the floor."

Silas Smith returned.

He shook his head and his voice had regained some calm. "I can't call out. Phones are out from the storm. We're running on our own generator even."

"My CB's broken," I said. "Any cell phones?"

Nobody responded.

"The cellular sites usually take the first hits on the mainland," Smith said. "This is a bad reception area anyway."

"Well, send somebody," I said.

This handsome woman whose face was ashen shook her head. "The two sheriff's deputies are on the mainland for shift change." She hiccupped. I'd watched her last night. She'd been the center of a small party in the lounge. A "divorce party" Silas Smith had told me. The pregnant woman and the old lady were part of it, her friends, this intriguing woman, helping her celebrate her divorce. It had seemed to me more like a wake; however, she'd grabbed my attention with a bold look. The lady hiccupped again.

If she was March on a swimsuit calendar, you'd never get to April. She was wearing a pair of prairie shorts, made of

Chamois leather, revealing an acre of tan legs. A loose blouse of the same material exposed a strip of slim and tan waist. Last night she'd worn a lip-licking yellow cross-back knit dress with a swirl-like skirt. She hiccupped again.

One of the camo-dressed guys said, "The bridge washed out a little while ago."

As usual paying attention to what's happening around me and especially intriguing women who show a lot of class, I knew that the star of the divorce party was named Mary Lynn and, with a couple of the others at the party, hadn't gone home last night because they had too much to drink and didn't want to drive in the building storm. So they got rooms at the Inn.

Looking around at the different people, I thought at least there was room at this Inn. Which gave me an associative thought and I eyed the pregnant woman. She was standing there staring, her breathing ragged. Well, Gonzáles wasn't his old self. Not everybody gets to view a newly dead governor.

Trooper was just standing there; face scrunched up, eyes watery. Realization had paralyzed him.

The only person moving was the old lady. She was already on the first turn of the broad stairs heading upwards.

Well, at least somebody had something on the ball.

To Trooper, I said, "You'd best insure nobody disturbs the evidence for now."

"What are we gonna do with him?" Trooper's voice was a plaintive cry.

Edging through the crowd, I hit the stairs, my Nikes doing better than the old lady's pumps.

We made it to the third floor at the same time.

Nothing.

An overturned table against the wall, a busted railing, and a puddle of water, most likely from Gonzáles standing there dripping. I thought again of a life snuffed and the gorge rose once more.

The old lady was eyeing me and moving around looking at things.

"Maybe we shouldn't be up here messing around," I said, words serving to repel the fluctuating nausea.

"Says who?" she asked with an eye cocked at me. "Did the governor leave you in charge before he died?"

I shook my head. "Just common sense."

"You're the one they call Shortcut, aren't you?"

"I am."

"You're not from around here, are you?"

"I'm not."

"You talk and dress like a cowboy. I didn't think there were any cowboys left."

"I used to be; I'm not any longer."

"What are you now?"

"Unemployed," I said and thought, and running from a woman.

"Why is it that you look like a gill-caught fish?"

"Beats me." I shrugged and finally controlled my emotions. "I was shocked at the governor's death, that's all. I'd just been talking to him. He was a living, breathing person and now he's a corpse."

"Ghoulish, aren't you?" Her other eye nailed me. "You were talking to him? You saw it happen?"

"No. We were coming down the corridor after letting him off at the front door."

"You and that tall cowboy?"

"Yep. He's not a cowboy any longer; though once you clamp a steer's ear or dip a cow, I guess it stays with you. He's a mothballer."

The old lady shook her head. There was a beehive of gray hair neatly atop it. Her face was not wrinkled like you'd think. And she was a shade taller than me, not a hard thing to be.

"A mothballer? Surely you take advantage of an old lady."

"No, it's true. In Tucson, for the Air Farce. He decommissions aircraft and prepares them for what's called the Boneyard."

"Let me get this straight," she said, springing fingers up. She began ticking them off one at a time. "You're unemployed, yet on this semi-remote and relatively unknown island for some unknown reason—"

"Not at all, we were visiting the lighthouses."

"Right," she said and ticked another finger down. "You know nobody, and you were with Henry B. just before he died. It's all very suspicious."

"Who are *you* and why all these questions?" I said.

"I, sir, am Angela Maple," she said with a harrumph in her voice. "Who are *you*?"

"Shortcut."

"I mean, what's your name?"

"Shortcut."

"I need all the information I can get."

I groaned. "Why don't we leave the investigating to the authorities?"

"What authorities?" she asked.

"Beats me. Trooper?"

She harrumphed again. "Trooper's an alkie. Henry B. kept him on because of loyalty to a friend; he's not much of a bodyguard."

Suddenly, I realized I was dealing with a pretty shrewd woman. Aggravating, but intelligent. She'd been thinking while I was reacting. "You know, Mrs. Maple—"

"Mizz."

"Sure, whatever. If we've no authorities and we're stuck here, we've a problem. We've a dead governor, the outside world doesn't know it, and he's not going to get any, ah, fresher the longer he lays down there."

"Lies," she corrected. "But we've got the lieutenant governor here, too. And Henry B.'s chief aides."

"Then it ain't our problem," I countered. "Let 'em sort it out."

Gingerly she stepped to the broken railing. "He's down there now."

I figured she meant the lieutenant governor.

We were both waltzing about, not saying the one thing we both thought.

Ms. Maple looked at me. "I wonder who killed him?"

"And why," I added.

"There's the other thing, too," she said.

"No authorities, no crime scene investigation; when the storm passes, everybody will be gone."

"That about sizes it up," she said.

Somebody had deliberately murdered the governor of the fourth largest state in the United States and was going to get away with it—more than likely—because a storm was bottling us all up, and keeping others away.

On the wall next to the overturned table was a rack from which hung several tennis racquets.

She started down the steps. "Let's go see what the future governor has to say."

"Right." As she went down, I knelt and studied the floor. No clues. In all the movies there's always a clue. Shows to go you real life ain't like they show us on the big screen—or the small screen, for that matter. By now Perry Mason would've had Paul Drake headed in the right direction.

I flipped my finger in the puddle of water, absently tasted it, and wiped my finger on a wrinkle in the wall-to-banister rug. No pack of matches with a bar name, no cigarette with lipstick, no feather, no boot mark, no nothing.

Ms. Maple was standing a few steps down the staircase, her face level with this landing, watching me intently.

It occurred to me this was something me and Tapes didn't need to get involved in badly. We were outsiders and most of these people were local; that's a no-win situation.

But Henry B., she'd called him.

I'd worked a while in Tallahassee and never thought much about the governor. I'd disagreed with much of his politics— hell, I disagree with most politicians' politics. Politicians are people we pay who hire other people to spend our money.

But he'd sat right there in the crowded cab of my GT and sweated from running and talked about the weather. Everybody talks about the weather.

3 : MONDAY, 7:30 A.M.

Everybody watched me descend the stairs. I felt like a cockroach on a bald man's head.

Tapes, of course, was head and shoulders above the crowd. His eyes showed something which translated into a "Be careful" warning.

John Dellum Ionata, the lieutenant governor and soon-to-be head man, fixed me with his grizzled visage and tracked me all the way down. He wore khaki shorts and a khaki safari shirt with shoulder straps.

Near the bottom, I said self-consciously, "Not much up there." I thought again of Henry Beauchamps Gonzáles, looked at John Dellum Ionata, and kind of liked the late governor's penchant for three-named people.

Ms. Maple was standing in front of Ionata. "Very suspicious, John. That man is an itinerant, and here for no reason. He won't give his name." She was looking accusingly at me.

"There's an old saying," I told her, "about the more people I meet, the more I like my dog. And I don't have a dog."

She stared a challenge at me.

"He gave his name to me," said Silas Smith, fingering a pockmark on his neck. "It's Billy Birthday."

One of the guys in the camo hunting fatigues snorted loudly and elbowed his buddy. "Get that, Orlo? Billy Birthday." All three hunters, or whatever they were, laughed.

Nobody else did.

Mary Lynn, the recent divorcee who'd intrigued me last

night, watched me with one blue eye and one brown eye, compelling me to wish I could put some fire in those same eyes. I'm a grown man, but I sure dream like a boy. Once last night, I'd got close to her; her auburn hair smelled faintly of gardenias. Besides, I could never resist a pony tail. And, what the hell, Rebecca was in Tallahassee and we'd parted ways. Mary Lynn had stopped hiccupping. She'd also hiccupped last night during her speech, but it was in a corner of the lounge and I couldn't hear her words.

"Your honor," said the big one in camo known as Orlo, "them two strangers ain't from around here. The old lady says they coulda done it." His voice was low and caused me the proverbial chill. "They was the last one to see him." Orlo was as large as Trooper and had linebacker eyes.

Why did Orlo want to pin a murder on me and Tapes?

The pregnant woman burped, turned aside, and vomited against a plastic potted fern. Served it right.

Mary Lynn hurried to her side. "This is no place for you. The shock could—"

"The shock *did*," said the woman who looked like she was gonna explode from the middle. I guess dead bodies lying around and people conversing over them would make you sick if you were about to have a baby.

John Dellum Ionata took charge. "Mary Lynn, get her to her room and see that she's comfortable. You help, too, Angie." He looked at the old lady and she nodded. He was obviously trying to defuse the situation.

The geek was still standing alongside the staircase whimpering.

Ionata fixed Orlo and his two cronies with a command glare. "Everybody is innocent until proven guilty."

Hell, I could've said that.

The three simply watched him, one drooling a bit from the corner of his mouth. I wondered if he wasn't one of those guys you read about who was a result of his mother and father being brother and sister. But, for once, I kept my mouth shut. We didn't need any more trouble.

Ionata turned to Trooper. "Sober up. Coffee and a cold shower."

A great gust of wind shook the whole building and most likely did damage to one or more of the upper stories of the wings. Everybody turned their gaze upward for a moment.

Not me. I watched Mary Lynn leading the pregnant woman off. Mary Lynn had a fascinating walk, too.

Angie Maple was walking hesitantly; probably afraid she'd miss something.

The lieutenant governor ripped his gaze downward. He reminded me a little of Poppa Smurf, what with his gray beard and piercing eyes and all. His voice wasn't Smurf-like, though, it was pure Florida cracker.

"Silas," he said, "get a camera and—"

"I don't have one, sir—"

"I do," said Ms. Maple and hurried off.

Back then cell phones didn't have cameras.

"Then," said Ionata to the Inn's manager, "go find a doctor or a nurse or a midwife."

"It's too dangerous out in the storm," I said, not caring about Silas Smith, but knowing that to be a fact.

"Are you a weatherman?" asked Ionata softly.

"No, sir, but I was out there a little while ago and it's gotten worse," I said, showing a bit of testiness in my voice. Ionata angered me with the weatherman comment.

He continued to stare at me. He was probably thinking I had reason for no one to leave the Inn. "Are you willing to attend to a birth?" His voice was warning me,

"If I have to," I said, edgy at the prospect.

"You a doctor?" said Ionata.

Orlo snorted and his two fellows followed suit.

I shook my head. "No, sir, but I've delivered a baby."

"Where?" demanded Angie Maple returning with a 35mm camera, flash and all.

"In Colorado, if you must know. An emergency situation like

this. In the bed of a pickup under a tarp. This'll be a snap." I snapped my fingers. It wasn't any of their business, but I'd let the them-against-us crowd get to me.

Ionata addressed everybody, several of whom were now sitting in overstuffed chairs and whom I hadn't had a chance to catalog yet. "If anyone here knows anything about childbirth, or knows anyone else here at the Gaspar Inn who does, please come forward."

I didn't like the immediate silence that followed. I wouldn't of said anything had I not been challenged and probably subliminally or subconsciously or whatever the hell that word is, needed to stake out a position of importance and input into the situation. That is, I should have kept my big mouth shut. Not to mention wanting to impress Mary Lynn who had stopped to watch the byplay. At that moment thunder crashed and she turned and continued on with the pregnant woman. The probability of spending time with Mary Lynn at the expense of assisting in a birth was worth the effort.

Ionata spoke again. "Please, ladies and gentlemen, nobody leave the hotel?" He looked straight at me.

"It occurs to me," I said softly, "that as lieutenant governor, you've got the most to gain from Henry B.'s death."

The entire place fell silent except for a couple of deep intakes of breath.

Ionata surpised me. After giving me a scathing look, he nodded. "That's one way to look at it."

Ms. Maple began flashing pictures from every conceivable angle. Henry B. would be immortalized on film in a rictus of death. When she was finished, she climbed the stairs slowly and flashed pictures up there.

After she completed her task, Ionata wrapped the tennis racquet murder weapon in a plastic garbage bag. Blood stained the clear plastic immediately. I'd guessed that whoever did it would probably have had the foresight to wipe it clean of prints before dropping it over the railing, but you never know. Then I noticed the handle had a cloth sleeve. So much for prints.

A real pencil-necked geek I'd seen but didn't know escorted the whimpering fellow away down the corridor. Somebody whispered that the two were the governor's aides. "Late governor," somebody else pointed out.

Ionata addressed me and Silas Smith because we were the closest to him. "What do you do with a body? We can't just leave him here."

"I don't know, Judge."

"Put it on ice," I said, eying Henry B. who was getting stiffer by the minute. Ordinarily, a recent corpse will allow fluids, solids, or gases to escape through various channels, so to speak. But Henry B. was countering the norm.

"Stands to reason," said Ionata, rubbing his gray beard. He looked at me through wire-rimmed glasses, showing suspicion. "Is this more of your expertise? You've both medical and funeral experience?"

I know I looked guilty. I glanced at Tapes for help, but he was characteristically silent. I'd gotten myself into this and, since it wasn't physically dangerous now, he'd let me get myself out of it.

"The woman I assisted in giving birth?" I said. "Her husband was there and he was a mortician. I learned some things."

"Sure he was," said Ionata. "But what Mr. Birthday says is not contra-indicated."

"I smell a bureaucrat," I said.

Ionata stepped to Orlo and friends. "Would you help carry him?"

"Where, your honor?" Orlo asked uneasily and looked at the body.

"To the freezer at the back of the kitchen," said Ionata.

"Urp," said Silas Smith and swallowed, his Adam's apple bouncing like a ping pong ball going down a windy mail chute.

"Our freezer?" he asked timidly.

"Well, then," Ionata said slowly, "let us just chuck him out on the front lawn." He paused a moment. "Maybe we should just leave him here and wait for the sheriff's department in a couple of days."

"I can make room in the freezer," said Silas Smith quickly.

Orlo looked at the body. "I ain't touchin' no dead body. How 'bout thee, Axe?" he said to the one drooling from the corner of his mouth. At the time, I thought Orlo's reluctance was natural.

Axe shook his head widely but said nothing.

Tapes had disappeared but reappeared down the hall carrying a blanket. The rest of the world talks, but Tapes acts.

He laid the blanket out beside the late governor and stood at the corpse's head waiting.

Gritting my teeth, I strode over and grasped Henry B.'s ankles above the Nikes. Tapes took his shoulders and we scooted him onto the blanket. Each of us grabbed two corners of the blanket and straightened.

"Lead the way, Silas," I said.

We went down the corridor of the north wing, past the elevator and public rest rooms, past the first kitchen doors, to the rear kitchen doors. Inside were several walk-in coolers and freezers. We headed for the closest one, Gonzáles not getting any lighter.

Silas Smith hurried in front of us. "No, no, not that one." He pulled open the door of the center cooler and indicated a place atop some crates.

I shivered.

We covered the ex-governor with another blanket.

4: MONDAY, 11:30 A.M.

"Geography bee," I said. The dog was making me angry.

"Spelling bee," Tapes said.

"Geography bees make you think, know things. Spelling bees you memorize a few rules and a few exceptions and that's it." I crossed my arms.

"Spelling bees require discipline and presence of mind," he said, putting down his Bud on the table. "Geography bees, you just got to know places; then memory tricks and associations bail you out."

"Geography bees," I said emphatically, "open the entire world to you. Stange and foreign places. Mystic lands. You know geography, you have a good start on knowing people, peoples of this good Earth—"

"Don't get deep on me, Shorts," he warned. "Next you'll be using iambic pentameter—"

"I don't do metric," I shot at him.

"Anyway," he said around a mouthful of roast beef, "you can tell a lot about a person by the way they use the language."

"Ain't that the truth," I said.

"You talk like you ate a dictionary," he accused.

Tapes and I were sitting in the lounge eating sandwiches and potatoes I'd nuked: Silas Smith had sent the few remaining staff home last night. A move which I thought strange. Of course, the day shift had never arrived this morning.

Orlo and his two buddies were there, too, eating steaks they'd cooked.

Silas Smith entered through the double-wide doorway. I was becoming used to his sallow face and bad complexion. They say beauty is only skin deep, but Smith proved the old adage that ugly is clear to the bone.

"NOAA radio," he said, stopping at our table, "just reported that winds are up to seventy-three miles an hour."

"That makes it a tropical storm," I said. Two more MPH's and we'd have a hurricane. Shutters rattled as if to underscore his news.

"And it's stalled right out there in the Gulf by some kind of weather front," he finished.

Just like Henry B. had said.

"We're in for it," I said. "I hope your Budweiser holds out."

"Storm party!" shouted Orlo and his buddies guffawed. They were giving good beer a bad name. But they were paying attention to Smith.

The Rottweiler with the red bandanna for a collar lapped beer from a plate at Orlo's feet.

Silas ran his hand down his scarred neck. "We're stuck for at least a day."

"How's—what's the pregnant girl's name?" I asked.

"Kowalski," he said.

"Sandra Dee Kowalski," said Ms. Maple coming through the doors with a couple of rolls and a grapefruit on a plate. "She's still in labor. It will be a long day."

Another three-name person. "What is this, a convention?" I said and nobody paid any attention because a series of thunderclaps shook the entire building like successive incoming mortar rounds. I wondered about Sandy's mom.

Angie Maple wore a half-sleeve pullover shirt Tapes was staring at. One of his things is adorning shirts with weird and wonderful sayings, like "Pit bulls need love, too," or "Get insight, eat a cornea."

"Hi, Granny," I said without thinking.

She didn't respond, but she made sure we could all see her shirt. An elderly lady graced the front. She carried a big Uzi, and wore crossed bandoliers adorned with grenades and ammo.

Above her was the word "GRAMBO" and below her the caption read: "TAKE AWAY *WHOSE* SOCIAL SECURITY?"

Granny Maple was a Gray Panther if nothing else. She sat at the table next to us and buttered a roll and tinkled iced tea.

Silas Smith was looking awkward. "Thanks for, ah, carrying the governor back there and—"

The dog growled at him.

"No sweat," I said. "What's Mary Lynn's last name?"

"Messenger," he said.

"None of your beeswax," said Angie Maple.

Smith looked funny and backed out the door, warily eying the beast. "Your accommodations are free and so is the food if you remain. By doing so, you release the Inn from any liability."

I drank some Bud and leaned toward Ms. Maple. "Why isn't it any of my business? I'm not intruding."

"She already had one bad experience with a man and doesn't need to get started on another."

"Granny, I'm beginning to resent—"

"I saw the way you were looking at her last night. You're trying to catch her on the rebound, just for your own nefarious purposes."

"Yeah, and I might be a murderer, also," I said. Hell, I was vulnerable, too. I'd just broken up with Rebecca and wasn't too happy with the opposite sex. But, I stopped short in my reverie, Granny might be right. A kind and bold look last night from a pretty woman, sort of a soft touch which wormed into my heart a little. I shook my head. Tapes was correct, next thing I'll be writing poetry and I like poetry only a little more than death marches and cholera.

"You remind me of somebody...," she said and I ignored her.

Orlo and his buddies were drinking beer and paying close attention to us.

I stared wrath and hellfire at them and, lo and behold, they averted their gaze. I guess Rebecca's defection had burned me more than I thought. The dog returned my glare. Beer dripped from his mouth.

"You might well be," said Ms. Maple.

"Be what?" I asked.

"The murderer."

"That's the least of my worries."

"I'll find out and when I do—"

Things added up then. "Just one minute, Granny, you've been watching too much television—"

"Somebody's got to uncover the culprit."

"They send you a badge with your AARP kit?"

"Shortcut," Tapes said warningly.

"Well, she got to me."

"The old Shortcut wadn't that touchy," he said.

"Okay, okay. Granny, I apologize for my remark. It was insensitive."

"It was," she said, "especially coming from someone who puts peanut butter on his baked potato."

I put the knife down. "It's good for you—"

A noise at the doors interrupted. Trooper entered. He was wearing his full uniform, light brown with a darker trousers-stripe, and had shaved and appeared sober. He wore his revolver, a flashlight, and a pair of handcuffs tucked in his belt at the small of his back. He went straight to the bar and behind it; he drew himself a draft Bud like Orlo and the other two stooges had.

Trooper drank the entire beer without the glass leaving his mouth. He sighed and drew himself another draft and set it on the bar.

He looked around the room, surveying it as if for the first time. He ran a finger around his collar and stretched his neck uncomfortably.

I was watching him with interest and he began watching me watch him. He pulled a flipover notebook out of a rear pocket and came around the bar. He stopped next to me, towering bulkily there as if to intimidate me.

He found a mechanical pencil and licked the tip. "Give me

your name please, last name first, first name last, then middle initial."

"Why?"

He frowned and sighed. Surprisingly, his voice softened. "You're a witness, mister."

"He's a suspect," Orlo said from his table over his dog's head, "ye'd better read him his rights."

"I do my job as I see it," Trooper replied.

"I don't see any way around it," Tapes said.

Nor did I. "Birthday, Billy. NMI."

"Let me see your driver's license please."

Angry with him towering over me, I stood and moved aside. I still had no choice.

I pulled my wallet out and the dog lunged at me.

My wallet went flying and cards and plastic and cash fluttered about.

Since my Nikes were drying in the room, I was wearing my Tony Lamas. With pointy toes.

I'd been waiting for something to happen and had seen Orlo nudge the dog and whisper in its ear.

Executing a perfect swivel that helps me win club racquetball championships, I swung around and the pointy toe of the boot slammed into the Rottweiler's throat knocking him aside.

Before anything else happened, Tapes had his Buck knife flicked open and was heading for the dog.

"Deacon!" shouted Orlo.

The dog scrambled back and stood poised at Orlo's feet.

Tapes stopped.

"That sumbitch was fast," said the one called "Axe."

"Both them sumbitches were fast," said Orlo, looking at me and Tapes with a new appreciation.

I was waiting for an apology or an explanation I never got. The third camo-dressed guy was on his hands and knees in front of Trooper and me scooping up the stuff from my wallet.

"Lookit, Orlo," he said over his shoulder. He held up some of my cards. "Libary cards. A million of 'em."

"Twelve," I said.

The guy had black, greasy hair and one of those little pigtails tied by a rubber band. He was reading the cards. "Tucson, Tallahassee, San Antonio, Dallas, Florida State, Trinity, Davis-Monthan Air Force Base, El Paso, Uvalde—"

"We've established you can read," I said, anger creeping into my voice. I snatched them out of his hand. Angela Maple was staring at me quizzically. I was changing everybody's opinion of me.

Trooper was still standing there stoically. Not helping, not making a gesture one way or the other.

Tapes clicked his Buck knife and it disappeared.

"Orlo," I said. "You still hungry?"

"What?"

"You want to eat that dog, you turn him loose again."

"Me? Eat the Deacon?"

"Balls first. You're lucky: you already cut off his tail." I will never, ever understand why people de-tail dogs. It can't be for aesthetic reasons because most dogs are too ugly to change.

Orlo studied me under lowered brows. "I'd like to see that come to pass." His voice was soft and speculative. He continued to stare at me. "I call him 'Deacon' because if he comes after ye, ye'd better say thy prayers."

I'd figured something like that.

Shuffling my stuff, I handed Trooper my driver's license and put everything back in my wallet.

"Arizona," Trooper said, writing in his notebook. "How long did you say you've been in Florida?"

"I didn't."

"How long have you been in Florida?"

"Seven months."

"You should've got a Florida license, and tags for that old junker you drive." He wasn't as nonobservant as he looked.

"It was my intention to return to Arizona before this," I said.

"Ye surely should have," Orlo said in that same piercing, soft voice.

"Mizz Maple said you were unemployed and itinerant," Trooper said.

"Granny says a lot of things," I said. She might be more damaging to me than Deacon, who was still poised and locked onto me like MG-10 radar in an F-102 (when it worked). I sincerely hoped the current USAF inventory aircraft had better radar.

Tapes interrupted by handing Trooper his license.

Trooper looked at the two licenses and paused in his writing. "Same Tucson address." He squinted down at me. "You homosexuals?"

I shook my head. "No, but if we were, it wouldn't be any of your goddamn business."

"Fags," said Orlo and I wondered why he was creating conflict and pushing the situation toward flash points. He made the traditional limp wrist.

The dog growled.

"You like mustard, Orlo?" I asked.

"Why is that?"

"It'll make that dog taste better."

Orlo looked puzzled for a moment. He glanced at his buddies then back to me. "Ye? A short little shit? Taking on three growed men?" He laughed. "Too Tall and Too Small."

"I admit the odds are against you," I said. I turned away from him. I was already tired of listening to him and shouldn't have sparred with him.

Trooper returned our licenses. He nodded to Angie Maple. She found her purse and silently handed him her license.

When he was finished with her, he moved over to Orlo, ignoring Deacon. Trooper was doing his job and not letting anything threaten him. "Your names and licenses, please."

Orlo stood and in that same chilling soft voice, he said, "And if we do not so choose?" He caressed Deacon's head. Orlo was every bit as big as Trooper. He faced the Highway Patrol officer. "Deacon?"

You could tell the animal was ready. At the slightest signal he would attack. His neck strained against the red bandana.

Orlo's two friends stood also, the one with the pigtail poised on the balls of his feet.

Trooper said calmly, "I don't know you. You're not from around here. But I have seen you here some time ago. There is something funny about you I can't place, but I will. Twenty-five years in this business and I got the feel."

Deacon growled low in his throat.

Trooper continued. "That dog makes one move toward me, he's a dead motherfucker, understand?"

"There's no call for any of this confrontation stuff," I said.

"Shut the fuck up," said Trooper.

"Yes, sir," I said.

Trooper broke first, right then, and his hand went for his gun high on his hip.

The dog shot at him and Trooper wasn't as quick as I had been. Deacon had Trooper's arm in a nanosecond and Trooper screeched in sudden pain and fell to the side, the dog jumping at his shoulder now.

Angle Maple screamed.

Orlo stepped in and kicked Trooper in the temple with a fat boot. Pigtail began kicking Trooper in the back.

If he hadn't told me to shut the fuck up, things might have been different. In about three heartbeats he was no longer defending himself. Likely the first blow to the temple had knocked him out.

Tapes was quicker than me. He kicked the dog about eleven feet into a table spilling a full ashtray and knocking over the table.

I took Pigtail out with a hand to the throat and a boot to his knee. Instantly he was on the floor next to Trooper making noises like his larynx was crushed which it wasn't and like he was trying to breathe and couldn't and I didn't care about that.

Axe was still standing there drooling. He wasn't much more than a kid anyway.

Tapes had his Buck knife out and to Orlo's throat. "Call it

off."

The dog was scrambling back this way.

"Now," said Tapes, voice not worried.

"Deacon," said Orlo. "Freeze."

The Rottweiler stopped in place as if turned to stone.

"Hold it!" said a commanding voice from the entryway.

Lieutenant Governor John Dellum Ionata walked in. "What the *hell* is going on here?"

Orlo spoke quickly, disregarding Tapes' knife tickling his throat. "Your honor. The cop threatened me and Deacon, my dog, verily he did not understand and now, I think, everything is straightened out."

"Angie?" the next governor said.

"Everybody in here was at everybody's throat. However, these three, ah, gentlemen, were not cooperating with Trooper and his investigation." She looked at me. "Possibly because Mr. Birthday had already started an argument with them and with Trooper—"

"That ain't exactly how—" I began.

"Trooper needs help," Tapes said mildly. "Here's the way it happens. Orlo, you tell one of your friends to take the dog out, understand?"

"I do," Orlo said and tried to nod. He hadn't shaved in a week and looked like a pirate. Tapes' knife scraped his throat at the base and Orlo grimaced. "Deacon. Go ye with Axe. Axe, ye put the Deacon in the van, hear?"

"Yessir, Orlo, I heard. C'mon, Deacon." Axe simply walked off and the beast didn't follow. He still had the blood lust upon him.

"Orlo?" Tapes prompted with a gentle flick of his knife.

"Deacon, now, baby. Go with Axe." Orlo motioned with his left hand.

The dog obeyed and the tableau remained frozen. He trotted to Axe waiting at the entrance to the lounge.

Mary Lynn stood there. She'd been watching. She hiccupped twice.

I saw Axe pull the side doors to this the south wing open and the wind and rain burst in. It didn't bother Axe. He leaned against one of the screen doors and pushed hard, not an easy task. The door opened and he held it for the animal. The weather didn't seem to bother either.

The rain and wind poured in. Ionata went through the entry to the saloon and shouldered the heavy doors closed. The lashing rain soaked his slacks and the front of his white shirt.

"I don't know if you'll have to answer for assault on a lawman or not," Ionata said to all of us. "But I want that knife out of sight right away."

Tapes caressed Orlo's neck for a split second sending a message, and thumbed the blade closed and the knife disappeared.

Angie and Ionata were bending over Trooper.

Tapes was watching Orlo.

I stepped over to Pigtail. He was lying quietly on the floor, apparently concentrating on breathing. But his color was good and he'd recover soon. One of his hands was rubbing his knee I'd kicked. I hoped he'd have a lifetime limp.

"Now that's what I call rapid dissipation."

"He's unconscious," Angie Maple said. "I suspect he's got a concussion from that kick to the head."

"Trooper's tough," said Ionata. "We'll put him in his room and maybe you can keep ice on his head, Angie?"

"You're going to run out of nurses soon," I said.

Mary Lynn Messenger shook herself and hurried into the bar. Her eyes were wide and I wanted to drown in them. "Sandra Dee's having contractions. Her baby's coming."

"Oh, shit," I said.

Something is always interfering in my love life. Tapes saw my look at Mary Lynn and his eyes narrowed. He knew I hadn't had time to get over Becky and was prone to fall in love anyway.

I didn't know what the hell to think.

All I knew was that I didn't want to deliver a baby, not a bit; but if that's what it took to be in Mary Lynn's presence, I'd do anything it took.

"Come on," Mary Lynn urged. Her eyes drew me like a hypnotist.

Two quick witticisms jumped to my lips but I found myself suddenly tongue-tied.

The three hunters were after blood, my blood, not to mention their attack beast. There was absolutely no law to stand between us and them. I thought about their van. Most hunters have guns to hunt with.

It also occurred to me that there was a murderer running around loose, too.

I looked at Mary Lynn Messenger and felt very vulnerable.

5: MONDAY, 3:00 P.M.

"Tapes argues in favor of steel bridges," I was telling Mary Lynn. "He's very precise, mathematically oriented. He allows that steel bridges are engineered and designed to an inordinate exactitude." I wondered if there was such a word as "exactitude" but I didn't let it stop me from keeping Mary Lynn's attention. "I, on the other hand, prefer wooden bridges. They're better looking, rustic while functional, and usually develop their own character."

"I have to listen to this?" asked Granny from Sandra Dee Kowalski's bedside.

Mary Lynn glanced at Mizz Maple.

"Besides," I continued desperately, "your average wood bridge lasts seventy years and—"

"How in Heaven do *you* know that?" demanded Angie Maple.

Mary Lynn looked between me and Granny.

"Statistics show it," I said, an edge coming into my voice. "Road salt corrodes steel bridges and—"

"Excuse me?" said Sandra Dee Kowalski, retching to the side.

Granny held a pie plate out to receive the bile.

"I want a drink of water," Sandra Dee said.

"Give her some more ice," I directed. We'd been through this a couple of times.

"Yes, *sir*," Angie Maple said, voice dripping.

"Gimme a break, Granny. Look, we're almost done with the first stage of labor—"

"First stage?" asked Mary Lynn, rubbing her eyes. Which told me she'd never gone through childbirth herself.

Pointing, I said, "She's had what you call your 'show'," which was the bloody discharge occurring after the mucous plug goes, "and sometime recently the membranes which surround the amniotic fluid have ruptured—"

"She broke her water," Mary Lynn said.

"Well, yeah, if you want to put it that way."

"You certainly know the terminology," she added.

"Call it malarkey," said Angie, wiping Sandra Dee's brow with a wet cloth.

Ignoring the elderly "Granbo," I nodded to Mary Lynn. "After I assisted in the emergency birth that time, I went to the library and read up on it. I, um, kind of have a didactic memory for some things."

"You can say that again," said Angie.

"Damndamndamndamndamndamn," said Sandra Dee.

"You better check again, Billy," said Mary Lynn. Her pony tail bobbed, distracting me for a moment.

Wishing I really did know what the hell I was doing, I checked again. I was wearing a pair of disposable plastic gloves from a package Tapes had found in the kitchen. He'd microwaved 'em for a few seconds to insure their sterility.

"Drop your knees to the side," I directed Sandra Dee.

Granny shot me a scathing look; but Sandra Dee was in too much pain now to be modest. Soon she'd pay any price to be done with the labor.

Awkwardly and reluctantly, I felt around in there. "The infant's head's right there waiting. Her—" I regrouped. I wasn't playing to an audience, even though it included the fair Mary Lynn. I should be concentrating on the one person who really needed my help. "Your," I corrected, "cervix is dilating well. You certain you never had a baby before?"

"Yes, I, damndamn, mean no, I mean, damndamndamn, I don't know what the hell I—"

"I know what you mean," I said, and pulled the sheet down

over her. "You're close to ten centimeters—"

"What's that mean?" asked Sandra Dee panting.

"Beats me," I said. "I don't do metrics."

"About four inches," said Mary Lynn.

I bent down there again and mopped up a bit of discharge. "The border between the first stage and the second stage begins when you get full dilation of the cervix. Your contractions will become stronger and more frequent."

"Damndamndamn that's reassuring," Sandra Dee gasped. Her brown hair was splayed out on the pillow, framing her pale face. Her lips were almost bloodless.

"It's not really any of my business," I began, wondering. "But why are you here?"

"Any of your business?" Granny Maple said.

"It's my fault," said Mary Lynn.

"Nononono," said Sandra Dee. "I live over in Placida, just across the bridge. I came to support my friend—damndamn damn."

Not being familiar with divorce parties, I didn't know the protocol about how you support a friend by attending a party in honor of the formal dissolution of her marriage.

"It's about ten miles," said Mary Lynn. She took the pie plate and went into the bathroom and rinsed out the accumulated bile, etc.

"I'm a licensed cosmetologist and, damndamn, esthetician," Sandy explained.

"That must mean something," I said.

"I wax, ohnoohno, Mary Lynn's legs about once a month...."

"I'll trade jobs right now," I said.

"See," she moaned a bit, "after waxing, the new hair is softer than razor stubble—"

"I'm fantasizing," I said.

Mary Lynn returned from the bathroom and my eyes froze on her legs for a moment.

A series of strong winds buffeted the hotel and the lights flickered and we all held our breaths at the same time and I saw the pure panic in Sandra Dee's eyes.

The lights steadied. "No problem," I said.

"*You* say," said Angie.

"I do."

"Mary Lynn needed her friends, it was—damndamndamn damn—as simple as that."

I put my hand gently on her bulging lower stomach. "Sandy, push during the contractions. Use whatever muscles you can control; think abdominal wall, think diaphragm."

"Her name is Sandra Dee, not Sandy," said Granny.

"It doesn't mat—damndamndamn."

"Push a little this time."

Things quieted down for a few minutes.

Mary Lynn moved to the other side of Sandra Dee and held her hand while looking at me. "My husband was ten years older than I am. We were married for ten years. He became enamored of someone ten years younger than I am." She dropped her head and hiccupped softly. She still wasn't over the trauma. Her pony tail wavered atop her bowed head. She raised her head.

"Some guys don't know what they've got," I said softly.

She eyed me, slightly off balance from what I said, and then said, "Several of my friends decided to help me over the hump. The first night of official singleness—some call it freedom." She stopped as if she didn't consider being single being free. "It was their idea to celebrate—"

"Damndamndamndamndamn," Sandy breathed hard, "we wanted to show her she oughta be glad to be shut of that sneaking sonofa—"

"Now, now," smoothed Angie. She looked crossly at me. "It's none of his business anyway."

"Just curious," I said. "Not prying."

"Sure," Granny said.

Sandy's legs spasmed, rippling the sheet. "God*damn*." Her hair was bunching up around her head and Mary Lynn methodically straightened it.

A firm knock came at the door. Tapes.

I held up my gloved hands which I'd taken pains to keep from touching anything other than Sandra Dee Kowalski.

Angie went to the door and opened it a slice.

"Shortpants, it's for you."

"Shortcut," I corrected. At least I was taller than Michael J. Fox and maybe Tom Cruise.

She held the door open and I walked out, hands elevated like you see on television.

Tapes was wet around the edges; he'd been outside, but in his foul weather gear.

"Thought you ought to know," he said, glancing up and down the corridor. He spoke softly and the thick floor mat or rug or whatever the hell they called it in 1920 absorbed much of the sound.

"Damndamndamndamn!" came through the cracked door.

"Close?" he asked.

I shrugged. "That's what I'm telling her. It could take a couple more hours. This is her first."

"You need any help?"

"Nope—got too much already. Maybe you could figger out a ruse to get Angie Maple out of there?"

He shook his head. "I ain't getting involved in your love life—"

"What should I ought to know?" I asked, irritated. If your best friend since childhood refuses to help you, what are you going to do?

"I had a look through the windows of several vans before I found the right one."

"I bet Deacon didn't like that."

"Not a bit. But Deacon can't work a door handle."

Tapes would've killed the dog had it attacked.

"And?" I prompted again.

Tapes pulled out his tin of Copenhagen, opened it, touched a wet finger to the tobacco, and put that little taste onto his tongue. He sighed.

"That kid in there's going to be in first grade before you get out with it," I said.

"The weather's bad and they got that dark tint on the windows." He moved his tongue around in his closed mouth contentedly for a minute.

"You could look through the front windshield," I said.

"Highbacked seats. But I did. Shortcut, there's something weird. I saw a couple of gator hides. And there are big containers along the sides of the van. I leaned against the outside and about froze my arm off."

"Ice?"

"Probably. Could be dry ice, I don't know."

"Why?" I wondered aloud.

"Beats me, but it could be poaching." He dipped into the pocket of his jeans under the parka and took out a little six-foot tape measure made in Taiwan. He dragged about eighteen inches worth of steel out and let it retract back of its own accord, smacking eerily in the empty corridor.

The idea had leapt immediately into my mind too.

"Damndamndamnohshit!"

Mary Lynn's worried face appeared at the door. "Billy?"

"Be right in," I said, suddenly self-conscious.

"Billy? Billy?" Tapes said, eyebrows raised. Nobody calls me Billy. Except women when I fall in love.

"Don't start," I warned.

Mary Lynn had disappeared back inside.

"Don't me start? Come on, Shortcut. You fall in love so fast and so complicatedly that—"

"You're going to tell me I'm on the rebound from Becky—"

"Rebecca," he corrected automatically, then realized, "I mean Becky. Hell, I forget what it's supposed to be."

"Forget the whole thing. I ain't on the rebound. It's just that me and Mary Lynn are kind of alike what with our same similar circumstance and all—"

Tapes groaned and drew the tape measure as far as it would go and released it. The damn thing snickered and crinkled for a second as it wound in.

"We're becoming special friends," I said defensively.

"DamndamndamndamnJesuspizzus!"

"Billy!" an imperative from Mary Lynn, but I knew Sandy had a while yet.

I looked at my gloved hands held in front of me and noticed they were kind of gunky. Well, I still had a dozen more inside. "Got to go." Then I stopped and turned. "Remember that other freezer that Silas Smith didn't want us to put Henry B. in?"

"I'll go make me a sandwich," Tapes nodded, pocketing the tape measure. "Want anything?"

"Nah. I'll be busy for a while. Besides, it ain't polite to eat in front of sick women."

When I got back inside, I washed up again and pulled on another pair of gloves.

"It's about time," said Angie Maple.

"You ever have any children?" I asked the old lady.

"Nope." She looked at me warily.

I shook my head. "Then don't be so goddamn sure of yourself."

"Well!"

I shook my head again. "A room full of women and not one knows anything about childbirth."

"Damndamndamndamnsonofabitch!"

"That's right," I said, "push, slow and steady. Control your breathing." I glanced at the wall across the room. "You need a focal point. See that picture of a sailboat?" Framed, short waves, some spray, blue background, the obligatory scuttling clouds.

"Nonononono, not that—"

"Whatever turns you on, Sandy. How about—"

"Sandra Dee," said Angle Maple.

"—that old tapestry on the wall, that crossed thing in the middle?"

"Finefinefinefine, it hurts like bees." Her eyes were as green as Vermont and as wide as Texas.

"Then push at the right time." It would still be a while. Her dilation was coming along, but not quite finished.

"I'mumah trying."

"Your husband is going to be surprised," I said, positioning a few clean towels.

The immediate and freezing silence told me I'd stuck my foot in my mouth. Was he dead?

Mary Lynn's face was serious. "Sandra Dee doesn't have a husband."

"Oh. Ah. Um. Forgive the intrusion, Sandy."

She was breathing shallowly as if in fear of another contraction. "It's okay, Shortcut. You didn't know damndamn. Obviously God is a man."

"Why do you say that?" I asked.

"If He were a woman, women wouldn't have to go through this shit, damndamndamn."

She had a legitimate point.

Her face scrunched up in pure pain and I wished I had some kind of anesthetic for her. "Who'd want to kill Henry B.?" I asked.

"Not me," said Angie Maple.

"Darn," I said.

"What's that mean?" Angie said, suspicious.

"DAMN!DAMN!DAMN!DAMN!"

"Push harder," I said, ignoring the old lady.

Sandy's tummy rippled and I lifted the sheet to top of her stomach.

"Is it time?" asked Mary Lynn.

"Close," I said, checking and adjusting Sandy's legs wider. "Each of you help hold one leg apart." I knelt at the foot of the bed. "This here is what you call your second stage of giving birth." Sandy's perineum was bulging out. "Sandy, right now your pelvic muscles are rotating the baby's head so that her chin is pointing down for the classic delivery position." I so fervently hoped. If not, Sandy and I were in trouble.

"This cowboy knows some big words," said Angie tugging on Sandra Dee's left knee.

"I got a GED." I paused, thought and to lighten up things,

said, "Alexander was talking about Callisthenes when he said, 'That vain pretense to wisdom I detest/Where a man's blind to his own interest.'"

Mary Lynn's blue eye stabbed me with curiosity.

Angie said, "What's *that* supposed to mean?"

"Never mind." I wondered if I wasn't trying to show off in front of Mary Lynn to disguise the fact I had only a GED. Oh, Shortcut, thy vanity is education.

Mary Lynn was looking at me. "Do you know it's a girl?"

"Nope. It just figures that a boy would have been on time and not made us all wait."

"That's sexist," accused Angie.

"That's funny," said Mary Lynn.

"Damndamndamnitall!"

"Keep pushing at the right time," I said.

"I am, goddamnit. You want to switch places?"

I drew back dramatically. "Not me." To divert her, I said, "how'd you come by the name Sandra Dee?"

"Her mother," said Angie.

"I didn't ask you."

Angie glared at me.

"My mom," said Sandra Dee. "She was a child of the sixties."

"I guess it's better than Elvisaria."

"Sexist, *and* insulting," said Angie.

"Diverting," said Mary Lynn.

I spared Mary Lynn one eye and gave her an imperceptive nod. I could like this woman a lot.

The kid's head was beginning to show. The perineal tissues were really stretched, I mean stretched.

"Keep 'em wide," I directed.

"Goddamngoddamngoddamngoddamn...."

"I think I'd like your mom," I said. I was still kneeling on the floor and we all scooted Sandy toward me a few inches.

The head stopped moving and I began to panic. The head had not yet emerged, but simply showed a clump of matted hair and gunk.

I started running my fingers around the opening, edging skin and tissue aside. I'd read sometimes the tissue tears of necessity. If the kid didn't recommence his trip, I hoped that would happen automatically because I sure as hell didn't know how to cut the tissue, nor was I prepared to do so.

Sandy was breathing rapidly now, retching a bit. Mary Lynn wiped saliva off her mouth. "Mom loved movies and movie stars oh God I feel like they're wrenching my guts out and she had me after a movie and that's why she named me ohChrist my guts are ripping out like in that movie *Alien* when the monster jumps out of a guy's guts into Sigourney Weaver's face and ohshitGodhelpme—"

Her stomach actually vibrated and her head jerked up and down and her harsh breathing whistled through her mouth and nose angrily and her feet tattooed the edge of the bed and I had an empathy attack.

I put command into my voice, "Control your breathing and push synchronously." Was the word "synchronistically" instead? Granny gave me that odd look again. "Her head's coming out," I said, relief evident in my voice. When the weight of the world comes off my shoulders, ofttimes I become verbose. "As her head comes out, it will turn back to realign itself with the rest of her body."

"Didactic is an understatement," said Angie.

"Yet I avoid moral self-righteousness." That ought to shut her up. I didn't want to argue with her and this was distracting me.

My hands were edging and tugging and pushing and helping and the head was emerging and I was trying to help it go back to the right position all the while making the exit easier and get this damn thing over with.

"You're doing this like a pro, Sandy."

"Damndamndamn." Her voice was much weaker. "I like the way you say 'Sandy,' Billy."

"All delivering mothers fall in love with their obstertricicans."

"Or whatever," said Angie.

"Pushpushpush," I said.

"Ihurtohsomuch." Sandy was leaking sweat.

"It'll all be over soon."

"Come on, Sandra Dee, you can do it," said Mary Lynn. "Follow my lead." Mary Lynn began to breathe in and out in an exaggerated fashion, pausing to push at the right moment. She was a quick learner.

My hands continued to fly and the damn lights went out.

Oh, shit, I thought.

"Oh, shit," said Mary Lynn.

"OhmyGodohmyGodohmyGodohmyGod."

Angie acted swiftly and soon two flashlight beams pierced the dark. I might not be prepared for in-depth surgery, but the 7-P principle came to my aid. I'd been prepared for power failure.

"No problem," I said calmly. "We don't need power anyway." The kid's whole head was emerging. "Thanks, Miss Maple."

"Mizz."

"Whatever. Sandy, your daughter's head is turning back into the correct position regarding the rest of her body."

Angie snorted. "You can add pedagogic to didactic."

"Irregardless of that—" I began.

"Humpf," said Angie.

"Okay, disregardless—"

"SHE'S COMING DAMNDAMNDAMNDAMN."

"Just like in the textbooks," I continued. "One shoulder at a time within the next few contractions."

Great gusts of wind buffeted the building and windows blew out and gables rattled, whatever the hell a gable is. The flashlights wavered in Angie's hands.

Again, we all held our collective breath—except Sandy.

"You can name your daughter Storm," I said.

"Damndamnda...." Her voice was weary and weak and I could feel her body wanting to give up.

"Just another minute, hon, hang in there." I put as much confidence as I could into my words.

Her body rippled again and the kid *surged* out into my scrambling hands.

"OhJesusGoddamn."

"Yeah, me, too, Sandy. The kid's out." Just in time, for I believed that Sandy was becoming too weak to help and that wouldn't have helped a bit.

The most important thing is to get the infant to breathing. I was holding her half upside down and cleaning gunk out of her mouth.

Nothing.

In the light of the flashlights, I couldn't tell if the kid were turning blue or not but I sure as hell imagined it to be so.

The room was stifling; with the power off, the great paddle fan wasn't turning and all four of us were sweating like we were on a death march and the kid still wasn't breathing.

"Angie! The basting bulb. Now." Tried to keep my voice calm.

The lights jiggled and the beams slewed aside.

Slap, and the basting bulb was in my held-up hand and I stuck it in the baby's mouth not very delicately and pumped and withdrew it and stuck it back in and pumped and withdrew it and repeated and the kid was breathing like she'd been doing so for years.

"Nothing to it when you know how." My voice was lame.

"They were right," said Angie. "You are quick."

"Not in everything," I said absently and looked at Mary Lynn who was bending over in the pale light to check the kid.

Mary Lynn turned her head and stared at me, her special bold look again, shook her head, and looked at the kid again.

I felt like I'd been through a war. My hands were not shaking—yet.

I was still holding the baby but turning her around for Mary Lynn.

"It's a girl, Sandra Dee, you've a daughter." Mary Lynn's voice was light, just the right touch.

"I told you so," I said unnecessarily.

"And she has ten of everything," Mary Lynn went on.

"Thank God," whispered Sandy. She was so weak I knew we'd just made it.

Near the kid's tummy, I snapped a number 2 Hunt clip onto the kid's umbilical. We'd got several of the strong metal clamps from the front desk. Mary Lynn had boiled them in the kitchen.

Then I put the kid on Sandy's stomach. "For warmth and bonding," I said.

I thought Sandy cooed, but it could've been an exhausted sigh.

"We've got maybe ten minutes," I began and my hands started shaking and mercifully Angie moved the light away from us all.

Mary Lynn must've sensed my reaction, for she started talking.

"You wonder who killed Henry? Check with cuckolded husbands. He's wealthy, very much so. Or I should say, was wealthy. A womanizer on the grandest scale."

"A charmer, Henry was," agreed Angie, still holding the two flashlights aimlessly pointed at the floor. "One who leaves lives shattered in his wake." There was a story behind Angie's words.

I should be working, but the reaction was still pulsing through me, the shakes still assaulting me.

"He had it all," Mary Lynn went on. "Wealth. Looks. Intelligence. Olde local family, don't you know? Political power. National image."

"If you spend too much time polishing your image, you'll tarnish your character," I said.

In the splash of light, Mary Lynn favored me with her brown eye.

"He had his health, too," said Angie, "and I suspect he was very happy with himself."

"He had to be," said Mary Lynn. Her voice turned a bit angry. "You have to be somewhat amoral to be a good politician; so, hurting women wouldn't bother him. Using women didn't bother him. I doubt much of anything bothered him."

I was now controlling my breathing. The reaction was

passing. "A tennis racquet bothered him to death."

"I believe he died from the fall," Angie said, returning the flashlights to the proper position.

It was stifling in here and suddenly this wing of the building shook under a heavy gust and a window somewhere blew out and wind screeched down the corridor and sucked the stifling out the opened transom and the cool breeze made me feel better until someone slammed a door and the breeze died.

"How is it in there?" came a distinct Florida cracker voice. The lieutenant governor.

"Fine. The baby is doing well." Angle's voice was relieved, too.

"Let us know if you need anything."

Angie didn't answer.

I cut the umbilical with a boiled sharp kitchen knife near the office clamp.

I breathed deeply. We weren't out of the woods yet. "The third stage of labor takes up to ten minutes."

It didn't. It happened right then.

"Goddamngoddamngoddamnnotagain!" Voice very weak. I don't know how women take it, and Sandy was having a difficult time. But she'd live through it.

"Placenta, Sandy. Push a little. This is natural." The mess came right out in my hands. Soon, I had it wrapped in a towel and dumped into a plastic garbage bag. Talk about your maggot gaggers.

Wishing for real lights, I made do with the flashlights. This was critical. While I had several needles ready and threaded, I knew zilch about sewing up vaginal bleeding. I cleaned as well as I could—

"Sandy?" my voice demanded her attention.

"Billy?"

"Relax, hon. Breathe evenly. Think about your daughter, not your pain. Relax."

Mary Lynn and Angie had caught my urgency.

"Another clean cloth," I said quickly and Angie supplied one.

I mopped around, Angie moving the lights over my shoulders as I shifted position to keep the light on.

Mary Lynn hiccupped and wiped Sandy's brow with a cool wet cloth and spoke softly to her.

I wasn't sure what the hell was going on. Something I'd read—and I read a great deal. The uterus has to contract properly or blood—

I held the cloth on the source tightly for two long minutes.

Sandy perceptively relaxed and the trickle of blood which had me in a panic stopped. Carefully, I removed the cloth and the bleeding did not recommence.

Then I cleaned Sandy and Mary Lynn cleaned the baby.

When I finished, I went into the bathroom, thought about vomiting, but didn't. I peeled off the gory gloves and washed up to my armpits in the old fashioned shower.

When I left the bathroom, I went straight to the dresser at the side of the room. There was enough splashover from the flashlights to enable me to find what I was looking for.

The 7-P Principle in operation again. A liter of Jim Beam from the bar. Even though I don't do metrics, I made an exception.

I upended the bottle and gurgled happily for a moment.

"Ahem." The voice startled me.

Mary Lynn reached out and took the bottle from my hands. She did not upend the bottle and gurgle. But she did take two healthy slugs of the amber liquid before she returned the bottle to me. Her hiccups were gone.

A pounding came at the door.

"Hello in there." The lit gov.

Angie opened the door and explained that it was over.

"Good," said John Dellum Ionata. "Mr. Birthday, would you step out here for a minute?"

Angie stood aside, her flashlights swinging awkwardly, and I walked out still holding the bottle of bourbon.

The corridor was lighted by a gas lamp Silas Smith was holding. The tall geek and the short geek were standing to the side.

Tapes was standing in front of them with his arms crossed. He was livid. I didn't need ESP to pick up the emanating danger signals from him.

"Mr. Birthday," Ionata began, "you have the right to remain silent, you have the right to—"

"Tapes, what the hell is going on?"

Ionata said quietly, "You both are being placed under arrest for suspicion of murder of Governor Henry B. Gonzáles."

I drank quickly from the bottle. "Just washing a bad taste from my mouth. Ionata, you take dislike a long way."

"You also have the right to an attorney present—"

"You aren't a cop," I pointed out. "You can't arrest or charge anybody."

His Florida-cane voice was assured. "I am constitutionally sworn to uphold the law. I am de facto governor. The governor is in direct chain of command of the state law enforcement agencies, including the Highway Patrol." He said highway patrol as "ha-way pee-troll." "Which gives me all the authority I need."

Angie applauded awkwardly, flashlight beams swinging. "Very good, John."

"You'd best back off, *Mrs.* Maple, lest you be stung by my words." The vehemence in my voice caused her to step back.

I was tired and shaken by tending to Sandra Dee Kowalski and child. For once, I was out of words.

6: MONDAY, 7:00 P.M.

"You're full of it, Shortcut," Tapes said angrily.

My steak was searing on the gas grill and I was sautéing mushrooms. "Nah. The hot oil seals in the moisture."

"Slow cooking is best," he repeated. "The flavor is a hell of a lot better because much of the water's gone." He meant the mushroom taste was stronger.

"Fast cooked mushrooms are crunchy and chewy," I pointed out. "Not soft and mushy."

"Richer flavor," he said eyeing me with disdain.

I tipped the Jim Beam bottle over my fresh glass of shaved ice until it spilled over the rim. I sipped it until the overflow was gone. "Too bad you don't know what the hell you're talking about—"

"Olde Worlde cuisine," he replied, "versus that California nouveau—"

"*I'm* the one does most of the cooking anyway." I gulped another slug of iced Beam. "Ah."

The oil was smoking in the frying pan and Tapes watched the smoke boil off. "Most of the burning, you mean."

"Oops." Inspiration struck and I dumped the rest of the iced Beam into the frying pan. It didn't catch fire, but the oil and ice damn near exploded and steam came off like Hiroshima. The crackle sounded like a forest fire. I hit the switch on the hood and the exhaust grabbed the cloud and sucked it out.

Tapes shook his head and stormed out. The back of his T-shirt read, READ A BOOK, NOT A SHIRT. He wasn't gonna eat anyway. I had to, for I sorely needed something to absorb the bourbon. I needed refueling, what with all the psychic energy I'd just burned delivering the kid.

Another burning smell grabbed my attention. Over at the gas grill where the JG Inn cooked their steaks, more smoke was boiling off.

"Damn." I hurried over and flipped the steak. The flames had burned the bottom black. "Screw it," I said and went back to get a refill of Beam.

The kitchen was big and interesting and old and, at the same time, modern. Butcher block tables, lots of counter space, pans hanging rustically from hooks and organized by size and type. Stoves, ovens, gas grills, sinks, dishwashers, shelves, cypress cabinets. In the back, a great room-sized pantry. On the other side near the rear exit was a short hall off of which sat several walk-in coolers and freezers—one of which was currently the residing place of the late Henry B.

I'd avoided that cooler and found the meat locker. The chef's proclivity for organization continued. I grabbed what was probably a boneless sirloin wrapped in freezer wrap and brought it into the kitchen. Not paying much attention, I fired the gas grill and had a drink and then unwrapped the steak and tossed it on.

Now Tapes was gone and I was more than half drunk and the mushrooms were burnt and I needed another drink while my steak seared on the other side.

I dug my tumbler into the ice machine and filled it up with Jim Beam. The generator was back on, saving the ice.

I'd managed to maintain my control while attending to Sandra Dee's delivery; but now the reaction was setting in. My hands were no longer shaking, having to do with the Jim Beam, I'm sure. Anything could have gone wrong and Sandy and the kid could well be nearby now, right next to Henry B., laid out like a family, Poppa Bear, Momma Bear, and Baby Bear; would that have shook up Goldilocks or what?

Another drink and my head was disoriented for it felt like the building was shaking off its foundation. I looked at a shuttered window trembling against nature's onslaught. Maybe the building was shaking off its foundations.

My steak was burning on the other side but I didn't care. Good thing Tapes had fixed the generator out back. He'd be out of dry clothes soon, though he did have maybe a thousand T-shirts.

Another drink and I didn't know whether I was afoot or on horseback.

Rummaging around, I found a stack of clean plates, took one, and dumped the bourbon-sizzled mushrooms thereupon.

I cracked a couple of eggs into the frying pan. Steak and eggs, one of my favorites. And to my now jaundiced eyes, not being of uniform size and color I was used to, they looked like fresh eggs.

Juggling the glass of bourbon and the plate, I flipped the steak once more for luck. While I hadn't used any spice, it could pass for Cajun-blackened now. I decided I needed something green. I put the plate and booze down and dug into a large stand up cooler.

"Ah." Fresh spinach, right next to the fresh mushrooms. I wasn't sure whether it was washed or not but I dumped it on a plate anyway.

"Hello, Billy," came a throaty voice. Mary Lynn walked in.

I gave her my best smile and had a sip of my drink. Time to get on my best behavior. "Hi," I said creatively.

Something in my voice caught her attention and she looked closely at me. "What's wrong?"

"I burned my steak. Creatures are people of habit, too. Or is it 'Habits are creatures of people, too?'"

"It's that way, is it?" She leaned against a counter and crossed her arms.

I started to say something, and then I decided I wasn't going to defend myself. It'd only make things worse.

"You were very, very good with Sandra Dee," Mary Lynn said.

"Yeah." The eggs were smoking. I killed the burner.

"Tapes tells me you're like ice in a crisis."

"Tapes talks a lot." He doesn't really. I dumped the eggs onto the steak and they seemed to bounce.

"He told me about one time when you were in Laos—"

"The Plain of Jars—"

"You fixed an oil line using a brake line on an airplane—"

"C-47, AKA the Gooney Bird or DC-3."

"And just in time because the whole communist army was coming—"

"Pathet Lao guerrillas, mean sonofabitches—"

"And held them off with M-16s while the pilot took off—"

"CIA pilot, almost burned out the battery whining for help—"

She shook her head, pony tail flapping around entrancingly.

I found an industrial sized container of bacon bits and dumped a ton on my spinach, couldn't find any already hardboiled eggs so a half-dozen dollops of crunchy peanut butter would have to suffice. Which was okay because the peanut butter helped the tomato cubes stick to the top of the spinach and not slide right off.

"And everybody's heard of the incident at the rest stop," she continued, her eyes searching mine. Or was that my bourbon induced imagination?

Me and Tapes had interrupted some bad guys gonna rape and plunder and murder some people they were holding in a women's restroom and took 'em down. Only one of them walked away. We'd declined the publicity and the papers had kept our names out of it. How come Tapes was all of a sudden building me up to Mary Lynn? He'd been against her before. Did he recognize I'd need something, someone if I went into one of my reaction-funks? Jeez, if I got any deeper I'd—

"I wonder who killed the governor?" I said, hunting for a fork.

"It wasn't me," said Mary Lynn.

"I didn't mean to infer it was. Or is it imply?" I sipped my drink. "Want a drink?"

She shook her head. "Who do you think did it?"

"It wasn't me," I said.

"I never thought so," she said, "regardless of what John Ionata says."

"Ionata's crazy. Why's he got me and Tapes on house arrest? This sounds like teevee."

"He's afraid you'll run out."

"In a hurricane, on an isolated island, with nowhere to go?"

Mary Lynn made a face. "You two are as likely suspects as anyone."

"'Round up the usual suspects,' said Claude Rains." I looked at my plate.

"*Casablanca*, I love that movie." She eyed my plate. "I'm not supporting John Ionata, but just about everyone else here is familiar and...well, he thought that since almost all the people here except you two knew Henry B., that they'd have much better opportunities to murder him." She shivered. "I still can't believe he's dead."

I was busy thinking. "Knowing Ionata only a little, I suspect he wants to show immediate and strong leadership to enhance himself when he ascends to the governor's office."

"A case could be made for Orlo and his friends. But Silas Smith spoke for them." She eyed my plate again. Pretty soon I was going to have to eat.

"The three stooges? Something's weird there, I agree. Tapes thinks they're poachers or selling illegal fish like redfish. Not being from Florida for very long, I'm not sure I understand all I know about that."

While I assembled my meal she explained.

"Redfish almost became extinct years ago. They are tasty and the blackened-redfish craze accounted for the depletion. The current rules allow no commercial fishing, and only one redfish per-day limit for private fishermen. There are size limitations, and you can't fish for them from March to May. There are big fines and jail time for repeat offenders."

We were standing on opposite sides of a butcher-block table and I cut into my steak and ate a bite. I'd burned it badly, me who thinks rare is too done. Have another drink, Shortcut, I told myself.

"So Orlo and company are selling illegal redfish to the chef here?" I asked.

She shrugged. "Beats me. It's possible. But is that a motive for murder?"

I speared a mushroom which had been cooked to almost nothing.

Mary Lynn watched with interest.

"Mushrooms don't burn easily because of all the water in 'em," I said unnecessarily. I tasted the mushroom and the flavor of burned butter invaded my mouth. I nailed a chunk of steak and dragged it through some of the peanut butter on the spinach salad and that tasted a whole lot better. Maybe the meat had been in a cooler with fish and absorbed that flavor.

"If you say so," she said.

I resisted the urge to have another drink. "How about the old lady?"

"I've known Angie Maple for years."

That was all she said, leaving something unsaid. "She's nosey, cranky, and gets on my nerves," I pointed out.

"I noticed," said Mary Lynn. "She's cranky because she's a vegetarian. She has a fetish for broccoflower—"

"Say again?"

"Broccoflower. Half broccoli and half cauliflower. She grows it in her backyard. But it makes her flatulent—"

"It figgers."

"A Dutch seed company developed it."

"It's got to taste better with peanut butter on it," I said, "especially crunchy."

"Angie's set in her ways. You just have to get used to her."

"Not me." Another bite of steak. I shouldn't have drank—drunk?—so much, for it didn't taste like a sirloin. Of course, I'd burned the hell out of it. Peanut butter helped it, so I spread a thin layer over the steak, pushing the eggs aside.

Mary Lynn unconsciously tore a piece of spinach loose from

my salad and munched on it while watching me wide-eyed.

"And the lieutenant governor," I said. "He becomes governor."

"The motive's too obvious," she said, eying my steak.

"Well, he's formally arrested me and Tapes for murder. He well could be trying to divert attention."

"That was neither a wise nor an appropriate move," she agreed.

Still feeling the booze, I said, "No statesman he, no disciple of Solon the Lawgiver. Solon was supposed to be a humanist in his ideas and thoughts. And he was supposed to be a wise man—even though he did write poetry. Too bad wisdom is no longer required to be a politician." I needed to sober up before I made a complete fool of myself.

"Poetry?" Mary Lynn asked.

"Great men can be forgiven many things," I said. "Only about 250 lines of Solon's poetry remain. They ought to make this a limit for all poets. Pick your best 250 lines and that's it."

"You're not fond of poetry."

"As fond as a mongoose is of a cobra, Pepsi of Coke, Ford of—"

"I get your point." She held up her hand.

I chopped off a slice of steak, stuck my fork into it, and held it out to her. She leaned forward and took it in her mouth, an oddly intimate gesture.

"Sorry it ain't rare," I said. "Actually, prime rib red is one of my favorite colors."

"What're your other favorite colors?" She was chewing on the steak appearing to roll it around in her mouth. "Not even peanut butter can save this meat."

"Red, white, and blue. U.S. Treasury mint green. Jack Daniels black."

She swallowed. "I can do that, too. How about Johnny Walker Red, sterling silver, key lime, sparkling diamond, powder blue?"

"On you, I can imagine powder blue with lots of lace," I said, emboldened by the drink past my natural modesty.

For a long moment she stood frozen looking at me. Slowly

she said, "I will take that as a compliment Billy; I choose not to regard your comment as salacious."

I knew I was coloring, like a celery stalk in a kid's science experiment. "You'd be right," I stammered, all the while wondering at her strange choice of words. But I wasn't gonna apologize. I turned and dumped the rest of my drink into a nearby sink. Fortunately for my reputation, it was practically empty. "Sometimes afterwards," I said carefully, "a great and strong reaction overwhelms me. It's a combination of 'What if's?' and the shakes—"

"But you did what had to be done first." She was avoiding my eyes, for I'd bared my soul and she didn't know how to respond.

"Tapes, he's the one made of steel. Why, he can nail Jell-O to the wall and freeze it there with one look—"

"Tapes is nice," she said, now locking onto my eyes. "But we're talking about you."

"What is this? A counseling session?" I ate a big chunk of steak and eggs and followed with a forkful of uncut and floppy spinach, bacon bits falling like dandruff,

"It is not," she said crossly, leaning over the table, straining at her chamois leather blouse. She stopped when her face was ten inches in front of mine. "You done good and saved a friend of mine. I came to express my appreciation. I liked you since I first saw you, even if you do appear to hide your inner feelings with a weird kind of flippancy—"

"Humor and wit," I said.

"—and interrupt everybody half the time. But your actions speak louder than your words, Billy Birthday. I saw how you rescued Trooper in the saloon from Orlo? I saw you take charge when Henry B. died. And I saw the fear in your eyes through the sweat when you delivered Sandra Dee's baby." She took a deep breath. "You try to cover your actions with words, Billy. I want to find the real you."

I didn't know what to say, so I said it anyway. "That was almost professional."

"Don't say it, Billy. Don't say anymore." She leaned back.

She didn't want to think about something. I assumed it was her failed marriage. She took my empty glass and poured some Jim Beam into it and drank it neat.

"I won't if you won't," I said.

"What?"

"Say it. Say anything to ruin our relationship."

"What relationship?" Her voice was suspicious. "Don't assume something that isn't there."

"Never mind," I said.

I ate and she drank.

In twenty minutes, she was tipsy and I was full. Mary Lynn had eaten half my spinach peanut butter salad and part of my steak and eggs.

"I like your tailor," I said.

She looked down and colored a bit. "I was afraid I'd drink too much and not be able to drive so I brought a change of clothes."

As I dumped the dishes into the garbage—it seemed to my askewed mind a waste to wash them—I said, "It could be Silas Smith who done it. Do you know him?"

"As a passing acquaintance," she said, now sipping on the remnants of the Jim Beam. "He's managed the José Gaspar Inn for a few years now."

"He could have been cooking the books and the governor discovered it."

She thought for a moment. "That's possible. Anything's possible. But, but...all these are possibilities, not major reasons to kill someone, and on top of that, risk the electric chair. Well, nowadays an injection or three."

"That's true," I said. "We don't know enough. For instance, Orlo could be a repeat offender and any felony could send him to hard time for a long time."

"Why is it *you* care?" she asked suddenly. "I mean, what's it to you? You're not from around here—"

"Texas originally and Arizona now."

"You don't know these people. Most of who are sitting in their rooms not contributing while you are helping out, doing everything. Why? What is Henry B.'s death to you?"

"We talked about the weather and he said something about 'rapidly dissipating'."

Mary Lynn Messenger looked at me as if I were crazy.

"We connected on a level different from the norm, and right away, too. He liked three-named names. Me, too." I paused. "There's Mary Lynn Messenger, for instance. And Sandra Dee Kowalski."

"And John Dellum Ionata?" she said.

I shrugged. "Every rule has exceptions. Me and Henry B. got along." Henry B. had kind of liked a cowboy quoting Plutarch.

"You aren't telling me everything," she said.

Was I not sober enough to hide my feelings? Not to mention that she was prying. "You're prying," I accused.

"It's my nature," she shot back.

"Got it," I snapped my fingers. "You *are* a professional. You're a counselor or a shrink—"

"What are *you* hiding from me?" she said. "I don't believe it has to do with Henry B.'s murder."

"No it don't. He was just nice to me when he could've been uppity." I needed to sober up bad. "I hate elitism, intellectual arrogance worse than anything except maybe murder, rape, and plagiarism. Pillage and plunder comes way after. Gonzáles had the opportunity and office in life to stick up his nose at me and Tapes, but he didn't; he seemed like a regular guy." I tried to pout but blew it. "So there. Now you know." I felt drained. But I'd clouded the issue enough I didn't have to fess up about Becky.

She was silent for a minute. Then she cocked her attractive blue eye at me. "You know? That's the strangest thing I've ever heard in my life. Knowing you now, it has to be true." She paused and drank. "Some people march to a different drummer. You march to a different band."

I shrugged, not sure about this. Maybe I'd exposed too much about myself. When I do that, I become vulnerable; and since Rebecca's defection, I didn't want to be vulnerable more than I didn't want a lot of other things. I think I understand what I just said.

Mary Lynn had been very perceptive. Perhaps she was a soul mate. I took a shot. "What's *your* secret?"

Startled, she stared at me. Then she finished her drink and sighed. "Sister Mary Lynn. I was a nun until my husband to be swept me off my feet and I quit the order and married him. He was a carpenter, very well built, a Tom Selleck mustache, and a way with words. For ten years I told myself I hadn't made a mistake and given up my vows when I shouldn't have. Then he woos somebody ten years younger than I am and he's gone and I'm all alone, without the Church, and probably better off without my husband. Make that ex-husband."

Empathy flowed like wine for a few moments in time.

"With nowhere to go," I said softly.

She was fighting tears and won. She nodded so she didn't have to speak.

"I suspect down deep you realize you're better off without the sonofabitch," I said.

She shrugged and went over and got the dishes out of the big can and rinsed them and placed them on the sideboard.

Women such as Mary Lynn should not be wasted on men who do not appreciate them.

I scraped out the burned mushrooms from the pan and washed it, standing alongside Mary Lynn.

She started a Mr. Coffee. While I don't usually drink coffee, I could this day. The hotel continued to shake under strong, killer winds and I wondered if the building would outlast the storm.

"*Who* are you?" Mary Lynn asked.

We both were leaning against a counter watching coffee drip into the pot.

"Billy Birthday."

"Who is Tapes?"

"Wallace Francis Fidgle."

"What is it with you two?"

I shrugged. My shoulders were going to hurt tomorrow from

all this shrugging. "We grew up together."

"Tell me more."

"Me and Tapes. We grew up in West Texas. Maverick County. El Paso County. We were friends. Momma, God rest her soul, loved Tapes. She and him shared a penchant for advanced math. Momma worked for the paymaster at Fort Bliss in El Paso. When Tapes' father, who is an inveterate gambler, left after Tapes' mom passed away, why Momma just took him in and we been like brothers ever since. We lived in San Antonio when we were in high school. We quit in the middle of our senior year and joined the Air Farce." I didn't tell Mary Lynn it was on accounta a girl and I quit and joined up and Tapes followed because I needed someone to watch over me and besides we did everything together, didn't we?

"You're well educated regardless," Mary Lynn said.

"You patronizing me?"

"'Penchant?' And 'inveterate?' And Solon and Plutarch."

Me and my big mouth. "Well, I got a GED in the service," I said. "Anyway, me and Tapes buddy-systemed through boot camp right across town at Lackland Air Force Base and tech school up at Wichita Falls, just south of the Oklahoma line, thank God. The buddy-system assured us of the first assignment together, which was in the Philippines." I filled the booze glass with water and thought of a couple of girls in the PI. "We worked on Deuces—F-102s."

"After that?"

"F-4s, in Da Nang."

"Together?"

"Sure. Air Force personnel system. If you volunteered for the mystic shores of Southeast Asia, you got your choice of assignments. So we could stay together. We then went to Takhli Royal Thai Air Force Base, near a town named Tak Raheang in western Thailand on the road to Chaing Mai. I was a crew chief on F-105s, Tapes a crew chief on them ear-splittin' EB-66s, which were electronics countermeasures aircraft. Then our four years expired. What's the difference between the Air Force and the Boy Scouts?"

She shook her head not sure what I was leading to.

"The Boy Scouts have adult leadership. Then we worked for the CIA as crew chiefs for a while, and that's where that story about the Plain of Jars came from. We came back to the land of the big BX and worked for Braniff at DFW on the night shift parking 727s and stuff and Braniff went belly up for the first time so we returned to what we knew best in Uvalde: poking, punching, nudging, pampering, everythinging cows—back to our roots, what we done as kids; if you can, with finesse, brand a steer's ear, put a ring in a cow's nose, or trim a bull's horns, you got a job in West Texas anytime—"

"You can stop and breathe whenever you want."

"Well, you got me started—"

"Go on," she prompted me back to the subject.

"Then we moved to Tucson," I went on, not mentioning the fact that a girl had broke my heart and I'd decided to run away again and Tapes had obligingly went along. "We had jobs as civilians for the USAF mothballing aircraft at their so-called 'Graveyard' over at Davis-Monthan Air Force Base. Tapes still works there."

"Angie Maple said you were unemployed."

"I am, and ain't drawing unemployment either. It's a principle with me."

"Orlo says you and Tapes are gay."

I could imagine what Orlo had said, and was saying. For some reason, he was agitating. "Orlo can say whatever he wants. We never had time to be gay. In West Texas it's said that if Custer had Shortcut and Tapes, he'd of been alive and president instead of bald and dead. If Bob Lee had Shortcut and Tapes, grits'd be the national food and Grant's Tomb would've been occupied years sooner. If Colonel Travis had us at the Alamo, then Santa Anna would be taking a dirt nap instead of Crockett and Bowie and the rest."

"Why'd you and Tapes, after all those years, wind up apart?"

"Um, ah, lemme see." It was on accounta women, of course.

Tapes was in love with Kelly in Tucson and I had fallen for Rebecca in Tallahassee. "I, uh, got an interesting job offer in Tallahassee," I said convincingly. "I was assistant supervisor of the Junior Museum, which was part zoo, part museum, part historical showplace. But, um, I got sort of tired of ordering panther feed and assigning guys to fix the wire cage of the aviary, so when Tapes came to visit I quit and we decided to drive the circumference of Florida and visit all the lighthouses before we went back to Tucson...." I rushed the last words to cover my embarrassment regarding Rebecca and our recent split.

All of which made me feel more vulnerable.

"Lighthouses. It fits." Her voice was back to soft and throaty.

Mary Lynn must have sensed my vulnerability, for she linked her arm in mine. She was my height and our eyes locked.

"Oh, no," I said.

"Oh, no," she said.

Through our attached arms, I felt her body tremble.

I was suddenly sober.

My whole body went as rigid as a priest's collar.

And the damn power failed again and it was dark in the kitchen and quiet as a candle until the sounds of locomotives crushing winds before them intruded and she melted against me and my body lost its rigidity and molded against her.

My face felt as if on fire, hers was cool and oh so smooth and I wanted to rub cheeks forever had not the urgency of her lips and body drawn me to her like a moth to a flame.

7: MONDAY, 10:00 P.M.

Mary Lynn Messenger was the kind of girl Conway Twitty sang about.

The generator came back on the line, lights flickering eerily until they steadied.

Which was all very distracting but not enough to stop the kiss.

I was going to ignore how hard the butcher block table was, forgetting in my passion that the kitchen was likely a high-traffic area, when the double doors slammed open.

My eyes snapped up in time to see Orlo stop wide-eyed.

It was like we forgot what we were doing. There was no more soft, moist feeling shared between us, no more passion building. We split apart quickly.

"Goddamn," said Orlo. "Looky what I interrupted."

He'd shaved and his hair was slicked straight back, making it ragged at the back of his head and giving him a piratical appearance.

Mary Lynn almost choked trying to control her breathing.

The shared intimacy disappeared, but the memory lingered.

"Ye would have found the tile a mite chilly," Orlo said. "I come to fry up a batch of them fresh laid eggs, but, hell, I get a floor show to go along with it." His black eyes seemed larger than life.

"Don't push it," I warned.

"Billy," Mary Lynn warned.

"Ye haven't got a chance," Orlo warned. "Ye want, have at

me, now there is no big cowboy to back yer play."

"I—" I began.

"Let's go," said Mary Lynn, tugging at my arm, a visible aura still emanating from her.

"Shrimp like ye whet my appetite," said Orlo.

Mary Lynn pulled my arm again and my passion directed me to go with her. Usually I'm tough as a two-dollar steak and don't avoid a challenge.

As we passed through the doors, I said, "Soon, Orlo, I'm going to determine why you're behaving in the fashion you are."

"What the hell is he talking about?" Orlo asked Mary Lynn's back and the doors swung closed behind us.

"Good thing I'm mature enough to ignore people like him—upon occasion," I said as we walked down the corridor and past the elevator.

Mary Lynn snuggled her hand into mine as we turned left into the intersecting corridor along which were all the rooms.

I was still rarin' to go, but I'd lost some of the immediacy of the situation. I wondered if Mary Lynn were under the influence of the Jim beam she'd downed.

She looked over at me and the sense of urgency overcame me once again.

"Your room or mine?" she asked.

"Whichever is closer," I said. "Oops, I'm bunked with Tapes. How about yours?"

"Let us stop wasting time," she said, pulling me along which she didn't have to do for long as I was in as much hurry as she was.

We had to pass our room to get to hers and something occurred to me. Protection. What an awkward thing to address.

"Um, ah, er," I said. The delay had made my thinking clearer.

She stopped and put her arms around me and rubbed noses with me. "Um what?"

"You reckon, I mean, er, ah, what I'm trying to say is that maybe, um perhaps—"

She cocked her head back and looked at me. "Perhaps what?"

She wasn't making it any easier.

"I mean, ah, how to put it? Um, I've never even had a cold in my life, so I'm not worried about that, ah between us—oops, pun not intended—um, what I'm trying to say is," Christ on fire, where was the celebrated Shortcut glibness?, "is it possible you might, er, get, um pregnant?"

She leaned forward, her body straining against me, her breath against my cheek. You can't tell me spontaneous electricity does not exist. The loose leather blouse made my palms itch overwhelmingly.

"You mean safe sex?" she whispered.

"Um, sure, that's what I was trying to say."

She squinted, obviously counting. "I *could* get PG, now that you mention it." She squinted her eyes. "It's been a year and months and months since...and, at any rate, I no longer take the pill."

A vision of an unwed Sandra Dee Kowalski giving birth decided me. "Let's not take a chance."

She squeezed against me with more urgency. "Let's not take a chance, but let's not take a chance quickly."

I was melting against her.

"Humpf!" came a grumpy voice.

Unnoticed by either one of us, Angie Maple had stopped beside us. I wondered how much she'd overheard.

"Now I know who you remind me of, it's Alan Ladd."

"Whatever you say, Granny—"

"I'm no grandmother, you know that from the conversation in Sandra Dee's room."

"Sure, if you'll excuse us—"

"Yep, Alan Ladd. Except that your shoulders and forearms are bigger."

"Alan Ladd probably never worked out except for the axe-and-stump scene in *Shane*. I bench press 280 three twelve rep sets in a row," I said. "Not to mention a ton of forearm curls." To Mary Lynn, "Let's go."

The elderly lady "Humpfed" again and went down the

corridor the way we'd come.

I was beginning to believe that me and Mary Lynn were not meant to take an aerobic nap together.

"Do you have any?" Mary Lynn asked.

"Any what?"

"Protection."

"Ah, actually no. Tapes might. Let's check." I hoped Tapes wasn't in.

We went a bit along the hall and I opened our door glancing guiltily back down the corridor. Yep, Angie Maple was standing there watching us. "She's going to kill your reputation," I said.

Mary Lynn tossed her head. "I don't care." She sighed. "Hurry up."

I walked into our room and there was Tapes sitting on the end of the bed with a dry shirt on, the one which has TALL PEOPLE HAVE HIGHER STANDARDS on the back and the shot smiley face on the front—the one with the bullet hole in the middle of Smiley's forehead and blood running down from it.

I groaned.

"Hurry up for what?" Tapes asked, just being conversational. He was watching an old black and white movie on television and drying his hair with a towel. A Sears six foot push pull tape measure in a red case sat next to him on the bed.

"Um, ah, er, that's it!" I was stammering. "I have to make a quick pit stop." I hurried into the bathroom, closing the door behind me.

I also searched Tapes' dop kit for condoms. My luck was running true to form and he had no condoms there.

What the hell was I going to do? Much longer and I'd forget how to do what we started to do.

I went out the door exaggeratedly wiping my hands on a towel.

Tapes was talking to Mary Lynn, both staring at the television where King Kong was menacing the natives atop the great wall.

"Now Shortcut," Tapes was saying, "he prefers *Mighty Joe*

Young. But *King Kong*'s got the drama of the Empire State Building—"

"Joe has real character, though," I pointed out.

"If it was so good, how many remakes and sons of Joe Young movies did they make?" Tapes sucked on a bruised knuckle. Another knuckle was skinned.

"Well, Joe rescued all those crippled orphans. Kong was never that altruistic." I never was real fond of Kong and I always felt a moral compulsion to stand up for Joe Young.

"Kong had Fay Wray *and* Jessica Lange," he said like "So there." He picked up the tape measure and absently pulled it out and let it auto-retract.

"Did I mention Joe rescuing all those crippled orphans from a burning orphanage?" I said.

"Joe Young was a rip-off of the Kong movie."

"Imitation is the sincerest form of flattery," I said, "did I mention those orphans were crippled?"

"Billy!" hissed Mary Lynn.

"Oops. Forgot. Right with you, hon." How the hell was I going to ask Tapes for a condom—or two—right here in front of God and Mary Lynn and everybody?

She still had that dreamy look and I took a deep breath and swallowed hard. "Um, Tapes, the ah, operative word is that Joe Young *protected* those young-uns. They needed *protection*."

Usually he knows what I'm thinking before I do; but our Shortcut/Tapes ESP Center wasn't working well. He hopped up, a considerable distance as tall as he is. "Sure, Shortcut. I understand." He went to the door. "I'll sort of stand around outside and make sure nobody bothers you." He must have been distracted because ordinarily he's got more discretion.

"That's not exactly what I was referring to—"

"I am *not*," Mary Lynn said, "going to be in here and, well, you know, while somebody stands around outside waiting."

"Uh, oh," Tapes said, "I kind of said the wrong thing, huh?" His concern was evident. Tapes is a ladies' man and he was born silent and discreet. He gave Mary Lynn sort of an apologetic smile and the stiffness left her.

"Look, Tapes," I tried again, "what we want to do is prevent the birds and bees from, um...."

Tapes' face screwed up while he attempted to decipher what I was saying.

"For God's sake," said Mary Lynn. "Just ask for what you want. Will you excuse me?"

I nodded and she went into the bathroom, intelligently and neatly solving my problem; wish I'd of thought of that.

Tapes was beginning to understand.

"Now that I've tripped all over my tongue, you finally get it. Thanks a lot, buddy." I folded my arms.

"It ain't my problem," he said. "If you could speak English on occasion—"

"I don't need a lecture, and she'll be out in a second and I don't want to be embarrassed again."

"How many you want?" he asked.

"By the time we get to it, I'll have to be retrained," I said. "I don't know—"

He was digging around in his bag, pulling out a Stanley 100-foot tape measure and dropping it on the bed, and then he came out with a three-pack and handed them to me.

"Glow in the dark?" I said, humiliation washing over me.

"It's all I got left."

"You're weird, Tapes."

"Maybe if you don't expose them to light they won't glow," he said.

"Jeez."

He brightened. "Lissen, don't forget to check the serial number."

"Yeah, sure." He was making the old joke about you have to roll the condom *all* the way down to see the number. Well, it is an *old* joke.

The bathroom door swung open and Mary Lynn came out. I slipped the package of condoms into my pocket, feeling self-conscious.

Mary Lynn saw me and looked away and color crept up her neck.

Tapes murmured, "Amateurs."

I just shook my head and reached for the door.

Mary Lynn followed me out.

"Later," said Tapes.

Neither one of us answered. Grimly, I took her hand and we walked down the hall.

"All this kind of takes the edge off, doesn't it?" said Mary Lynn with a crooked smile. She was as self-conscious as I was.

"It's a real error of comedies," I said.

This wing of the hotel shook and lights flickered again. Mary Lynn squeezed my hand and some of the electricity returned. I looked at her and her eyes got bigger as we locked eyes. Anticipation was growing again.

We made it to her room uninterrupted and she opened the door. At the time I didn't think anything of her not having her room locked.

Without glancing back down the corridor, I followed her inside and closed the door and leaned on it. "Finally."

She turned to me and moved up against me. Our hands clenched together, our arms stretched out beside our now-locked hips. Her cheek was cool.

"Umm," she said.

"It was worth the wait," I said after a moment.

She pushed against me with more vigor, her mouth clinging tenderly to mine. We were a bit clumsy, not being used to each other and all, but enthusiasm made up for the awkwardness.

I surveyed the room, located the bed in my mind, hit the overhead fan switch, and killed the light. Fortunately her room was laid out like mine and all the switches were right there near us at the door.

She slumped against me and both of our breathing became pronounced.

The pronounced breathing almost drowned out the pronounced pounding at the door.

But the vibrations of the emphatic knocking transmitted through the door to and through my torso into her more interesting torso.

"Uh, oh," she whispered.

"Me, too," I whispered as quietly. "Damn," I thought.

The knocking continued and, if anything, increased in intensity.

"I know you're in there," came Angie Maple's voice accusingly. "I saw the light."

I didn't know what to say so I didn't say it.

Mary Lynn tucked her head onto my shoulder and I could feel her lips opening into a grin.

"Maybe it wasn't meant to be," I said into her ear. My hands were on her hips. She had the most intriguing hips.

"Mary Lynn?" called the elderly woman through the door. Her mouth must have been up against the wood panel.

Mary Lynn didn't answer.

"With our luck," I said, "today's not the day to play the lottery."

"I know you're in there. I saw the lights go out," said Angie. The darkened-glass transom, I thought.

"Mr. Birthday? The governor wants everybody in the kitchen."

"The governor's dead," I pointed out, realizing too late she'd tricked me.

"Hah," she said through the door, telling me I was dumb enough to fall for her ploy. "Something happened to Silas Smith in the kitchen and Mr. Ionata wants everyone to come at once."

"Why me, Lord?" I said.

8: MONDAY, 11:00 P.M.

As we went down the corridor following Angela Maple, others came from their rooms.

I felt terribly self-conscious. But Mary Lynn walked alongside of me with sort of a half-smile. Much as I've tried, I doubt I'll ever understand women. Upon reflection, I'm not altogether sure I *want* to understand women. Never mind the so-called mystery—I figger women are just like men: they're real people, but they see life from a perspective alien to me.

At the intersection of the corridors and lounges where the staircase wound its way up and the late governor had found his way precipitously down, Angie Maple turned left to go through a waiting room to see who was in the saloon to bring them.

"Paul Revere was a stoolie, too," I said.

Nobody paid any attention to me.

Duly, we all went down the corridor past the elevator and then the formal dining room and through the big double doors into the kitchen.

Lt. Governor Ionata was there, along with Orlo, Axe, and Pigtail. Also there were the two geeks, aides to Henry B., a couple of people I'd seen but didn't know. Shortly, Angie Maple came in with a couple of stragglers. The numbers were down. The governor was in the ice box, Trooper was laid up in his room, and Sandra Dee Kowalski and daughter were resting. I made a mental note to check in on them.

Silas Smith was sitting on the very butcher block table I'd eaten at and was holding a towel wrapped around ice against his jaw. Ionata had a wet cloth and was swabbing blood from Smith's forehead. Smith's face was puffy and both eyes were beginning to color; he was favoring one arm and was hunched over obviously in some internal pain.

Tapes, Mary Lynn and I stopped at a counter near the Mr. Coffee which Mary Lynn had fixed and we had sort of neglected in our mutual haste. I poured each of us a cup, though I wasn't really a coffee drinker. Remembering from my earlier rummaging around, I found what I needed. I put five M & M's into my coffee.

"I noted," I said to Tapes, "that the chef maintains his fresh tomatoes in the refrigerator."

"It figures," he said. His standard position was that tomatoes were not really fresh if ever refrigerated and/or gassed like they do in grocery stores. On the other hand, I maintain a chilled tomato is better in a salad than a warm one, never mind the fresher flavor Tapes claims.

Ionata turned to face all of us clustered around counters and sinks watching him minister to Silas Smith.

The lieutenant governor studied all of us, one by one, slowly. "I want," he said in his best projected voice, "to know exactly what's going on here."

Of course nobody answered.

Then I said, "What happened?"

Right on the tail end of my words, Orlo said, "What've ye got in mind, Yer Honor?"

Ionata had been a circuit court judge or something similar, but Orlo was the only one who used that honorific.

"Someone savagely attacked Silas," Ionata announced pontifically.

"He appears to me to still be breathing," said Orlo and the two geeks stared at him and stepped back at the same time.

"I am going to get to the bottom of this," Ionata continued, setting aside the bloody cloth.

"Who did it to him?" I asked.

Ionata turned to Silas. "Do you feel comfortable in talking

yet?"

Silas shook his head and winced. "No." His voice was a harsh whisper. "I came into the kitchen and the lights had gone off."

"And then," said Ionata, "somebody attacked him viciously in the dark."

"Why'd they want to do that?" I asked.

"Maybe they thought he was another person," Orlo said matter-of-factly and grinned at me.

"It could have been the killer," said Angie Maple.

"Do you mean," I asked Silas, "that the generator had gone off again, or that someone had turned out the lights?"

He shrugged and pain shot across his face from the arm resting in his lap. "Likely the generator."

Mary Lynn and I had been in here when the generator had a power interruption. Earlier, the power had gone off for a longer time. And Silas had obviously come into the kitchen after Mary Lynn and I had left. And Orlo had been in here then. Silas was lying, or too groggy to remember correctly.

"So why the dog and pony show?" I asked Ionata.

He didn't answer, but came around the counter and looked over most of us. Finally, he came back and stopped in front of Tapes.

Tapes was deceptively loose. Something was going on and he was prepared.

Ionata reached out and took Tapes' right hand and the lieutenant governor didn't know how close he was to harm's way.

Ionata held up Tapes' hand. His skinned knuckles were evident.

"Now, is there any question why I charged these two strangers with murder?" Ionata said.

"Even if he did beat up Smith, it doesn't make us murderers," I pointed out.

"Billy!" protested Mary Lynn.

"I didn't mean to say he did it," I said. "He didn't do it."

"He didn't," Mary Lynn said.

"Tapes skinned his knuckles fixing the generator," I said.

"Everybody owes him thanks, not accusations."

"Can you prove that?" asked Ionata.

Tapes was too angry to talk. In these circumstances, it was probably for the better.

"Yes," I said. "I was in here cooking and eating—"

"I knew something smelled bad," Angie Maple said.

"It ain't broccoflower," I said to shut her up.

I glanced at Orlo and knew I couldn't hide the fact Mary Lynn had been in here too. Orlo was grinning at both my predicament and worry about what he would say.

"Orlo can vouch for it," I said. "He came in after I was finished. Before I left, we exchanged a few words. Is that not correct, Orlo?"

He didn't like that. It put him on the spot—and likely to have been in the kitchen when Silas got stomped. If he admitted it, he could publicly expose Mary Lynn and me. If he didn't admit it, he was in essence admitting some culpability. He had a personal dilemma to solve, and do it swiftly.

"Well?" prompted John Dellum Ionata.

"What he says," Orlo began, jerking a thumb at me, "ain't necessarily such." He looked around at his audience. "I entered and the short guy and the woman was fixin' to make a union. They left with the short thing threatening me." Which, as I recalled, I had. Orlo went on. "I grabbed a snack and left real quick like. I suspect the short one dispatched his tall partner to inflict personal damage to me." Orlo's eyes had turned right cagey. "Likely the tall one found the lights out and thought the manager was in fact myself."

"You'll note," I observed loudly, "that Orlo's knuckles are thick with scar tissue and calluses from dragging on the ground and therefore will not show small damage from Silas Smith."

Nobody said anything.

"And like I said earlier," I continued while I had the floor, "for what reason would someone want to whip on poor Silas?"

"Mistake," said Ionata. "It could have been a mistake."

Orlo smiled widely.

"I will admit," I said, "there are people here who need whipping more than Silas." I paused. "Everyone here seems to possess a nose; that proves they should have been able to distinguish the difference between the two." Maybe I had not sobered sufficiently yet.

It didn't take Orlo long to grow angry.

I turned to Ionata. Orlo was not the issue here. Yet. "Suppose it was not a mistake."

"Birthday, there are five men here capable of savagely beating Silas Smith. You and your friend are two of them."

I waved my arm around the room. "Why do you need an audience, then?"

"They may contribute. Do not forget, I've officially read you your rights and made you a suspect subject to—"

"How about due process for openers?" I asked.

One of the geeks nodded.

I suspect Ionata might need the support he would perceive coming to him because of his position.

"I'm just doing my job," Ionata said.

"Unless of course," I said in measured tones, "you are the killer and doing everything in your power to shift suspicion, to cover up your own culpability."

"Culpability?" said Orlo.

Suddenly, I was disgusted. "I don't need to be part of anymore grandstanding." I turned and walked out. Tapes and Mary Lynn hastened to follow, and the rest of them were leaving as we turned the corner past the stairway.

"Something strange is definitely going on," Mary Lynn said.

"That's a fact," I said. "Listen, I'm dying for sleep. I need to check up on Sandra Dee and—"

"Me, too," said Mary Lynn.

Sandra Dee was fine, the kid was fine.

I saw Mary Lynn to her door and, in a very mature fashion, went to our room and fell dead asleep.

Until Tapes woke me a couple of hours later.

He'd been silently snooping around, as is his wont, for he has insomnia upon occasion. "Orlo just slipped out," Tapes told me. "I'm gonna follow him. I just wanted you to know." Smart of him, Orlo being Orlo and all.

I was groggy and whipped; all I wanted to do was roll over and sleep a year or two. Hell, it had been an eventful day.

"Not without me, you aren't."

"I figured as much."

9: TUESDAY, 2:30 A.M.

I dressed in a New York second, wet Nikes and jeans. Dark rain parka.

Tapes was already gone, afraid we'd lose Orlo.

I hurried down the corridor and slid out the door. It was just before three in the morning and, surprisingly, the storm winds had abated. It was merely breezy and not even raining. Having on a dark pullover shirt, I dumped the parka in the back of my pickup parked right by the east wing entrance. I watched for a signal from Tapes.

He'd been paying attention for the slice of light escaping from the corridor door and a flash from his pocket light showed me which way to go.

Occasional flashes led me, though it wasn't difficult.

The José Gaspar Inn was sort of in the middle of Boca Grande, the town on Gasparilla Island. At its widest, the slender Gasparilla Island wasn't much more than three-quarters of a mile thick by my reckoning. Here was probably the widest point. Which, in the midst of an incipient hurricane, was not all that reassuring. Boca Grande maintains some of its quaint age, lots of palms and old timey houses, big stucco fences. All of an era long gone.

I've noticed where many lament the end of eras, especially in Florida. They talk about the old days, about the way it used to be, and how sad that much of the natural charm was gone. And that's been replaced by plastic and glass and concrete.

Well, hell. I don't believe all that. It's nice not to have to dodge water moccasins, rattlers, coral snakes at every step. It's nice to pull into a quick stop for a Coke and cheap gas; in the old days you'd have to stop at some sleepy station where you couldn't pump your own gas and it cost twice as much. You'd have to find a cafe and wait for a Coke and a sandwich and probably wave the flies away while you were waiting. And these lamenters, where do they shop? What roads do they drive on? They certainly take advantage of all the modern amenities. And they probably all live in condos on the beach. And most of them are likely refugees from the cold northland.

Hell, I like Big Macs and interstate highways. And it is wonderful to have a bookstore or a liquor store within five minutes of wherever you are. Though, I will admit, the lamenters do have a point; it's just you can't do anything about it.

On the other hand, if they start screwing with Southwest Texas like they have with Florida, I will take immediate and drastic exception.

I caught up with Tapes on a fairway of the golf course.

The wind freshened.

We went south along Grande Bayou and over a little bridge.

On this slope of the bridge, actually just an overpass of Grande Bayou, Tapes halted. "He's acting funny."

"What do you mean." I peered into the darkness without success.

"He stops and goes, just like we are." Tapes was tall enough to see over the hump. "Let's go." He moved out.

"Orlo is following someone himself?"

"Looks like it."

"Go figure."

We crested the bridge and I caught sight of Orlo against a lighter background. He was cutting down a shell road toward what could charitably be called a marina. Several boathouses and a series of docks.

This was facing east, and bordered on Charlotte Harbor. Thus it was protected from the rampaging Gulf—or what I'd last seen appeared rampaging. Wave action was less here? however, boats were being tossed about. Many were lashed between two docks with at least four ropes tying them loosely to pilings and cleats.

One of the boathouses had light coming from it.

We stopped alongside another boathouse and water slapped over a seawall next to us.

Orlo was a shadow pasted against a greasy window of the lighted boathouse.

Wind was picking up again.

"I thought the storm was abating," I said.

"Abating?" Tapes was pulling my chain again. "That was the eye of the storm." His voice was pitched low. He shook his raingear. "You should have brought yours. You're going to get soaked soon."

"Damn."

We watched Orlo watch through the window of the boathouse. The weak light inside indicated a battery operated lantern.

The wind was beginning to whistle now. I felt water being whipped off the harbor.

"What do you think?" Tapes had to bend over now so I could hear him without him shouting.

"He followed somebody. Light on in a boathouse." I was talking to the side of Tapes' bent over head. "Who the hell is sneaking around at three in the morning in a marina? Obviously, somebody is doing something they don't want anyone to see."

Tapes turned his head and looked at me.

"Doing away with another body?" I said, not believing it. "Nah. It doesn't add up." I searched with my eyes; the wind dried them and the dark inhibited my field of view. "I'll be back."

Heading back inland, I had to lean into the wind. It appeared to be coming from a different direction, more north or northeast.

Keeping low, I ran up the shell road and paralleled the marina for a minute, then cut back toward the harbor again. I was angling toward the lighted boathouse from the south, opposite the side where Orlo was watching.

I had to go out on the dock to approach the boathouse. It took me a couple of minutes to insure I wouldn't be seen, scooting along the dock from davit to davit to piling. I could almost see into the boathouse. It was one of those which overhang the space between two docks, where you can keep your boat inside under cover, or hanging from davits undercover. There was a garage door like affair in the front so you could get your boat in or out.

However, this side of the building had no door, no window, no access. I peeked around the corner in the back and the wind, which had been intercepted by the boathouse, lashed at me, making my eyes tear. I jerked back not being able to see and worried that Orlo was there. He'd have little compunction about putting me away out here in the dark if he thought he could get away with it. I'd made an enemy for life.

So I crouched and peered around the rear of the boathouse, figuring no one would think to look that far down.

Nothing.

Darker than before. Boiling clouds occluding what enfeebled moon and star light had helped before.

On hands and feet, I scurried like a dog toward the far corner and promptly got a splinter in my hand from something. The ground was rock.

There was a door here on the west side of the building, but no window. I continued to the far side of the boathouse.

Again, near the ground, being pressed down by the wind and now some stinging rain, I inched my head around the corner.

Orlo. Pasted against the door with the window in it.

The spillover of the light etched around his large frame. He was wearing a slicker.

The wind and rain stung my eyes and I ducked my head to wipe them clear.

At the same time, I was aware the light went out and a crushing pain crunched my left hand. Which stopped the pain from the splinter.

I started to jerk it out and stopped.

Orlo. He'd stepped around the back of the building so's not to be seen by whoever was in the boathouse—and likely leaving now.

Orlo's slicker flapped in my face and I cursed silently. I imagined I could smell Orlo's sour odor but I knew it was in my mind for the wind was whipping too fast. My own mouth tasted like rotting seaweed.

The door slammed and a flashlight beam led off up the path and onto the shell road.

Mercifully, Orlo followed almost immediately and I sat and shook my hand. Carefully, I moved each finger, starting fearfully with the one which went weewee all the way home to the thumb. Fortunately, they all worked, though with some pain in the palm. Great, just great. I rose and walked against the wind and rain to where Tapes was standing alongside the next boathouse.

He acknowledged my presence with a nod.

"Did you see who it was?" I asked him.

Orlo was out of sight now in the dark, but the flashlight rose and disappeared as the carrier went over the bridge.

"Silas Smith."

"Well, pour me a glass of sheep dip."

"I have more questions than you would believe," Tapes said.

"Me, too. And very very few answers."

"Might be some answers in that hut," Tapes said.

"Boathouse," I said absently, my nautical knowledge being depleted with that and "davits."

Of course, the door was locked.

"Just a minute," I said, and went around to the back of the building. My hand hurt worse when I passed the spot where Orlo had stood upon it. I found the shard of lumber which had provided the splinter and returned to Tapes at the door.

Using the board, I smashed the glass. "Lookit the wind did with this board," I said.

I reached in and unfastened the lock by turning the door handle.

We slipped inside and Tapes took off his parka. He handed

me his pocket flashlight and held the parka against the window so light wouldn't give us away.

It took only a few seconds to find the battery lantern on a workbench against the wall. I turned it on.

Like I said about my nautical knowledge, the onliest thing I know about water is to mix it with bourbon or how to use it to make ice.

A boat, which I would call a cabin cruiser, rolled in the water. It had been backed in, and was tied with five or six lines to various cleats. If the wave action here in the protected part of the harbor did not reach mammoth proportions, then the boat would be safe. The name on the back was etched in orange and blue and read *HBG'S GATOR GAL*. The thing was wallowing and snapping tie down ropes and had a big open bridge above the cabin. It was close to being a luxury yacht.

"How long you reckon this thing is?" I asked Tapes. He's got calibrated eyeballs.

"Fifty-one feet, not counting the ladder hanging on the rear—make that stern." With that and port and starboard, I'd just remembered enough sea-lingo to double my vocabulary.

I smelled fuel. "I smell fuel," I said.

Tapes pointed.

Over towards the stern of *HBG'S GATOR GAL* sat a couple of fifty-five gallon drums. I went over and kicked them. "One's empty. The other about half full." I pointed to the dock beside the barrels. "Hand pump and lines. Silas Smith just refueled the *GATOR GAL* by hand."

"My turn," said Tapes.

We switched off and I held the parka against the window and wind and rain blew in where I'd broken the glass.

Tapes jumped onto the *GATOR GAL* and went down into the cabin. When he reemerged and jumped back onto the dock, he said, "Duffel bag. Smith's ready to go someplace."

My arms were getting tired, me not being as tall as Tapes and all, I had to hold the parka up above my head. "Stands to reason. He said the bridge was out, so as soon as the storm dies down enough for him to make a run for it, he will. I wonder why that is?"

"It could be because he murdered Gonzáles and is afraid he'll get caught." Tapes prowled the boathouse for a moment. "Nothing else."

"If Silas is the murderer, then why did he murder the governor?"

Tapes came back toward me and shut off the lantern.

Gratefully, I dropped my arms and handed him his rain slicker.

"I looked in the boat," he said from the darkness as the wind and rain began to soak me, "and I couldn't find a raincoat or anything."

"Thanks." I pried the door open and peered out. "If Silas done it, who beat him up?"

"Beats me," said Tapes. "He probably knows who whipped upon him, he just isn't telling."

"Could be. A conspiracy? More than one person killed Henry B.?"

I could sense Tapes shrugging. "With that tennis racquet and all, it sure looks like what they call unpremeditated, a spur of the moment thing."

"A crime of passion," I said. "But if that's so, how does Silas fit in?"

"There's a boat full of fuel and fresh clothing and a tooth-brush, that's a bunch of evidence."

"You've got a point, Tapes. Damn near everybody at the JG Inn has good and plenty reason to do away with Henry B." I paused. "He must have been a real jerk. I didn't dislike him at all, though we didn't spend a lot of time with him."

"He's a politician. They train themselves to be personable. We going to stand here and jaw or get back to the Inn before the storm blows any worse?"

"You're just saying that because you've got rain gear."

"The 7-P Principle," he said smugly. Proper Prior Planning Prevents Piss Poor Performance.

"Thanks, buddy. I wish it was a nice starry night, no wind or moon."

"Full moon," Tapes said brushing past me, "dominates the sky. It serves as a beacon, big and powerful."

"A sky chock full of stars and no moon is more attractive; it stretches your imagination."

"Gimme a break," he said and slipped out of the door.

"Einstein said that imagination is more important than knowledge, so there." I followed, cursing myself for leaving my own rain gear in the truck.

No moon or stars were visible. I was partial to a starlit sky; out in the waste lands of Southwest Texas and Arizona, you could look up and see millions of stars like through a clear glass. This Florida humidity impairs your vision, and only bright stars penetrate the atmosphere.

We wound our way back to the Inn, me being soaked clear through.

The storm was returning with a vengeance.

We stopped at the pickup alongside the Inn for me to retrieve my rain parka. This pretty well concealed us from the doorway.

Which accounted for the person leaving not noticing us.

Axe slipped out, holding the door tightly, and then closed it gently. A flashlight beam snickered out in front of him.

Obviously, he did not expect to be seen during the storm at this time of night. As Orlo had been, Axe was dressed in a dark poncho.

He walked off toward Charlotte Harbor.

I climbed onto the bed of the truck and watched the bobbing light until it went out of sight.

Leaning down for a change, I shouted into Tapes' ear. "He's following the same track we were just on."

The wind tore away my words.

10: TUESDAY, 4:00 A.M.

I was in clean, dry jeans and pulling on my dry Tony Lamas.

"Likely, Orlo sent Axe to check out the boathouse," I said. "He was following Silas and didn't want to lose track of him."

"Makes sense," said Tapes. "Does Orlo strike you as one who cares who murdered the governor?"

I had to admit Tapes was right. "Maybe he's acting like a detective."

"Which brings up a point," Tapes said. "Why are we doing that very thing?"

I thought about Henry B. discussing the weather. I thought about "rapidly dissipate." "We're not, really. We're just sort of paying attention a little more than normal."

"Then how come we're fixing to go find Silas and question him?"

"Our duty as citizens." I thought for a moment. "If we don't, he might rapidly dissipate from this here Inn leaving us as the lieutenant governor's prime suspects."

"If Smith runs off," Tapes said slowly pulling on a new T-shirt, "that would make him suspect number one."

"Maybe, maybe not. But he won't be here to explain a lot of things which need explaining, things which perhaps he's the onliest one who can explain. Things that would give the real authorities motive to investigate."

"As long as Silas is around, it will help keep the heat off us and maybe your sweetie," Tapes said, looking at me keenly under his eyebrows.

After a moment, I shrugged uncomfortably. "She ain't my sweetie and she didn't kill Gonzáles any more than we did."

Tapes was wearing an old shirt showing an Arab on a camel in the desert which said "NUKE THEIR ASS AND TAKE THEIR GAS."

"But none of that is why," he continued.

"Why what?" I asked.

"Why we're running around trying to solve the murder of Governor Gonzáles."

"You're going to say something about the ephemeral liking I had for the man—"

Tapes gave me one of his looks. "No. What I think is that you want to show up John Ionata and rub his nose in it in a less than ephemeral fashion. You want to beat everyone to the punch—"

"I don't do hero stuff—"

"That ain't what I'm saying, Shorts. I'm saying that you've taken an instant and gratifying dislike to Ionata—"

"Not a difficult thing to do."

"—and are determined to make him look like a fool—"

"Not a difficult thing to do."

"—and make you look better than him in the process."

"Well," I said slowly, "he pisses me off."

"I noticed. You might also have another reason, and that is to stay around as long as possible and develop the lovely Mary Lynn."

That had kind of crossed my mind. "Umm, so what?"

"So, you're not even over the fair and lovely Rebecca yet. Surely that has a bearing on your current feelings for Mary Lynn."

"How do you know what my current feelings are?" I was indignant.

"Lookit your sleeve."

I looked. "What do you mean? Oh." I couldn't meet his eyes.

"How long we been together, Shortcut?"

"Too goddamn long."

"Well, I know you. I've followed your love life with quite an interest. It's worth observing someone who fucks up their love life all the time, almost like self-destruction."

"You're full of shit, Tapes." I was angry. "You know that is not true. They're the ones break it up."

"Not all the time. Think about it. And when the girl is the one who dumps you, you chose her in the first place."

"Either way, it's my fault?"

"I didn't exactly say that. But that ain't my point anyway; not here, not now. You're a grown man with your eyes wide open— well, sort of. You see through rose-colored glasses all the time. But as soon as some lass drops her hanky, there you are falling in love. Look." He began springing his twenty-five-foot Unilok tape measure. "We got some lighthouses to see. We got to get back to Tucson and all them starry skies. We're stuck in an old hotel in a storm on a now-isolated island with a killer running around loose and three goons wanting to mix it up—"

"Not to mention loco politicians, medical emergencies, danger and so on. What are you trying to say now?"

"We got things to do. Maybe you don't need an affair right now. It kind of complicates matters."

I grinned. "It makes love taste better, living on the edge. It makes you appreciate the human female a bunch more. It sharpens and heightens life. It—"

Tapes snorted. "Don't get started. Your—what do you call it?"

"Tolutiloquence."

He shook his head and brought out his tin of Copenhagen. "You eat all them books you all the time reading?" He tapped the top of the tin with three fingers three times. He opened it and took a tiny pinch and put it between his cheek and gum. He sighed and looked very satisfied. That stuff has more of a nicotine hit than smokes, so it's harder to break the habit. "It occurs to me that once Axe returns, then they're gonna head straight for Silas Smith."

"And we should get there first?" I said.

"Yep. Especially considering those three most likely were

the ones who stomped Silas earlier."

"If you're waiting on me, you're backing up," I said. "Like they say in the Mystic Far East, it's difficult to get off the tiger once you get on."

11: TUESDAY, 5:30 A.M.

"I'm beat," I said, topping the third flight of stairs.

The third floor of the José Gaspar Inn was laid out along the same wing lines as the first floor, except that in place of dining rooms, lounges, kitchens, offices, and reception areas were VIP and permanent resident suites.

Tapes behind me, I pounded on Silas Smith's door, ignoring the fancy brass knocker.

No answer.

I thumped the door again.

"It's near dawn," said Tapes. "Maybe he's downstairs already."

I turned the door handle and it opened. "No thievery expected here."

"Just a killer," Tapes said. "You'd think he'd keep his door locked under those circumstances."

I walked in. "Unless he's the killer and doesn't have to worry about it."

Tapes followed. "There's that."

Big sitting room. Television, VCR, CD set-up. Rattan couch and chairs. Sliding glass door onto a balcony, closed with rain beating upon it. Desk with a computer and printer taking up a quarter of the area in the sitting room. Green and scarlet floral pattern cushions—not my style, but to each his own. Big ceiling fans making the room feel more comfortable.

Tapes had gone through an open door. "Bedroom," he reported. "Big one. And a bathroom. Bed slept in, and unmade.

Electric razor, still warm, recently used. Wet toothbrush."

"He's around, Tapes. It's still too nasty out there to make his break." I thought about the scars on his neck. "Guess I'd use an electric razor, too."

Tapes grunted acknowledgment. He knew what I was talking about.

"There's something strange here."

"What?" he asked.

"Let me think."

I went over to the desk and pulled out drawers.

"Careful," Tapes told me. "He'll know someone was in here."

"So what? It'll be like stirring the pot if he does. Maybe he'll panic. Who knows?"

JG Inn stationery and envelopes. Stamps, pads, pencils, generic desk stuff.

Atop the desk was an empty disk storage box. "Disks are gone, you can tell it had some disks in it from the dust pattern. He shouldn't have kept it open and let the dust in."

"Tell him that," Tapes said.

In the far corner was a counter and on the other side were a refrigerator, stove, dishwasher, and some cabinets. Salt, pepper, and napkins on the counter. I went through the cabinets. A minimum of cutlery, flatware, plates, and so on. A few pots and pans. "He's no gourmet cook." How wrong I turned out to be.

Tapes was standing in front of the sliding glass windows. "What's your point?"

"I don't know yet."

I went into the bedroom. Queen-sized bed. Chest of drawers with a pair of dirty socks on top. Telephones and books on bed tables. I checked the books.

Tapes came in behind me. "Figure it out yet?" He knew I'd come up with whatever had struck me as an anomaly.

I picked up the books. "Well, I knew he wasn't a deep thinker. Westerns."

Uh, oh. I'd started it again.

"That's your own intellectual arrogance showing now,

Shortcut, Westerns are a dip in history."

I hate to disparage *any* books, but I couldn't avoid our traditional argument even though I like Louis L'Amour westerns and absolutely love Lou Cameron westerns.

So I argued by avoidance of the disparagement, known as Shortcut's Avoidance. "Science fiction is best, it tickles your mind and stretches your imagination."

"Stretches your imagination is right," Tapes said, dropping to his knees and looking under the bed. "You use that line for every argument."

I went to the walk-in closet and turned on the light. "In science fiction you can look into the future; hell, you can look into many futures."

"Westerns are patriotic, they're about the growth of this great land of ours—damn, I'm beginning to sound like you." He shook his head and pushed himself to his feet.

I rummaged around in Smith's closet. "Westerns are about good guys in bad towns, cattle rustling, or the new foreman on the ranch with the woman rancher."

"You left out the Indian plot," he said. "And how many aliens on Earth or humans on alien planets you read about?"

"Some," I admitted. "But, those ain't the only plots." There was a suitcase on the shelf, and an empty space where it was possible that Smith's duffle bag had been folded.

"Besides, westerns show the character of our nation." He wouldn't let it go. "They capture our pioneer spirit, showcase how we built the country from the ground up. Real history."

"I forgot the rancher's daughter thematic statement."

"Also, westerns highlight the diverse peoples and cultures which mixed to produce what we've got today."

"Jeez, Tapes, I didn't mean to step on your toe."

"You got me started," he accused. There isn't much he'll wax long and loud about. "It got to me personally—"

"That's it." I turned and walked out of the closet and pointed around. "What don't you see?"

He looked at me suspiciously.

"See," I said. "You said it. Personal. Character of a nation. Well, show me a bunch of personal stuff in these rooms. Show me something more than a couple of cheap western novels that gives us a peek at Silas Smith's character."

We walked into the sitting room.

"None," Tapes admitted. "No family pictures. A couple of prints hotels use for paintings. Hotel furniture. Dirty clothes and an unmade bed. No transistor radios, no biographies, no personal mail, no *Sports Illustrated* annual swimsuit calendar, no bowling trophies, no nothing."

"That's what I was thinking. Let us go find Silas."

"Where?"

"Downstairs maybe?"

We went downstairs. I don't trust elevators normally, much less in a storm with electricity provided by an outside generator.

In the corridor before you reach the lobby was the door to Smith's office. Locked door, that is.

I cocked my head. "Tapes, listen."

The door was wooden and Tapes put his ear against the upper panel. "Listen, nothin'. Feel. There's a hellacious draft coming from under the door."

"Isn't that 'an' hellacious?"

Tapes gave me one of those looks which I ignored as I hurried down the corridor into the lobby. No one was in the lobby. We went behind the old-fashioned counter and past the alcove where the old fashioned switchboard was and to the other door for Silas Smith's office.

It was locked.

"Damn," I said.

"I brought my key." Tapes edged me aside and lifted his size thirteen boot and slammed it into the door jamb just below the handle. Surprisingly, it made very little noise.

Mainly because the storm made more noise and roared out of Smith's office into our faces.

"I'm running out of dry clothes," I said.

Tapes beat me inside.

Maybe twenty by twenty. An old fashioned Persian carpet rolled out on the floor. Under water now. A modern metal executive desk. A file cabinet. Built-in book shelves which held nothing, but apparently had supported a dozen or so framed photos of the José Gaspar Inn which were now blown off and smashed onto the floor.

Big lift-up window completely smashed in—or out.

Upon the desk and credenza behind it and under the window: several account books torn and ruined, open file folders and a couple of dozen disks. On the end of the credenza a PC desk top with the case removed and hard drive dangling from it and facing out and water pouring into it from off the credenza and the open window.

Wind and rain slung against my face. "I bet he's erased the entire hard drive, or crashed it somehow so the info is not retrievable."

"Mighty convenient," Tapes said loudly to compensate for the wind whistling through the room and into the phone operator's alcove. "I bet these are the good books, too."

"He'd have destroyed the cooked ones," I agreed. "And likely any memory which wouldn't match the books here."

Tapes peered out the window, his face streaking with water. He turned. "Let's go."

I scrambled ahead of him and closed the door behind him by propping the telephone operator's chair against the door handle.

"Lot of glass outside his window," Tapes pointed out.

"Oh?"

"Convenient again."

"Storms do weird things," I said, which made me wonder.

I dragged the phone operator's console away from the wall. It was one which had been designed and built before microminiaturization and computers.

"More convenience," I said. Wiring feeding from the back of the phone set-up had been neatly sliced where they mated into conduits which fed into the wall.

"I'm coming up with more questions and fewer answers,"

Tapes said leaning over the back of the console and studying the mess. "On the other hand, we're mere amateurs and we're figuring this stuff out."

"Are you suggesting that Smith is deliberately diverting attention for some reason?"

"I ain't saying nothing. That's your job."

"Thanks." I glared up at him. "One thing about westerns? They show so very little sensitivity; they lack any kind of subtlety. More than likely, those traits are also reflected by their readers."

"You're sitting there being critical and philosophical, which for you sometimes is the same thing—"

"I know, I know," I said, rising, "all the while we ain't finding Silas any quicker."

12: TUESDAY, 7:00 A.M.

"Crunchy peanut butter doesn't belong on split Oreos," Tapes said.

"I nonconcur. It's one of the good things about crunchy. And smooth doesn't go well on baked potatoes," I argued.

The two geeks were staring at us.

We were in the big kitchen waiting on Silas. The geeks, one pencil-necked and one very proper, had told us Silas had just left.

"He went with Lieutenant Governor Ionata," said the pencil-necked geek. He wore a long-sleeved white shirt, buttoned-down, open with no tie, but you expected one.

"They had to help Trooper to the bathroom and give him breakfast," said the very proper other geek who wore a pink long-sleeved shirt with a George Will bow tie. He was the one who'd discovered Henry B.'s body and had been devastated. He was maybe five eight, a shade taller than me, just a shade.

Both the late governor's aides were eating doughnuts and drinking coffee and orange juice.

I couldn't find any of my favorite apple-cherry juice and my opinion of the chef went down some. But I did a diet Coke instead.

Tapes and I were attacking a bag of Oreos, and a little peanut butter, and the cookies were rapidly dissipating.

"Real men don't eat smooth," I said with disdain.

"I do." Tapes fixed his gaze on me.

"Well, you're always an exception to every rule," I said diplomatically.

"We haven't been formally introduced," bow-tie said. He looked nervously at his companion. "He is Vernon Bernstein, the governor's legislative aide."

"Late governor," said Vernon Bernstein quietly. His neck was long and thin and his Adam's apple pronounced, but not nearly as much as Silas Smith. Bernstein was taller than his buddy, but thinner, almost awkwardly so. His face was sharp and gaunt.

"Hey, Vern," I said to the pencil-necked geek, while reminding myself that prejudgment of a person amounts to a form of elitism. It was difficult not to prejudge these two; however, I've been pleasantly surprised before—meaning I've been dead wrong.

"I'm—was," continued bow-tie, "Henry B.'s assistant chief-of-staff. I saw you act quickly and decisively when," his face fell, "I found," gulp, "the governor's body," gulp, "may the Lord bless and keep him."

"What's your name?" I asked.

He shook his head to clear it. "I, sir, am Pinkus Keanon Clapsaddle, III."

I just couldn't bring myself to say it, so I went over to him and offered my hand. "Hi, Pinky. I'm Shortcut and this here's Tapes."

But he nodded and the bow-tie bobbed up and down like Bernstein's Adam's apple. "I know full who you are, Mr. Birthday."

We shook hands all around and I went back to my Coke and the few Oreos Tapes left me. All the while, Bernstein's eyes followed me. This guy was slicker than a mayonnaise sandwich.

"It was scandalous," Pinky said, "the way John Ionata treated you."

"You mean by charging us with the governor's murder?" I asked. As usual, Tapes was letting me do the talking. "Practice makes perfect," he always says.

"I do. The Lord giveth and the Lord taketh away," said Pinky and Bernstein rolled his eyes.

"Pinky is very Born-Again, maybe you noticed?" said Hey Vern.

I didn't use the "I'm diagnostic myself" line because I was too tired to pull their chain. I felt like I was three Buds short of a six-pack.

Pinky nodded appreciatively. "I'm the one who holds up the John 3:16 sign when they kick field goals and extra points."

I groaned. I always wanted to carry a sign reading "Dolphins 18 Bucs 14" into church.

Tapes measured the diameter of an Oreo.

"We used to go to most in-state big games," Vern said, "since Henry B. was a football fanatic. He was a star for the University of Florida." Vern frowned. "He let Pinky come with us and thought it great fun to watch Pinky hold up the sign."

"What does an assistant chief-of-staff do?" I asked. I didn't want them to fight and cost me a chance to pump them for whatever information I could get.

"Whatever I'm told," Pinky said with a slight smile. "The chief-of-staff is generally concerned with political matters; Vernon is involved with heavy-duty matters of legislation and liaison with the legislature and legislators; there are other assistants out and about, but I usually handle energy affairs, environmental programs, the budget for the governor's office, catch-all items such as these." He dusted sugar off his hand and sipped some coffee.

We were eating at the butcher block table and they were standing on the other side of a counter facing us.

Hey Vern was silent and watchful, which to me added up to being distrusting. Of course, we had been sort of formally accused of murder.

I determined to pump Pinky at least while he was in a talkative mood. There were a thousand questions I wanted to ask and I wasn't sure where to start when his words reoccurred to me. "Environmental" popped out.

"Listen, Pinky, you said part of your duties included environmental matters. What are the penalties for poaching animals or taking them out of season?"

"Plenty, Mr. Shortcut. But it depends on what the animal is, and if the perpetrator has a previous record. For instance, there are perhaps as few as fifty Florida panthers left and they fall under the federal Endangered Species Act. Under this, you can get six months in jail and a maximum of $25,000 fine for possessing or selling or doing anything like that to a logger-head turtle. The U.S. Fish and Wildlife Service estimates there are fewer than a few thousand manatees left. These, too, are an endangered species. The feds can also convict those who would steal protected wildlife on federal preserves—they can be charged with conspiracy to violate the Lacey Act—"

"Which is?" asked Tapes.

"It's a law that protects wildlife. If the perpetrator is found guilty, it could cost him $250,000 and five years in prison. Now, keep in mind judges impose harsher penalties for repeat offenders—within the guidelines, of course—when they get the opportunity. Additionally, the Florida State's Attorneys can tag on other, Florida specific, charges of our own if the case warrants." Pinky appeared to be just warming up.

I knew what a manatee was: a sea cow, and they live in fresh water such as rivers and canals. Big goddamn mammals, ten to twelve feet long and weighing half a ton. A big cause here in Florida, often led by Jimmy Buffet. "I read that manatees are dying because of propellers."

Pinky nodded enthusiastically. "Most manatees have scars on their backs from boat props. Upwards of two hundred of them die each year from prop wounds. We're trying to regulate boat speed and identify more no wake zones to protect these wonderful creatures."

Tapes said, "How about a breeding program?"

"They're wild," said Pinky, "and don't mature sexually until they're about six years old. The plain fact is that the manatee does not reproduce fast enough. Females have a calf perhaps every three years."

"At two hundred dying a year and a couple of thousand left,

they ain't gonna make it as a species much longer," Tapes said.

Pinky held out his hands. "The Lord knows we're trying, and with His help...." Pinky adjusted his bow tie. "Proverbs 13:12 tells us, 'Hope deferred maketh the heart sick, but when the desire cometh, it is a tree of life.' Very appropriate, I believe."

I think I understood what he was saying. "How about alligator poaching?" The hides in Orlo's van.

"You must have a license and hunt gators during specific time periods in specific locations," he said specifically, sipping coffee and holding his little finger out.

"What's a gator hide worth?" Tapes asked.

"A medium sized one brings around two hundred dollars. And," he waved his right pointy finger instructively, "you can sell the meat, mostly the tail. Gators are mostly tail. Cooks nowadays blacken the meat, Cajun style, a great deal. In fact, in Louisiana as well as here there are alligator farms where people are actually raising gators for meat and leather. It is an industry we are encouraging; it's a clean industry—" He hesitated. "I'm getting wound up, aren't I, Vern?"

"As usual." Vern wasn't all that wordy himself. But his tone with Pinky was disproving.

I decided to change tracks. "The lieutenant governor? Why do you reckon he's so all-fired bent on nailing me and Tapes? And he calls everybody together every time anything happens. What's the deal with him?" I eyed Pinky in a friendly fashion to disarm him in case he didn't want to respond.

Pinky sighed. "It's a long story. John Ionata hails from the Panhandle. He ran against Henry B. in the primary; you see, John was a long term legislator and thus wielded much power. But Henry B. had national credentials and therefore more name recognition elsewhere in the state."

"Pinky," warned Vern Bernstein.

Pinky looked at him over the rim of the coffee cup. "I don't care, Vern. John Ionata is going to dismiss us in a couple of weeks anyway; he won't want any of Henry B.'s people near him."

"Sounds like Ionata and Gonzáles weren't the greatest of friends." I kept my voice casual so we could learn as much as possible.

"They were great enemies," Pinky replied. "The primary campaign was full of distortions of records, negative commercials, and other dirty campaign tricks."

Vern Bernstein nodded absently and grinned unconsciously. I could guess who Henry B.'s campaign dirty-trickster had been. And Vern had obviously been a good one, for Gonzáles was just into his second term.

"Not being from Florida," I said, "I don't know—but can guess—why they ended up on the same ticket."

"Exactly," Pinky said. He sighed. Pinky was being so sensitive I doubted that he could be the killer. But you never know. "Henry B. won the primary, but with a badly split party, one which was guaranteed to lose in November. One of Henry B.'s talents was accommodation." Meaning that he was a slimy politician? Or a true politician? "So, before the general election, Henry B.'s running mate, one chosen because he was from populous southeast Florida, resigned from the ticket and Henry B. had the party put John Ionata in the lieutenant governor nominee's place."

I finished my diet Coke. "So the party was united and the new ticket went on to win."

"That's what happened," Pinky said, nodding.

"But the two were still not on good terms," I said.

"Never. They maintained sort of a cordial enmity. And Henry B. used that against John Ionata. You see, the lieutenant governor has one major job: to become governor if the governor dies or is incapacitated. The Florida Constitution doesn't give him much else to do. Historically, the governor has assigned a certain portfolio of responsibilities to the lieutenant governor; but not Henry B. He did not let John Ionata do much of anything."

"And that really grates his ass," said Vern with another hawk-like grin. "It's effectively precluded Ionata from getting his name in the paper or on television." Bernstein laughed aloud.

"Also, it has kept Ionata from developing a power base and kept him from building a legitimate platform from which to express himself and his political ideas." Vern was right happy with the thought.

I stretched. "About five years of that would anger a man a great deal."

Both nodded in agreement.

So I hit them with the big question. "Would John Ionata have enough residual anger to kill Henry B.?"

Vern shrugged. He wasn't going to go out on a limb and answer that one.

Pinky surprised me. "I suppose a man in the heat of red hot anger will do almost anything, even things he might not ordinarily do."

"I know, I know. Husbands and wives knock each other off all the time and don't mean to do it." I peanut-buttered another half Oreo, the crème disappearing.

"That is what I was referring to," Pinky said watching me with fascination. After I ate the Oreo, he continued. "They had been arguing. John Ionata had come down here to have it out with Henry B. He had threatened to resign and embarrass Henry B. before the election; but Henry B. told John he'd make him Secretary of Commerce, or give him some other high-profile governor-appointed position. Well, um, Henry B. never fulfilled that promise."

"So a year later and Ionata is one year angrier."

Pinky lifted his shoulders. "Politics. What can I say."

"They eat their young," I said. "And that's part of the game."

"Exactly. I see you understand how it works. A variation of situational ethics."

"Ethics in politics?" Tapes said mildly.

"I personally don't think John Dellum Ionata killed the governor," said Vern.

"He's a possible suspect, though," I pointed out, "with more reason than either Tapes or me to croak Henry B."

"You've an entire Inn full of suspects," Vern said, Adam's

apple bobbing.

He was saying something more than the words expressed.

"What do you mean?" My voice was neutral.

Vern's eyes darted about conspirationally. "Everybody knows Henry B. couldn't keep his hands off women, and it didn't matter whether they were married."

Alarm raced through me. As did fear and apprehension. Followed by a sinking, sickening feeling. "You're not saying...?"

"I am," Vern said adamantly.

"Even," I took in a deep breath, "unlikely people such as Mary Lynn Messenger? And Angle Maple?"

"Unlikely?"

"Well," I said. "Mary Lynn knew Henry B. casually, I'm given to understand. They're both from Gasparilla Island. Angie Maple has been trying to solve the murder. How can she be suspect?" I'd brought up Angie Maple because I didn't want to seem stuck on the subject of one each Mary Lynn Messenger.

Vern laughed harshly. "Casual knowledge? Fill in this blank, Birthday. The Henry B. Gonzáles Gasparilla Island Reelection Campaign Chairperson was blank?"

"Oh, shit," I said.

"I told you about your sleeve," Tapes said quietly.

I was showing my feelings in public. I gathered myself in. "Angie—"

"And there are rumors," Vern continued, ignoring me, "about the real cause of the Messenger divorce. Wife much younger than carpenter husband. She a party activist and trusted political volunteer. You never know."

Sometimes you just want to up and quit, you know? It just ain't worth it. Things build up in importance to you and some sorry insensitive son of a bitch comes along and bursts your fucking balloon.

"You don't know that for a fact," Tapes said.

"I don't have to," Bernstein said. "I'm not a prosecutor or a judge. Birthday asked, I answered. Everybody knows the governor was running around with younger women last year.

Secret trysts, late night assignations here in the hotel."

That coincided with Mary Lynn's divorce.

Maybe what Bernstein said was not true. A straw to grasp.

And even if what he said was true, that Mary Lynn was having an affair with the governor; it didn't mean that she killed him.

My eyes sought the tiny stack of dishes that Mary Lynn had washed for me.

Bernstein looked around the kitchen and continued. "There's a scene happened here in the JG Inn lobby. Messenger and Gonzáles came down from *his* room. He was seen by several witnesses kissing her goodbye and giving her *cash* money."

I looked poison darts at Bernstein. He was as slimy as monkey brains on a plate of okra, the son of a bitch.

"Mary Lynn Messenger," said Hey Vern. "A superbly attractive woman. She'd draw our Henry B. like a moth to flame."

13: TUESDAY, 8:00 A.M.

My throat was so constricted it felt like a wolf had just ripped it out.

"How about Angie Maple?" Tapes asked, taking up the baton because of my lengthy silence. This fellow Bernstein was pure poison—but he knew some things we needed to know.

"She's a local gadfly," said Vern Bernstein.

Pinky adjusted his bow tie and looked sideways at Vern. "That's not an exact characterization I would use."

Bernstein poured himself some more coffee. "She's a Republican."

"Praise the Lord for that, too," said Pinky. His eyes were flashing. He was excited. "That would account for her running around and asking all those fool questions of all of us all the time."

"All right," I said. Pinky had a repetitive pattern that was driving even me nuts. "What do you mean?"

"If she could perhaps prove," Pinky said slowly, "one of us, specifically a Democrat like Vern or me or John Ionata, murdered Henry B. that would shake the party's foundations; the final fallout being the loss of the governor's chair in Florida, and perhaps some ancillary Republican gains in the statehouse and perhaps in Florida's Congressional delegation."

"Perhaps," I said, "but that's pretty hardcore political hatred." I saw Pinky's glance at Vern. There was something else here. "Mrs. Maple must have some personal stake involved, something which explains her hatred of Democrats—or this bunch of Democrats."

"Vern?" said Pinky.

Vern said, "Sure, Pinky. Look, Birthday. Do you know about Henry Beauchamps Gonzáles?"

"Some." I was still smarting from the revelations about Mary Lynn.

"Local rich kid," Bernstein said. "From right here in the city of Boca Grande and Gasparilla Island. Rich kid, I say again. Dad was into real estate, made money, so much so, that they invested money in numerous enterprises, including this old hotel, and, due to the enormous growth in Florida in the sixties, seventies and eighties, pyramided the family wealth. It's now run by an umbrella corporation of which Henry B. was in complete control."

I twisted the top onto the peanut butter jar. Crunchy is best. "So Henry B. had a ton of money."

"He wanted more," said Vern, "he went into politics. State legislator from this district to give him a stepping stone. U.S. Congressman which provided him statewide name recognition. He would have been U.S. Senator from Florida, except the incumbent was party and he didn't want to wait four years for the Republican's seat—the six year election cycle, you understand." Bernstein stopped cold there.

"Hey, Vern," I said. "This civics' lesson is all fine and good, but what's the connection with Angie Maple?"

He shot me a grin, albeit a slick one. "Henry B., while not unpopular hereabouts, was not the favorite son. There was a Republican representative named Howard K. Maple already occupying this seat, the 25th District of Florida. The contest was, by nature, dirty. Some aspersions were made, not really proven out in the final analysis, against Howie Maple. He lost, a very bitter man, and promptly died of a heart attack."

"Jeez," I said. "Isn't there anybody who did *not* have a motive to kill Henry B.?"

"Me," said Pinky.

"Me, neither," I said. "I heard of stuff earlier in Florida

history that in a fifties' U.S. Senate race, the opposition called Claude Pepper's brother or sister 'a practicing heterosexual' and 'a thespian' and so cost Pepper the race."

"That happened." Vern was in his element. "It was brilliant."

"But Henry B. came along later," I pointed out.

Bernstein grinned again. "Same chapter, different page. The game is a bit more sophisticated now. Whispers and open accusations suffice. When the target denies them publicly, he's in essence indicting himself by going public. Especially in local elections." He smiled happily. "You see, the brilliant thing about it all was that Henry B. was the rake and satyr. Everybody knew that. He'd been married a couple of times. That was a given. Now, if Howie Maple is whispered to be the same, it kills his reputation. Henry B. is rich and powerful and will look out for the district's interest better than some do-gooder who'll vote his conscience rather than vote on something that will financially benefit his district."

"That's true," I admitted. "Time tested, but that's the way it works. Honesty is usually a casualty of politics."

"You should see," Pinky said, "the United States Federal highways in Congressional District 25."

"And you'll notice a great deal of Federal money has been spent in and around Charlotte Harbor," said Vern. "The harbor, the keys, the passes dredged regularly. The U.S. Corps of Engineers has gone out of its way. There are several Coast Guard ships based here—clean industry, money spent on the local economy. Oh, Henry B. was a good congressman."

"And all that spells reelection," I said.

"It does." Bernstein nodded. "And power base and name recognition. Henry B. parlayed it into the Governor's Mansion in Tallahassee."

"With higher future ambitions?" I asked.

"Definitely," said Vern wistfully. He would have liked to gone all the way to the White House with Henry B. Now he was headed for the unemployment line.

I thought a moment. "So Angie blames her husband's death

on Henry B.?"

"To the penny," said Vern. "Howard Maple was idealistic and starry eyed. He was honest, legitimate, concerned, and dedicated to do the right thing regardless of political consequence." Bernstein chuckled to himself. "And he was a Republican. Can you imagine that?"

"I guess you could say he got what he deserved," I said dryly.

Bernstein nodded vigorously, his Adam's apple like a ping pong ball.

"It also explains Angie and all her fool questions," said Pinky. "If she did murder the governor, she could be diverting attention to everyone else, trying to find someone with motive and opportunity that fits the situation of the crime. And, failing that, if Angie is not guilty herself, and she can charge a key upper echelon Democrat, then she can vindicate her late husband and get even simultaneously."

It occurred to me that everyone with any motive to kill Gonzáles was probably trying to divert attention to anyone else—make that everyone else. This thing was getting more complicated than it originally appeared. I shook my head wearily. "Lying. Everybody has something to hide. They're not all telling the truth." A pain hit me. "Or by omission."

Bernstein smiled. This was his element. "The truth, my friend, is a commodity. You use commodities. You buy them. You trade them. You horde them. In this business, you use the commodities you have, whether it be truth, power, votes, whatever, but you use them."

"And the truth hurts," I said, hurting a little myself. "I often thought," I said quietly, more to Tapes than to them, "that there ought to be a physical law of nature like the Pinocchio bit, only different. Every time you lie, your pecker grows shorter. That would insure the truth."

"Probably insure a completely different world, too," Tapes said. "All the politicians would be eunuchs."

Pinky said, "'A man that beareth false witness against his neighbor is a maul, and a sword, and a sharp arrow.' Another

Proverb." Pinky was serious and I wondered what it meant.

"Leave us alone," said Vern.

I shook my head. This wasn't getting us anywhere. Henry B.'s death was causing a great deal to happen, and a great deal more to become exposed. "There are warts on people all throughout this hotel," I said. "How the hell could one man have alienated so many people, especially those close to him?"

"He worked hard at it," said Vern Bernstein seriously. While Vern was a cynic and a polished political hack, I think he was bright enough to have some personal insight to share.

"And those here at the Inn now are simply his close associates," I said.

"That's a fact, Birthday," said Vern warming to his subject. "There are spurned women all over this fair state." Mary Lynn? "And some that haven't yet been spurned. Old Henry B. had affairs going in every corner of Florida. It's a big state, from Pensacola to Key West. From Tallahassee it's over six hundred miles to Key West, almost five hundred to Miami," he pronounced Miami like Miam-ah, "two hundred and fifty to Tampa and a hundred and seventy or so to Jacksonville. Last but not least, close to four hundred miles to here."

"Geography pretty well compartmentalizes romance." I scratched my head, then thought of something. "There is something which doesn't add up, Vern. Angle Maple, activist Republican. Mary Lynn Messenger, Democrat and," I decided to stay away from her relationship with Henry B., "local reelection committee chair. The two should be mutually exclusive."

"That's what I thought, too," said Vern. "Pinky?"

Pinky swelled a little in self-importance at being deferred to by his higher ranking associate. "The two are friends. They share the same environmental and ecological concerns for Southwest Florida. Both were charter members of BIPS and GICIA—"

"Which mean?" Tapes prompted.

"BIPS is the Barrier Island Parks Society. It's a support organization for the four local state parks, all four on islands hereabouts. GICIA is Gasparilla Island Conservation & Improvement Association. It was primarily responsible for restoring the abandoned Old Port Boca Grande Lighthouse starting in 1985—"

"Great," said Tapes, cutting Pinky off before we got *all* the recent local history. "I suppose you were going to mention José Gaspar?"

"I'm not certain any of that myth is truth," Pinky said.

"The Chamber of Commerce is," said Vern. "And the headless woman dressed in white—"

"About Angie and Mary Lynn?" I said.

"Right." Pinky touched his tie as if for reassurance. "Mary Lynn Messenger was starry-eyed and young and easily caught up in a cause. She began as an environmentalist and therefore was a Democrat. She was a good party volunteer whenever the party needed help locally, and her rise to the Gasparilla Island Chair was natural. Keep in mind that she was island Campaign Reelection Chairperson, a largely ceremonial position answering to the party as well as the candidate; ceremonial, also, for this is Henry B.'s hometown, and the voters are going to vote for him regardless. Henry B. didn't even bother to campaign here for either gubernatorial election."

That made sense to me.

How was I going to face Mary Lynn?

I'd hung my hat upon her, so to speak. Or is it set my cap? Whatever, would I reveal what I knew? Could I pursue her in a romantic fashion still? Or were the stirrings I felt for her gone?

Even though Vern and Pinky had not said so, the scenario was easy to project. Mary Lynn had stayed over at the José Gaspar Inn for one of many reasons such as she'd had too much to drink, or the storm, or she'd planned it that way. She'd gone early to Henry B.'s suite, and not found him. Since he'd been jogging, she'd encountered him on the third floor landing, gotten into an argument because he'd dropped her or reneged on marrying her or any one of a dozen other possibilities, and, in a fit of passion, snatched the tennis racquet from the rack on the wall and smashed him. She could have intended to hit him with the strings, but he moved and the leading edge nailed Gonzáles on the forehead and bang through the railing and a quick non-elevator trip to the ground level.

I doubted it would be possible to establish where everyone was at the time of the murder.

Everyone's whereabouts at the time of the murder made me think of Silas, Silas who should have been finished helping with Trooper by now.

"What do you know about Silas Smith?" I asked. "He's a possible suspect."

"Silas didn't fall under any security program to research his background." Pinky was evasive.

Pinky's answer was what I was searching for, but why did Pinky address it from a security standpoint? "You spoke of Silas in terms of security checks. Why is that? I mean, as opposed to others we've just now discussed and their possible motives." Tired of leaning against the butcher block table I shifted position.

Pinky glanced at Vern.

Vern shrugged. "I think Smith is a fag, you know?" He shook his head disdainfully. Insensitivity I could understand from a politician's guru; but pencil-necked geeks ought to have a little bit more sensitivity than Vern was showing. "Smith lives alone and hardly ever goes out. When he does, he doesn't advertise his destination."

Pinky was looking at the ceiling. "'Judge not that ye be not judged.' Matthew 7:1."

"Since you believe Silas Smith's behavior aberrant," I pointed out, "it seems to me you've the wherewithall to order an investigative check on him without the governor's knowledge."

"Hah," laughed Pinky with genuine humor. "He's got you, Vern."

"I did," Vern said. "I could find no paper trail on him; and I couldn't very well ask Henry B. or Silas since they'd know I was going behind the governor's back."

"Everybody leaves a paper trail," said Tapes. "Especially in this day of computers."

Vern studied us for a minute. "It's bound to come out anyway. He gets no personal mail, including magazines. Those are all ordered in the Inn's name. He watches videos on television, that's about it. I ran his social security number and it appears that he applied for and was granted the number when he came to work for the Inn. No other hint or clue."

"Why wouldn't you ask Henry B.?" I wanted to know. "It's a logical step to protect your, um, meal ticket."

Vern nailed me with a glare. His moods and emotions were mercurial. "No diplomat you, Birthday. I did broach the subject with Henry B. He told me to forget it in no uncertain terms. So I did. I dropped the whole thing."

Pinky nodded. "Silas is—was—fiercely protective of Henry B. and vice versa."

"Boy, it's getting deep," I said. "And nobody knows why?"

Both shook their heads, one bow tie and one Adam's apple bobbing in unison.

"Tell them," Tapes suggested.

"What?" Vern Bernstein picked right up on it.

"Like you said, it'll come out sooner or later." I folded my arms and paused self-consciously, holding and drawing out the audience. In that extra moment, I decided not to say anything about Silas and his preparing a boat. "Tapes and I were looking for him and went by his office. He wasn't there." I didn't mention kicking the door open. "But someone had smashed the big window *from the inside*. Half the damn Gulf of Mexico, Charlotte Harbor, and rain were flooding his office. Conveniently, I'd suspect disks, files and accounting books had been busted, torn, and left out all over the desk and credenza under the window. Doubtlessly, all those financial records are ruined."

Pinky shrugged. "So what?"

Vern squinted. "So nobody can audit the books due to an act of God. Smith is the manager with total control over all the monies, incoming and outgoing. He could have been skimming the top, getting kickbacks from jobbers and not-so-low bidders. Dozens of possibilities occur to me."

"Got it," Pinky said, hand to his mouth. "The governor is murdered, meaning microscopic investigation of everything connected with the Inn. Malfeasance discovered."

"Exactly," I said. "Whether or not he killed Gonzáles, he'd be found out if he'd been cooking the books or whatever." And, I thought, Silas was doing a fine job of covering his back trail. Sometime in the next couple of weeks, *HBG'S GATOR GAL* would be sunk off some island in the Bahamas.

"We need to speak to Silas," Pinky said quietly as the wind had stopped rattling the shutters for a moment, "and insure his current presence subsequent to the termination of this meteorological anomaly."

"Gimme another break," said Vern. "At times he gets carried away." Vern sounded right fond of Pinky, his words only gently mocking.

"That's a good point," I said. "Where is Silas?"

At that moment, the lights went out again followed by an immediate dull explosion. The hotel shook a bit, but not near as much as at the height of the winds.

"I don't like that a lot," Tapes said, and his pocket flash sprang to life and settled on the kitchen doors.

Since it was daylight now, the kitchen took on a gray hue and I could see the outlines of the others.

Tapes was moving toward the doorway. "I've a bad feeling about this. Let's go, Shorts."

I hurried to catch up. "If you're waiting on me, you're backing up." I turned back and Vern and Pinky were following us. Tapes went out the back kitchen door down a short feeder corridor and into a courtyard affair open on two sides. A loading dock and a dumpster at the corner of the building and a shed attached to the outside kitchen wall.

The two sides of the building didn't help, because the wind was coming now from the north and east, blowing right in. It wasn't really raining, either; however, the wind whipped stinging droplets against my face. I hoped I had clean clothes left. I'd settle for dry clothes.

Tapes made it to the shed against the wall before I saw the fire. The shed contained the auxiliary generator which had been providing power to the Inn since the initial power outage.

Now one of the doors of the generator shed was banging open in the whipping rain and I could see the fire raging within the shed. The way it was burning told me it had at least been started by gasoline or fuel of some kind; I didn't know whether this generator was gasoline or diesel driven. If it was modern, it was probably gasoline.

When I got closer, I saw that the flames were leaping off the inside wall, that which the shed shared in common with the kitchen wing of the hotel.

Quickly, I turned to tell Pinky and Vern to get us some fire extinguishers from the kitchen.

They hadn't followed us outside.

A noise whipped past my ears and I turned back. Moving closer, I could see.

Tapes was pointing to an empty set of brackets on the inside wall of the shed next to the flapping door. The obligatory fire extinguisher was gone.

The wind was whipping the flames inside the shed into a frenzy.

"Hang on!" I shouted and spun. I ran against the wind and slammed into what I thought were closed doors, but which swung open as I began to hit them with my shoulder. I stumbled in and fell to my hands and knees.

Vern and Pinky were there and one of them must have opened the doors for me.

"What is it?" said Pinky.

"Light," I demanded.

Something clicked in the relative quiet of the corridor and there was Vern holding a disposable lighter.

I jumped to my feet and headed to the wall insert where I recalled seeing a fire extinguisher.

Gone.

I didn't have time to think of the ramifications.

"Into the kitchen," I said and hurried that way.

Vern caught up, his movement extinguishing his lighter. We went into the kitchen and I promptly banged my left knee.

"Light." My voice was demanding.

The lighter flicked on and I headed for the stove and the grill. A good place, I thought, for a fire extinguisher.

Vern followed me with his lighter. "What's wrong, Birthday?"

I fancied I could smell smoke and see paint peeling off the inside walls. "Fire. Somebody set a fire in the generator shed."

"The explosion?" said Vern.

"Likely," I said. "The flames probably ate through some wiring and bang the whole thing went. Blew out a wiring harness or something."

I was kneeling and throwing open pantry doors, drawers, anything large enough to contain a fire extinguisher.

"Here," said Vern and his light moved to the opposite side of the grill. Right there in the open attached to the wall above the dishwasher. Vern snapped the retaining plastic buckles and I snatched the red metal cylinder out of his hands.

As I ran toward the exit, I broke the safety wire and pulled the pin. I figured any fire extinguisher suitable for a professional kitchen would be appropriate for electrical and fuel fires.

Tapes met me as I ran into the courtyard.

Wind whipped flames against the building behind him. He grabbed the fire extinguisher from my hands and another explosion hit.

The shock wave knocked both of us against the wind. The matching door of the shed flew where our heads had been and clanged into the wall next to the door I'd just come out.

"Fuel tank or external supply," Tapes shouted in my ear.

We untangled ourselves. Diesel doesn't ordinarily explode.

"Whose idea was this anyway?" I asked, voice loud and complaining.

"You're the one who likes lighthouses," he accused. "I favor windmills."

We got to our feet and Tapes picked up the fire extinguisher again.

The shed was demolished.

Flames were crawling up the wall like a cat climbing a curtain, slowly but surely. Tapes ran, wind-aided, with the fire extinguisher out in front of him.

I turned and ran back inside to search out another unit. Again the door popped open as I reached it and, again, I stumbled in.

Vern was standing there holding another fire extinguisher.

Again I snatched the unit from his hands. "The whole side of the building might catch," I said as he looked over my shoulder. "Do something from the inside. If we're too late, you'd better warn everybody and get them out."

A chill ran over me when I thought of Sandra Dee Kowalski and her newborn. And Trooper was decommissioned, too.

As I went back outside, I wondered how much evidence, including the murder victim's body, would go up in flames?

14: TUESDAY, 9:20 A.M.

Wind whipped the flames and us. It was equally difficult to aim the extinguishant in high, swirling winds. The configuration of the hotel around the courtyard made for a nightmare of clashing elements, eddies and whirlpools of wind and rain.

High winds fan flames.

However, flames must have something upon which to feed; and the hotel, wood siding inside the courtyard, provided it. On the other hand, that wood was soaked from all the rain.

We sprayed the dry chemical at the base of the flames. It soon became obvious to me that the initial impetus of the fire, the gasoline, was the prime burning agent. Soda or whatever the extinguishers' contents flew all over the courtyard.

It was equally difficult to attack the fire because the bulk of the generator and the demolished shed hindered us.

Tapes' fire extinguisher quit and he stumbled aside. I moved over a shade and climbed on the cement slab at the end of the generator, then onto the generator housing itself. Tapes boosted me up.

Flames were blowing sideways and I concentrated on the base and worked my way along. Wind tore at me and I felt Tapes holding my ankles.

Fortunately, the flames I didn't kill just sort of petered out, the fuel feeding them exhausting. Whoever set the fire didn't know much about arson or fire dynamics.

I jumped down and Tapes steadied me. "Reminds me of the time you tried to barbecue a Spam loaf over a Tiki Torch," I shouted.

He favored me with a glare. "Let's go find Silas Smith and get some answers," he said, "before something else happens."

Back in the kitchen, we found Vern and Pinky actually helping. They had one of those small hoses you hitch up to your kitchen faucet and wet vegetables or water plants with, and they were spraying the wall on the outside of which was the generator and had been the threatening fire.

We could see better as they had set up a battery lantern.

I drew my pointy finger across my throat. "It's out."

"Thank God," Pinky said. "Make a joyful noise unto the Lord."

"And thank incompetence," I added.

We found some hand towels and dried off as well as we could.

"The generator's had it," Tapes said.

I'd known it. "Let us go and seek out the manager and make a formal complaint," I said. "What room is Trooper in?" I asked Pinky.

"One twelve."

"Let's go, Tapes."

We headed out, Tapes in the lead with his pocket flash. After a brief moment, Vern and Pinky appeared behind us, the battery lantern throwing out an unnecessary cone of light.

I stopped at Sandra Dee Kowalski's room and knocked gently.

Mary Lynn Messenger opened the door. A flickering candle behind her outlined her head, a few out-of-place strands were highlighted in shadow-relief. She saw me and a tired smile changed her face.

"I thought you were supposed to be asleep," I accused, for the moment forgetting everything else.

Her face tightened. "You, too." She looked me up and down. "Now you are soaked to the bone and there's soot and grime all over you." She put a hand on her hip and cocked her head, quite a fetching sight, I must admit.

"There was a small matter of someone trying to burn down the Inn," I said and explained briefly. "How's Sandy?"

"Mother and daughter are sleeping and doing well."

I noticed Angie Maple listening over Mary Lynn's shoulder. "Hi, Granny." I remembered Mary Lynn's position for Henry B., one she'd failed to mention to me. I also recalled Bernstein telling of her affair with the governor. "What is this, the divorce party reunion?"

Hurt leaped into Mary Lynn's eyes. "What's wrong, Billy?" She patted her hair down. Her eyes eemed to dance along with the flicker of the candle.

"You never told me you worked for Gonzáles' reelection."

Her eyes dropped, and then lifted defiantly. She paused, letting my accusatory tone sink in. "One, it never came up. Two, the position died naturally a year ago. Three, I didn't see where it mattered."

"It makes you a suspect in his murder," I said, letting my mouth outrun my brain.

She stood up straighter. "Is that what you think, Billy?"

"I don't know what the hell to think." I glared at her. "I heard about affairs, too—"

"Well, I forgot point number four," she said holding up three fingers and springing her little finger to make four. "Four. It isn't any of your business."

"You tell him, Mary Lynn," said Angie Maple.

Mary Lynn looked distracted for a moment, disappointed for another moment, and exhausted for a third moment. Then she closed the door in my face.

In the sudden quiet of the hallway, Tapes said, "That was real smooth, Shortcut."

"Christ, Birthday," Vern Bernstein's voice interrupted from the side. "What'd you do, hit her in the stomach? Did you see her face, Pinky?"

From behind Tapes, Pinky said, "Mr. Birthday, remember John three sixteen."

"Why me, Lord?" I said.

"That's not it," Pinky said.

Sometimes the only reason I open my mouth is to change

shoes.

I pushed past them and headed for one twelve, my emotions boiling. It was slowly occurring to me that I'd just royally fucked up. A dread crept through my gut into my brain. If Mary Lynn was guilty of murder, I'd lost her. If she wasn't guilty, I'd just lost her. My motor mouth had run ahead of my brain; I'd even begun accusing her of an affair with Henry B. It's hard to lose something, somebody you never really had to start with; but it sure as hell felt like it. I felt like my dog just got ran over. Like I found a bucketful of drownded kittens. Like I just got drafted. All of which X'd out some rosy future. It reminded me bitterly of Rebecca's recent defection. I decided to give up women and become celibrate. I shook my head. "Damn," I muttered.

Tapes' big hand settled on my shoulder and pulled me up. Vern and Pinky stopped alongside us.

"Shortcut, if you conduct the interview with Silas with as much finesse as you just used, we ain't gonna learn nothin'." Tapes sounded angry. Hell, I was the one madder than a pissed off armadillo.

I shook his hand off and headed on down the hall. "You don't like it, you do it."

The door to one twelve was propped open. Brilliant light spilled out into the corridor. Inside on the dresser was one of those halogen lights.

The room was practically the same as the rest of them in the east wing of the first floor. Large bed, television, hotel-generic framed prints on the walls, overstuffed chairs and overhead ceiling fan.

Trooper lay on the bed, propped up by a stack of pillows. He looked drawn but not quartered. His eye tracked us as we entered without knocking, settling on me.

On one side, stood John Ionata with his foot on a wooden chair.

On the other side of the bed, Silas Smith was sitting in a similar wooden chair edged up against Trooper's bed. He had a can of Campbell's Pork and Beans. He was holding it out to

Trooper.

Trooper had a spoon in his right hand. "Goddamn beans," he said. "I need a beer."

"I think his kidney is internally injured," said Silas.

Ionata was watching me. "They're not interested, Trooper. This has all the appearances of a lynching party."

"Shortcut just got some bad news," Tapes said.

"I'll say," echoed Vern from behind.

"We came to talk to Silas," I said, trying not to look as dark and brooding as I felt.

Smith's eyes bounced around like worms on a hot griddle. He said nothing, but held out the can of pork and beans into Trooper's face.

Trooper pushed the can out of the way and Silas sort of dropped his arm and rested it and the can on the edge of the bed.

"Just what is it you want?" Ionata asked, his voice soft, jealous of us, or me, initiating something without coordinating with him first.

"Somebody just tried to burn down the Inn," I said trying to be dramatic.

A startled look came over Silas Smith.

Ionata took his foot off the chair and stood up straight. For the first time he seemed to notice me and Tapes, wet and sooty and grimy. "What happened?"

"Perhaps we ought to ask Silas," I said.

"What *are* you talking about?" Silas said, eyes gaunt and bleak in this harsh lighting.

"The generator was sabotaged. And fuel was splashed over the insides of the generator shed," I said, "indiscriminately, and ignited the outside wall of the kitchen."

"Oh," said Silas.

"Who would do that?" said John Ionata.

"Silas," I said, answering his question and prompting Silas at the same time.

The manager of the Inn looked down then up. The bleak light highlighted the scars of his neck, creating small pockets of shadow. His Adam's apple wiggled a bit.

"Well, Silas?" I said.

He looked up at me, eyes shifting to Tapes who was leaning against the wall and tapping his can of Copenhagen.

The lieutenant governor cleared his throat. "It is apparent you know or suspect Silas of something. Please explain yourself."

I wasn't going to answer. I wanted to use what I knew against Silas if what he said conflicted with what we knew.

But Vern Bernstein stepped forward. "There's the fire in the generator shed, John. And the window in Smith's office was broken from the inside and all the pertinent hotel records have been ruined by the storm."

I shot Bernstein a hostile glare. He was trying to ingratiate himself with the future governor. Well, hell, it ain't fun being unemployed, a state I was currently enjoying. Idly, I wondered if they'd rehire me in my old job at Davis-Monthan Air Force Base in Tucson to mothball USAF aircraft. I'd quit when I'd fallen in love with Rebecca in Tallahassee. She'd been deep in business there and wouldn't move to Tucson. It bothered me for a nanosecond that love was geographically flinging me around like a tethered balloon in a wind storm. I shook my head to get back to the present.

"Hey, Vern," I said. "Remember our talk about integrity?"

"That was about honesty," he said, "in politics. So what?"

"You're right. So what." I shook my head.

"Oh," he said.

"Look, Ionata," I said, and should have addressed him more formally, I could tell from his demeanor and glare—but he'd already accused me and Tapes of murder and had high-handed everyone here. "Somebody killed Henry B. and since then, some strange things have happened. Silas Smith is in the best position to either have done them or know who done them—or why." I turned my attention to Silas. "Why?"

He watched me carefully but didn't answer. His eyes were cunning.

"Trooper," I said. "Did you know that they can't trace Smith back before he became manager of the Inn?"

Trooper had been watching the byplay. "No, sir." His voice was soft.

I nodded. "Bernstein quite illegally and unethically had Silas investigated. It was like he was born when he became manager of the Inn."

"Issat true?" Trooper asked Silas.

"I've my rights," Silas said. "My personal life is no one's concern." His scarred neck convulsed.

Trooper's left hand snaked out and grasped Smith's right elbow in a vise-like grip. Quick pain shot across the manager's face.

"Silas?" said Trooper.

"That hurts." He tried to pull his arm away, but Trooper's grip was unbreakable.

"Me and Henry B. been friends since college," said Trooper.

"That's a long time," I said.

Trooper nodded. "It is that. He was quarterback of the Gators up in Gainesville. I was the center. My job was to protect him. I hurt my back doing that in one game. It was in Jacksonville against Georgia. Then they got to Henry B. and knocked him out of the game and we lost." Trooper looked sad. "It was the first time I let him down."

Meaning the last time was when somebody killed the governor.

Trooper squeezed Silas' elbow with more enthusiasm. "I never graduated. Henry B. did and he had his daddy fix me up with a job with the state. Then me and Henry B. joined the Army. Went to RVN, that's Republic of. He was an officer and got me in his company and I saved his life and he saved mine and we made it through together. When we got out, Henry B. and his father used their influence and got me a job with the Florida Highway Patrol—I din't want any of the paper-pushing jobs they offered me with their company. I wanted a good-lookin' uniform and a glitzy job like the FHP. When Henry B. became governor, I was the natural FHP officer to be his bodyguard. Thanks to him, I got a nice retirement coming one day." He hesitated. "But now that don't seem to really matter anymore." He fixed his attention on Silas and squeezed. He jerked his thumb toward me. "You been good to me, Silas. You been seeing I get taken care of since them goons jumped me. But Henry B. Not only was he my job, but he was my friend, too. Talk, goddamn it. Answer Birthday's questions."

Silas shifted his gaze around the room. His eyes sank farther into their sockets.

"Well?" Trooper demanded.

Silas put the can of pork and beans on the edge of the bed. "I'm gay."

"So what?" I asked.

"If there came a big investigation, it would uncover that fact. I'd have to come out of the closet."

"I say again," I said again, "so what? Being gay isn't a crime."

Silas slumped back. "They'd uncover the fact that Pinky and I were having an affair."

"Oh no, no, no," said Pinky. "Oh, my Lord!"

15: TUESDAY, 10:10 A.M.

"So what?" I said again. "Who cares who you have an affair with."

Vern had moved over to Pinky. "A fudge-packer? You?"

Pinky just looked at his associate.

"Tell me," Vern went on, "that you are not a pecker-puffer."

"It's none of your business."

Ionata cleared his throat. "It is our business. Henry B. was severely prejudiced. If he discovered that Silas—or Pinky, for that matter—was gay, then he'd probably fire him." Ionata stood and pushed the chair aside. He fixed Silas with a glower. "Look, Smith. If Henry B. found you were gay and fired you right then and there on the third landing yesterday morning, you could well have flown into a rage and struck him with the tennis racquet."

"I did not."

"Then you do not deny it!" Ionata spat out.

"I do!" Silas said.

Vern was still staring at his friend. "Jesus."

"Hey, Vern," I said, "your level of tolerance is stratospheric. I'd think you're queer for snakes the way you operate."

"Shortcut," Tapes warned.

He was right. I calmed myself. Of course, none of it made any sense.

Actually, my intellectual curiosity was aroused. I addressed Pinky. "How do you reconcile being born-again with your homosexuality?"

Pinky's shoulders slumped. Then he raised his head and

looked me directly in the eye. "Are you religious?"

Which took me aback. I don't usually reveal my name, much less more personal information. "I'm diagnostic."

It didn't strike him as funny. He said, "I also sometimes drink wine or brandy and I don't reconcile that."

"Point taken," I admitted.

He went on, eyes glazing, "it is the simple folk who will enter Heaven before the remainder of us who have to eat our own jaded grapes."

I'd have to think that one through a while. I wondered if it wasn't a line in the Bible—but I didn't ask. Pinky was becoming a real person to me, no longer a bit player, no longer a geek.

Trooper was looking at Silas. "You're a homo?"

"No, sir, I am not. I am gay."

Trooper looked at his hand holding Smith's elbow as if for the first time. Then he jerked it away as if it were on fire.

"None of this follows," I said. "You're being gay has little or no bearing on the fact of the generator fire, of the destroyed computer, files and accounting books. I can see where it could explain your lack of past. But the rest doesn't add up."

Silas was folding into himself. It was a visible phenomenon.

"And it doesn't really explain somebody beating you up," Tapes pointed out from where he stood against the wall.

Silas raised his head and his eyes gleamed, a startling characteristic with his eyes being so far back in his skull. "I don't have to say anything to anybody. I have my constitutional rights, you know." He looked at Trooper. "And you have just violated them, using physical torture to make me talk."

The room was silent and I thought I could hear the halogen light crackling in the background, but it was just the wind pushing this wing of the old building around.

"He's got a good point," I said. "On the other hand, it seems to me that if you are not guilty of the governor's murder, then it would behoove you to cooperate."

"No, thank you." His eyes still blazed.

"One of the qualities I admire most in a person is reluctance,"

I said. "But you're carrying it too far."

"You become the prime suspect," said Ionata, shaking his head as if he didn't believe the murder just got solved.

"Silas?" I said. "It's likely you have much to account for, that's obvious. However, your failure to help us out does a couple of things, all of them bad."

"What's that?"

"It allows the real murderer time to escape," I said dramatically, looking around the room with concentration.

Silas caught my drift. "What else?"

"I suspect that Ionata and Trooper will lock you up, handcuff you to a bed or toilet or something. You'd be a prisoner, unable to move around, even when the weather clears a bit and the seas die down from the storm." I was doing everything I could to evoke the image of *HBG'S GATOR GAL* in Smith's mind. I was convinced he was going to use the boat to escape whatever malfeasance he'd committed here.

Vern was still standing in front of Pinky. "A bible-spouting, born-again, little-boy-chasing, chocolate-wick-dipping, faggot-humping—"

"Hey, Vern," I said, the animosity in my voice cutting through the air and silencing him. "Shut up or I will shut you up." I was looking up at him under my own lowered brows.

Bernstein nervously glanced around the room.

I turned my attention back to Silas. "Changed your mind about talking yet?"

He avoided my gaze.

"It's going to come out in the next day or so," I pointed out.

"Goddamn right," said Vern.

I looked back at Vern. "You're pretty vocal for about the only one who had no reason to kill the governor."

"Nuh, uh," said Trooper quietly.

"What do you mean?" I turned my head back to him.

Trooper's head sank into the mess of pillows behind him. "Henry B. He just found out Bernstein was a draft dodger during the war in 'Nam."

"So what?" I was getting tired of repeating myself.

"Henry B.," said Trooper building his voice dramatically, "hated draft dodgers more than he hated queers."

It occurred to me that everyone in the hotel, save maybe me and Tapes, had got together and killed Henry B. It would have been nice if that were true, but they were all at each other's' throats and stabbing one another in the back, so that sort of ruled out them working together. But that didn't account for Orlo and the other two stooges.

"Explain in more detail, please," said John Ionata, moving closer to the bed.

Tapes had to shift position to watch.

Trooper took a deep breath. "It turns out that Bernstein milked the student exemption route as long as he could until the lottery system was introduced into the draft. His birthdate came up in the first drawing. Somehow, he wangled a job with a Vancouver law firm which put him in Canada—"

"Very convenient," said Ionata.

"That's right," Trooper said. "He just ignored the draft notices forwarded to him. He only came back when Jimmy Carter pardoned all those traitorous mother fuckers. Shit. And he was a Southerner and a Democrat, too." Trooper shook his head. I supposed he was talking about Carter, not Vern Bernstein.

"Vern," said Pinky accusingly. "You weren't?"

Vern stepped back and drew himself up to his full height. "Everything I did was perfectly legal."

"Legal, smeagle," said Pinky. "I'm talking morally reprehensible—"

"Where were you during Viet Nam?" demanded Vern.

"Not old enough. But I tried to sign up anyway." Pinky spat the words.

"What's the matter, they wouldn't take queers?"

"Hey!" I shouted, imitating Richard Boone in *Big Jake*.

Everybody clamped their mouths shut and looked at me.

I looked over at Tapes. "Is this a three-ring circus, or what?"

"You lost control," he said.

"Hell, I never had control." I just wasn't thinking very well. The memory of Mary Lynn Messenger weighed heavily in my mind. I'd handled that situation equally as well. Cicero always maintained that justice will win out when you do things right. Of course, he hadn't said that in those exact terms, nor had he said it in the middle of a typhoon surrounded by a bunch of weirdoes. Cicero was a very knowing and tolerant man. It always amazed me that he put up with his name, Cicero. Coming from the Latin Cicer, it actually referred to a wart-like thing on Cicero's father's nose, and the appellation stuck. Marcus Tullius Cicero carried it well. But, like Plutarch, I digress. And, unlike me, Cicero was always eloquent.

"I want to get back to Silas," I said, and moved closer to Silas. "Look. Did you kill the governor or not?"

"I did not." He was emphatic and watching his sunken eyes, I could easily believe him—or, at least, thought he thought he was telling the truth.

"I believe you," said Pinky with deep meaning.

I shook my head. If I kept playing these mind games, we'd never determine who killed Henry B.

"Maybe you could fill us in on the strange occurrences now," I said. "Like the mess in your office, the generator fire, somebody beating you up."

"He's been in and out of this room," said John Ionata. "I thought it was normal managerial duties."

The manager's Adam's apple bobbed up and down, making me wonder who'd win a contest between him and Vern Bernstein. Smith's voice was plaintive. "I can't incriminate myself."

Tapes sighed loudly. "Whyn't you crack that tough nut, Shorts."

"Sure." I decided on the brass ball thing on the bedpost nearest me.

It was about the size of a grapefruit and I grabbed it with one hand and tested it. One hand wouldn't do. I wrapped both hands around it and snapped it off clean, the noise cutting through the room and momentarily blanking out the background noise of the storm.

Trooper's eyes widened like he had been shot.

I held the metal globe close to Smith's face. "And Tapes is twice as strong as I am."

Silas turned whiter, if that was possible, in the glaring light. "You can't touch me." He was hanging in there; I had to give him credit.

I looked around the room. "Would you all excuse us?" Then I realized Trooper probably couldn't move with the alacrity necessary to maintain the urgency of the situation. "That is, Tapes and I will take a walk down the hall with Silas." I grabbed Smith by the upper arm and jerked him to his feet. Before he knew what I was doing, I had his arm up behind his back with pressure on it and he had to do whatever I wanted him to do.

He glanced back over his shoulder at me, fear showing on his face for the first time.

I dropped the metal ball to make my point and it clanged on a chair leg next to the spilled can of beans.

I began marching him toward the door.

"You can't do this!" Silas squeaked.

"You're right, I can't."

Tapes stood aside at the door.

"Mr. Ionata, please!" Silas said in a panic.

To his credit, Ionata cooperated. He looked aside and folded his arms across his chest.

"Trooper," cried Silas, voice now desperate, "you're the law. You can't let this happen."

"I don't give a fuck what happens to no goddamn queers," said Trooper. I guess everybody has to hate somebody. But the sensitivity level at the Inn must be a national low. Trooper looked at Pinky. "You move and I'll kick your dick off."

Pinky looked stricken.

Vern looked happy.

We got Silas into the corridor and Tapes closed the door. The hallway was gloomy.

I did the thing with one of Smith's fingers while it was still behind his back, crooking it toward his palm and jamming it back and up into itself.

Silas Smith screamed high and piercing.

I had a momentary guilt attack, and then I remembered somebody had fucked up my relationship with Mary Lynn and did it again.

The resultant scream was music to my ears. On the other hand, if somebody hadn't of croaked the governor, then she and I might not have gotten together to start with. It was an interesting mental gymnastic. Me and Mary Lynn could have been riding out the storm together, delicately speaking, perhaps, and not be estranged by shenanigans and political bedfellows—the thought of which made me angrier and I squeezed Silas's finger again.

His scream brought immediate results.

The door to one twelve flung open and Pinkus Keanon Clapsaddle III hurried out.

"Stop! Right this instant! 'A soft answer turneth away wrath; but grievous words stir up anger.'" Another Proverb.

"Don't get your bow tie in an uproar," Vern said from the room.

"Tell them, Silas," Pinky said. "Please? It can't be any worse." He moved around to face Silas.

"It can," said Silas, "oh, it can." He was sweating now.

This terrible feeling overcame me. Just a bit of nausea and a lump in my gut. Worse than when I learned I failed algebra and had to take it in summer school where Tapes had tutored me through it. I dropped Smith's arm in disgust at myself. Worse? "Shit, I don't need this."

"Shortcut," Tapes said, voice commanding.

"Yeah?"

"Somebody's got to do it. You're the only one who can."

"Fuck it. I don't care who killed the son of a bitch. Look, Tapes, look what's it's done to me. Hell. Look what it's done to *everybody*. There's more dirty laundry in this goddamn hotel than at the laundromat on Saturday."

"What'd we learn in Alaska?" Tapes said. "The lead dog always gets bitten in the ass."

Silas was rubbing his arm and watching. Pinky's face was scrunched up like he didn't know what was going on now. Which he obviously didn't.

"I say again," Tapes said, "you're the only one here can handle all this."

"Let Ionata try."

"That dog won't hunt," Tapes said, and I knew that was a fact.

"You'll never forgive yourself," Tapes said. "For the rest of your life. You'll know you could have made a difference, but backed out when the going got rough."

I didn't respond.

Tapes grabbed Pinky and Silas by their shoulders and pushed them back into one twelve, closed the door extinguishing the slice of light. He turned to me. "Like you always say, if you're going to run with the big dogs, you got to expect to get some of those big fleas."

That is my favorite saying.

Tapes moved to me. "And year after year, you'll wonder about *her*." Mary Lynn. "What would have happened? What you could have made happen. You've got the opportunity."

I thought about what he was saying. I always got involved wherever and whatever. It was my nature.

"You could have done better with Rebecca," he said.

"I know that." Rebecca Ann MacKenzie. Tallahassee businesswoman who owned a rentatruck agency.

"And how about with Shimmer?"

Shimmer Cordell, daughter of a wealthy Texas rancher. A literary snob and a feminist. But we'd been in love—and fought often to prove it.

"Then there was Laura."

I'd called her "Beantown," Laura Hanover, a wandering journalist from Boston, who I'd known for a day and a night and we'd simply talked all night and then she drove out of my life.

I'd moped around for weeks.

"Marischino," Tapes said softly.

A young Filipina hooker who used to live with me in Angeles City.

"And Buttons."

Buttons O'Hara. My first real adult love. She reminded me of Olivia Newton-John. Ate doughnuts and read diet books.

"This ain't fair," I told Tapes, my mind in a torment.

"Life ain't fair."

"I feel like I've stepped on every cow pie in the pasture," I said.

"You have done that thing. There's still some more out there you haven't got to yet."

"Let 'em find their own killer."

"They might," Tapes said, "but maybe not in time. You're the only one with the brains *and* the initiative to handle it now, when it needs handling."

"Nah," I said.

"Your favorite fighter?" said Tapes.

"Archie Moore." I knew what Tapes was going to say.

"'Never run a mule at Santa Anita,'" quoted Tapes.

I think I liked Archie Moore because he hadn't been the biggest boxer in the business. Maybe my personal crisis here had been triggered by my insecurity and feelings of inferiority at not being tall. I wondered if there were a parallel between me and Alan Ladd. His shortness contributed to his own sense of inferiority; however, I'd read that very character trait had driven him to success in Hollywood. Later, he'd dealt with his problems by using and abusing pills and alcohol, and they killed him. Becky's defection had helped precipitate my personal crisis; on top of that, my inability to cope with Mary Lynn Messenger was also contributing greatly to this crisis. I usually deal with crises by extroverting, by not revealing my name, by getting involved with other people, by falling in love. I hoped these wouldn't kill me.

"You could still save it with her," Tapes continued, meaning

Mary Lynn. My Shortcut/Tapes ESP center was working over-time. Tapes really felt I needed to go through this, maybe for my own good? A catharsis?

"You do it," I told him.

"I got nothing that might can *rapidly dissipate*," he said.

Shit. "Okay, goddamnit, let's get on with it."

"About time."

We went back into one twelve. I moved to Silas. "Look, let's stop screwing around. You're cooking the books, you're into poaching, some damn thing. Out with it."

Ionata said, "What?"

"They're going to toss in murder on top of that," I said. "And now you're out of the closet. It just ain't your day, Silas. Fess up, okay?"

He stepped back, away from me.

"It's all right," I said, holding my hands up in front of me, palms toward him. "I'm not going to hurt you again. I shouldn't have done that thing in the first place. I'm sorry. However, you got a bunch to answer, how about let's get on with it?" I turned my palms upward.

Pinky said, "Thank you, Mr. Shortcut, for becoming civi-lized. Your behavior was inexcusable—"

"Cut the crap, Pinky, and help us out. It was your boss some-body took out. You can see how it would benefit Silas to coop-erate."

Pinky nodded. "He's correct, Silas." Pinky looked at John Ionata. "If there is a trial, will you testify that Silas cooperated fully?"

Ionata groaned, but didn't answer.

"Say 'yes,' John," I said.

He sighed. "Yes."

Pinky swiveled back to Silas. "As an attorney, I feel it would be in your best interests to be up front; if what Mr. Birthday says is correct, you will be prosecuted. Perhaps under the circum-stances, we could avoid prosecution."

"You just don't know," said Silas, "you just don't know it all."

"I know something," Pinky said. "More than just this." He waved an arm indicating the Inn. "I know something about California."

"Oh." Silas was crestfallen. He folded more into himself than he had earlier. Pinky knew something that Silas had thought was buried.

"You talk in your sleep," Pinky said, eyes bright.

Silas was down and out. But he said nothing.

Time for a nudge. I said, "Silas? If you don't make waves now, the sailing will be smoother later." Another attempt to evoke *HBG'S GATOR GAL* in his mind.

"All right," whispered Silas Smith. He was shrewd for he picked up on it. He fixed an eye on Pinky. "You aren't going to like it all."

Pinky reached out and touched Silas on the forearm. "I'll take that chance."

"Get on with it," I said.

"What did he mean, 'poaching?'" said Pinky. I recalled that Pinky was—had been—the governor's environmental expert.

Silas moved against a chest of drawers. He looked around apprehensively. He'd made a decision to tell all, or so we hoped, but it was hard to admit culpability in front of people.

"That's as good a place to start as any," I said.

Smith sighed again. "Gasparilla Island is home to many wealthy people. It's ten miles off the island to anywhere else. Other than the Inn, there's only a couple of seafood restaurants on the island. And the Inn is but a short walk from the marina. There are people with tremendous bank accounts all along the Intracoastal Waterway, all around Charlotte Harbor, Fort Myers, Sarasota, all who can access Gasparilla Island by boat." He stopped.

"Speeches are all well and good," I said. "Get to the point."

"Some of these wealthy people have eccentric tastes."

I knew what was coming. "This is where Orlo and his stooges fit in."

Silas nodded, pits in his skin rising and sinking in the glaring light.

Trooper propped himself on his elbows attentively.

"Usually, it's wild hog and deer," Silas said. "But we've quite a demand for alligator; although nowadays there are alligator farms. Once, Orlo killed a panther—"

"An endangered species!" Pinky huffed. "The Florida panther. Perhaps fifty remain. We've spent hundreds of thousands of dollars to save them—"

"Five thousand dollars," Silas said harshly. "I got a thousand, and Orlo four."

His words were brutal on Pinky. "God, no." Pinky was devastated.

"Two insurance men," Silas continued, "four retired yankees, a boat builder, and a car dealer from Chicago who lives here part time. Eight men who gather every couple of weeks and play poker or blackjack. We called it 'The Unique Dinner Club.' I was their personal chef. They've eaten a Bald Eagle. But their usual meal is manatee steaks."

You'd of thought Silas just shot Pinky. The assistant chief-of-staff sank to his knees. "No, no, no, no." You could hardly hear him. "That often!"

Silas looked at me. "I thought somebody here already knew this." His tone was quizzical.

"What do you mean?"

"Someone," he said, "got into the manatee steaks last night and—"

"Oh, shit," I said. Gorge rose in my throat. I remembered being three-sheets to the wind and burning the steak. That's what I'd blamed the odd taste on. Or there had been something about the steak absorbing a fish flavor from elsewhere in the cooler. I should have known better. I couldn't remember if I had basted the meat with mustard or peanut butter or both. "Oh, shit."

Pinky stared at me like he'd just found out I was a cannibal.

"You?" said Silas, his eyes widening.

"Him," Tapes chortled at my discomfiture. We were back to

normal.

I crinkled my mouth in memory. "Sure as hell not on purpose." I looked around to spit but managed to swallow and it tasted sour.

"Loggerhead turtle eggs were eaten, too," said Silas.

I felt like I'd just drank a gallon of emetic.

"Here," said Tapes, extending his hand to me. The tin of Copenhagen was open.

I don't do tobacco, not since I was a kid. But I took a big pinch and stuck it between my gum, lower right, and cheek. The nicotine hit me immediate and hard. The phantom memory I'd been experiencing since I'd given it up rose and grew, a full-blown thing. My mouth watered and I really needed to spit. I hustled into the bathroom and spit into the sink, fingered the tobacco out, and rinsed my mouth. Any longer and I'd be hooked again and I didn't need that worse than I didn't need a lot of things like the clap or a busted motor mount. But the stuff had wiped the manatee taste out of my mouth.

I came back to most everyone's amusement.

Pinky looked at me as if I'd just regained my humanity and that made me feel better.

Trooper was looking back and forth between me and the decapitated bed post, probably wondering if I was the same guy.

Again, Tapes had bailed me out. I was beginning to feel less sorry for myself and more interested in what was going on.

"The governor," Tapes prompted me and Silas.

Ionata fidgeted. There was more to him than met the eye. I remembered the political conflict between the governor and the lieutenant governor. Which leads to personal animus. But it was Silas Smith's turn.

"Silas," I said slowly, "you've told us about poaching and selling illegal game and all. It's obvious you were skimming or something similar off the top here. Was it the Inn? Or the restaurant portion?"

"Generally," said Vern, "it is both."

Silas nodded. He was pressing against the chest of drawers

and a vase upon it rocked.

I thought for a moment and added two plus two and kept coming up with eight and a half. I plinked off one finger at a time, remembering Mary Lynn had done the same. "One, you're homosexual. Two, you've ripped off the Inn. Three, you've violated gaming and state and federal laws about endangered species, plus likely they can get you for health code and kitchen violations. Now, from what I've learned about Henry B., he wasn't that stupid to be ignorant of everything."

Everyone sort of stood or sat up straighter. There grew an instant air of tension and anticipation in the room.

My clothes hadn't dried in the still, stifling air of the hotel. But the open door helped. I ran my hand through grimy hair. Not even in the stump-chopping scene in *Shane* had Alan Ladd's hair been as messy.

Pinky had settled back off his knees and was now sitting on his heels, scratching his head. He peered up at Silas. "What Mr. Birthday says contains a lot of merit, Silas. Was Henry B. aware of any of this?" Pinky's tone said if Henry B. did know, he, Pinky, didn't want to know the answer—but he'd been compelled to ask the question.

"He knew," said Silas.

16: TUESDAY, 12:15 P.M.

The room went dead. A thunder of wind slammed into the Inn and creaking and crashing went unnoticed. Everyone was watching Silas, whose Adam's apple was going up and down like the elevator at Sears on the day before Christmas.

Tapes moved first, but toward the door. He stopped at the doorway.

There stood Orlo.

Silas cleared his throat, accompanied by much bobbing. "I will not," he said harshly, "talk while *that* man is here."

"Give us the benefit of your absence," I told Orlo.

"If you will," Tapes said mildly and looked down at Orlo.

Orlo didn't back down. "Thee all allow that little shit-eatin' runt to boss things now?" He looked directly at me, then to Ionata. "Ye've not much authority, Judge. Two foreigners is tellin' all which to do. I do not understand."

The SOB had just insulted Texas. "Orlo," I said, "your mother and father were brother and sister and you misspelled 'evil' on your tattoo."

He glanced at the knuckles on his right hand.

"Not to mention 'mother' on your arm," I continued, not knowing why I was baiting the man. I agreed with Silas, I didn't want him here.

"I'm gonna bruise thy fuckin' ass," Orlo said and moved toward me, reaching out.

"No," Tapes said, voice full of warning. In his prime, Joe Louis could've took Tapes. Orlo was no Joe Louis.

Give Orlo credit, he was supremely confident in his abilities. He brushed past Tapes as if to attack me, but swiveled with his left elbow streaking for Tapes' midsection.

Tapes deflected the move, nailed Orlo in the knee with a quick boot, and hit him with two kidney punches before Orlo could grab his knee.

Tapes had hold of Orlo's shirt at his clean-shaven throat and was delivering what might not have been a fatal blow when the click sliced through the stifling air of the room.

Trooper was sitting there with his big .357 revolver pointing straight at the two. The hammer cocking nailed everyone's attention. And we all knew Trooper was dead serious, most of all Orlo. Orlo was right then regretting that he and his friends had jumped on Trooper. Tapes seemed relieved. Only he and I knew how close Orlo had come to permanent and disabling injury.

The sudden violence had paralyzed all the bureaucrats and Silas.

Trooper grew larger behind the big weapon, taking on a new role. In a quick moment, I saw what once had been. I saw what Henry B. had seen. One big, commanding, authoritative, poised, single-minded, tough and mean son of a bitch. Time had blurred that man into what he was today. Hours and minutes and days and years do different things to all of us, many things we do not want to acknowledge—especially to ourselves. Liquor, too, had dulled that razor edge which had once been Trooper.

"Okay," I said, moving slowly so as not to upset the balance of the universe, for I knew full well that if Trooper triggered a round into Orlo, who doubtlessly deserved more than one, we would all be irrevocably changed. The situation would deteriorate and never be straightened out. We would all be different because of it; I'd be somehow unfulfilled.

However, the major fear in my mind was that the man who was now Trooper would not be as accurate as he had been in the past and the powerful slug meant for Orlo would plough into Tapes, or go through Orlo into Tapes. Or Trooper would trigger all six shots, some of which might take out Tapes as well.

Which would require me to kill Trooper. Nobody screws with Shortcut and Tapes. I didn't want Trooper dead; he might know something we needed to know. And he was the only law enforcement we had to legitimatize our actions—as long as he and Ionata tacitly went along with us.

And I didn't really want Orlo dead—not right then—because there were too many questions he could provide the answers to.

And most of all and more than anything in the world, I didn't want Tapes dead. We'd grown up together and been partners our entire lives. Rarely we went our separate ways. Like now he was living in Tucson and I had been living in Tallahassee—but that circumstance was because of women and my hard-headedness.

Deliberately I stepped into Trooper's line of fire.

His words were level, but full of menace. "You stupid cock-sucker, move aside."

"No." I put my hands on my hips.

"You're fuckin' with fire, boy." Trooper's hands did not move, not a hair. The big, black gun was trained on me like an oncoming locomotive and it had about the same spellbinding power.

"You've had enough training," I said carefully, "to know that this will solve nothing. We need Orlo to find out who killed your friend."

Trooper's eyes wavered. His intention, I was certain, had initially been to stop Orlo, to break up the fight with Tapes. But something, some devil, had taken over his mind and was driving him. Orlo well could have made a major mistake when he and his buddies had stomped Trooper to inactive status.

Trooper drew himself up with new resolve. "Move out of my way, goddamnit."

"If you shoot, Trooper," I said, "the mirror ain't going to be the same."

His face twisted, wondering what I was talking about, but I think he figured it out.

I went on. "You will never, ever see what you want to see in it again."

I heard the whisper of fabric as Tapes released Orlo and stepped aside. Now I could move.

Trooper's face hardened, but shadows raced behind his eyes. "You know, Birthday, I ought to do the world a favor and blow a great big fucking hole out of you."

Tapes began moving and stopped abruptly when he figured out what Trooper had said.

Trooper aimed the weapon at the ceiling and eased the hammer down with his thumb, an affected John Wayne mannerism.

Silas was obviously hoping Trooper would shoot Orlo or Tapes would beat him to a pulp. Pinky was watching, aghast at the sudden violence. Vern Bernstein had stepped back into the bathroom door, not a stupid move for someone who hadn't any military training.

Orlo was half bent over, holding his knee with both hands. He began rubbing his knee, but Tapes had got it from the side, so Orlo probably wouldn't suffer any permanent damage, unfortunately.

Gradually he straightened and rubbed his side where Tapes had kidney-punched him.

Orlo surveyed the room. His words came softly and could have been a chant. "Last time I was hurt like this, I was on R and R in Bangkok. I tell thee this. There was a woman from Burma, an exquisite beauty, you see. She was blind and made her living giving massages." His voice became even softer. It was not difficult to imagine it was really José Gaspar standing there addressing us. "Her hands were supple, I tell thee. To this day I can feel them. She did not so desire, but I used her all night. In the morning, she was a broken, bleeding woman, inside and out. I tell thee."

Now I've been around and I know it is not possible, but I will say this and swear to it: the temperature in that hot, stifling room dropped twenty degrees and I shivered and something dark and black and deadly flittered away.

I should have been listening to what he was telling me, not

what he said.

But Orlo had been profoundly transformed by this. So, too, were we. But only Orlo and me—and maybe Tapes—knew he had had absolute complete command of the entire room one twelve and the six other people in it for the space of his few lilting sentences. Seldom, seldom have I ever been mesmerized. Maybe DeNiro could have carried it off, but I doubt it. I shivered again.

Orlo straightened and ignored his hurts, turned and walked out of the room without a hint of injury. The man was solid, but that?

For a long minute, no one spoke.

"Jesus," said Vern.

"The tender mercies of the wicked are cruel," said Pinky, quoting another Proverb.

Silas looked like he wanted to die.

I spoke to him. "Some things aren't as bad as they could be."

He must have mistook what I was saying. "I will say nothing else."

"I meant," I said, "that for you things could be worse. I suspect you've seen Orlo's wrath before?"

When Mary Lynn and I had left the kitchen because Orlo had come in. And there hadn't been much time between when Mary Lynn and I had finally made it to her room and the moment Angle Maple had interrupted us to join Ionata there. Immediately, I thought of Orlo and the possibility that I might have had to fight him in the kitchen with Mary Lynn looking on. Then I'd been supremely confident, pretty sure I could take him, strength, experience, quickness, and dirty tricks being sufficient for the task. I still thought I was faster, but as for the rest I now wasn't so certain. He could well have killed or maimed me and exacted a price for his anger from Mary Lynn. I'd been only half kidding when I'd said his mother and father were brother and sister. Some guys are like that, crazy and with no soul and conscience. They'll rape your dog and kill your wife. You'll be thinking about the law and the Ten Commandments and they'll be breathing hard, dirty breath on your dead, warm body. And if it's your wife or mother or sister or four-year-old daughter, whether they were dead or alive would not matter to his sexual preference, and probably both.

And now I knew why he hunted down and killed defenseless endangered animals. Orlo was a frustrated killer. A José Gaspar reincarnate.

And I wished I'd won the lottery last Saturday night and had stayed in Tallahassee to collect the jackpot instead of coming down here. But the most numbers I'd ever got were three of the six, batting .500 about summing up most of my life.

Trooper broke the mood. "Smith? You answer the questions from this stupid little cowboy so's we can all get on with our life."

Tapes glanced at me. While Trooper had not necessarily become an ally, he had, in a backhanded fashion, endorsed our effort to pursue the murder of his friend and governor.

I motioned Silas away from the chest of drawers, noticing that the vase had fallen over and the rose imprinted thereon had a vertical crack. I hooked a chair and dragged it away from the side of Trooper's bed.

Silas sat down heavily as if his legs couldn't make it any longer. Surely he'd been on an emotional roller coaster in the last hours, and especially the last few minutes, which had wrung him out. "All right."

Tapes moved over to the door, checked the corridor, and leaned against the frame.

"Start at the beginning," I said. "Where is the cemetery?"

"To the point," said Vern. Nobody else, except Silas, caught on.

"Cobbtown, Georgia," Silas said. "The original Silas Smith was born in 1940 and died in 1942."

Vern answered Pinky's unasked question. "You pick a dead kid, one born within a few years of you and one that's never had a social security number, and write to the state records office telling them you're him and requesting an official birth certificate. Then you become him. You take the birth certificate to the Social Security office and request a number. This all provides you with a new identity."

Pinky pursed his brows. "Then how do you get a driver's license? I understand you use the Social Security number for IRS W-2 forms and Forms 1099." He hesitated. "How do you explain to the driver's license folks and the Social Security issuers that you're over fifty and have never had a driver's license or a social security card?"

Silas shrugged. "I could have bought a fake out-of-state license and traded that to them. But they're government employees—most don't care and don't ask. When they did ask, I just told them I was an American who grew up in Hong Kong and worked in banks over there."

He'd said "banks," which must mean something.

"Surely someone remarks upon the unusualness of an American around fifty years old never having had a social security number or driver's license," said John Ionata.

Silas was slouching in the chair. "If they express interest like that, I simply tell them my family moved to Hong Kong when I was young and I'm just now returning. I tell them everybody's leaving Hong Kong because of the growing fear of chaos when the communists from Beijing take over. Most people are familiar with Britain signing the agreement with Beijing, and if they aren't, they pretend they are."

I made another couple of assumptions. "You used a small town graveyard because in a big city like Atlanta or Miami, someone else might have already used the dead child's name to get fake ID."

"That is correct. It took a couple of weeks of driving around rural Georgia looking at tombstones and grave markers. I'd write the ones down who were born within a year or two of me; and the marker would also have to show the locations where the child was born and died. Families don't put that information on the gravestone often."

At Ionata's questioning look, I said, "The kid had to be born in Georgia, for instance, but it'd be a lot better if he died somewhere else. The reason is, the states are getting wise to this way of building a false identity and they're starting to cross-reference births and deaths. So, Silas Smith was born in Cobbtown and died in another state and was transported back to Cobbtown for burial." I glanced at "Silas" for confirmation.

He nodded. "I also had to accomplish much research, for I did not want to go through all that trouble and find out the child was black or born with one arm and so on. The real Silas Smith died in Ohio, perfect for my purposes."

"And once you get a certified birth certificate, everything else falls in turn?" said Ionata.

"It does," I said.

"When I am governor," said the lieutenant governor, "I will introduce legislation to prevent that from occurring in Florida."

"I know just how to go about it," said Vern Bernstein, in what I thought was a particularly ingratiating manner.

Ionata didn't respond.

"You know," I said, "there're a hundred ways of building yourself a new life. We've established *how* you've gone about it, Silas. What we need to know is why. And what illegal activities you've engaged in here at the José Gaspar Inn."

He dropped his head and was silent.

"Not again," I said.

"Talk, you fucking gerbil-stuffer," said Trooper.

Silas said nothing.

"I think," I said, "we might as well just handcuff Silas to Trooper's bed and all leave."

Smith's head jerked up. "I was just thinking about how to say it."

"Try from the beginning." I shifted to my other foot. It wasn't all that comfortable in my now semi-wet clothes.

"It was California," he said reluctantly. "A small savings and loan. I'd worked my way up to president. A, a friend, came out of the closet and announced he was gay. He exposed three of us in a snit and in public. My family had never known until then, but it wrecked my life."

"Ah," Pinky said, "in Leviticus the Bible says, 'Thou shalt not lie with mankind.' In Peter, the Bible also says, 'Honor all men. Love the brotherhood.'"

"There is no God," Silas replied. "I lost my family." He shook his head and went on in a whisper. "I still cannot believe they deserted me." It occurred to me he must have at one time had a devoted family, him being so inordinately ugly.

I knew what else was coming, but I let him tell it. I tried to ease the telling, though. "California is ahead of the times. It's nothing unique to be gay. You don't have to hide."

He shook his head for the sixty-third time and seemed to fold in upon himself again. If he kept this up his head would fly off and his body would be a compact mass of flesh. "Not there. Not in that business."

"Where?" said Vern, oblivious to the manager's personal pain and in a hurry to get this over.

"Not in Orange County."

Vern nodded understanding. "They don't even like Democrats there, much less queers."

"Vern," said Pinky.

"I still can't believe it, Pinky," Vern said. "You. A homo."

Pinky seemed to draw himself up. "At least I can say I never dodged a draft or burned a flag."

"I never burned a flag, either," Vern said, visibly shaken.

"Well it's a blanket assumption, is it not?" Pinky said.

"But it's not true. That kind of talk will ruin me." Vern's Adam's apple was bouncing up and down like a yo yo being tested.

"Do you not think," Pinky said enunciating each word slowly, "that the same thing applies to the gay population?"

Vern thought about it for a moment. "I suppose you could say that."

"Fuckin' room's full of fuckin' queers and fuckin' traitors," said Trooper. "Fuck them. Get on with it, Birthday."

I shook my head. I was going to have a headache, too. I

wondered if Trooper ever paid attention to the human drama going on around him. Though, I will admit he was contributing his share to this human drama. I also wondered if his insensitivity actually helped him in his job of law enforcement.

"So you went from respected businessman to a pariah," I said. "People avoided you, your family deserted you, your friends shunned you, and your business acquaintances suddenly were busy all the time."

"The directors didn't say it, but they wanted me out and pressure began to build." A crafty look overcame Silas. "Well, I showed them. It was too late to play computer games with accounts and set myself up for life in the Bahamas," he glanced around quickly and I knew my guesses were close, "with embezzled funds no one could touch. There was no time to set up my own cover under different name or names and transfer funds around until they ended up in an anonymous offshore bank, laundered nice and untraceable. I had only a day or two in which to act. But I did manage to make sufficient transfers to the directors' accounts to muddy the water. When the payday cash delivery arrived the night before the thirty-first, I simply loaded the money into my car and left."

"How much?" Trooper asked quickly.

"A quarter of a million, give or take."

"Jesus shit," said Trooper.

I thought about *HBG'S GATOR GAL*.

"This is becoming quite involved," said John Ionata in an understatement.

"Wait till you become governor," I pointed out.

"Where's the money?" Trooper asked softly.

Everyone's attention was riveted on Silas.

"In a bank safety deposit box in Nassau," he said with a defiant flair.

Of course no one in the room believed him. Well, maybe Pinky and Ionata.

"But why did you not stay there?" Pinky asked. "Instead you're working here, actually working for a living."

"Hah!" Silas spat out. "Two hundred and fifty grand isn't an endless income. I'd go through that in a few years even being careful. No, even the Bahamas are not safe from Uncle Sam." He shot a look at Vern. "Safe enough, perhaps, for those who seek to avoid serving their obligation. But not sufficiently safe to hide from Uncle's paper-chasers. Once those guys are after you, you're a goner. They can even get into your Swiss accounts."

What he said was true. It was almost sad, Swiss banks no longer being sacrosanct and safe. Coke changing its recipe, the Berlin wall gone. Swiss banks no longer safe. What's the world coming to anyway? Some of us Americans value our privacy and, while we're not crooks at all, like to believe you can go somewhere and start over without some SOB and his computer knowing who you are and who you were and tracking you around the world.

I breathed deeply and wrenched my attention back to Silas. "What you did was to effectively hide out here on a little-known island, until the heat dies down. You'll go recover your quarter mil, and set up life somewhere else."

"That was my intention."

"Meanwhile," I continued, "you couldn't resist a little embezzlement here."

"I was building my nest egg," he said defensively.

"Sure," I said. "Skimming off the top and making tons of money feeding an immensely wealthy club of men forbidden fruit, as it were."

"Fruit, that's a good one," said Trooper. "Fuckin' fruitcakes is more like it."

"Give us a break, Troop," I said.

Surprisingly he nooded. Perhaps he was thinking about that mirror again. Perhaps Vern's silence had told him something.

All the while most of us were thinking about the additional cash Silas had skimmed and obviously stashed.

"You must have been taking off the top of the cash business," Vern said.

Silas' Adam's apple raced Vern's. "I did. It makes me angry

how many people use credit cards these days."

"Me, too," I said. Another bit of American privacy and wherewithal gone. One of Shortcut's Laments: the ATM card, the checkbook and the credit card are indeed the symbols of America in the '90s and beyond.

"Money came in also," Vern said, "from those rich guys eating proscribed meat. You must have been raking it in."

Silas shrugged.

Again, the rest of us were thinking, higher this time, of the money Silas must have made.

"However," I said, "we've still to establish why. Why did Henry B. hire you in the first place? Why did you steal from him? Especially when you were already on the run. I'd think that would be like waving a red flag. Not to mention spitting on the governor for hiring you. Good loyal employee." I was becoming angry. "And most of all, I am curious about your relationship with Henry B. Earlier you indicated he knew about your skimming."

Fire came from his eyes. "Why? I'll tell you why. Until very recently he did not know I was gay. Quite frankly, Gonzáles always denigrated homosexuality."

From what Trooper had said, I'd guessed it. "So that very fact negated your personal loyalty to the man that hired you."

"It did exactly." Smith's head was raised now and he was unfolding himself as if out of a shell.

"You limp-dick sonofabitch," said Trooper, the one person in the entire world who'd maintained his loyalty to Henry B.

"How'd you get the job?" I asked.

Silas smiled. "The best way in the world. I applied for it and was accepted."

"It figgers," I said. "I can understand your ability to construct the appropriate credentials. You falsified references, too?"

He nodded. "In Miami, I had printed stationery with several different letterheads. I merely typed or printed letters of recommendation on each different letterhead."

"With false addresses?" asked Ionata, trying to act like he

was conducting the inquiry.

"No," said Silas.

"Probably not," I said at the same time.

"You know," Silas told me.

"I do." I turned to the lieutenant governor. "In every city there are businesses which are called 'mail drops' in the trade. Usually, it's just a secretary and a desk, or somebody doing some other business and allows his address to be used. Again, usually, their address is something like Suite 301, such and such building. You come along and pay them forty, fifty bucks a month and use the address and they hold the mail for you. Right, Silas?"

"They'll even take phone messages," Silas said. "I've a drop in Miami, one in Orlando, and one in Jacksonville. Anonymous big cities. The business names I selected were 'Worldwide Resort Properties,' 'Bahamas Hotels, Inc.,' and so on. The governor's business aides sent letters of request for confirmation of my so-called resume and work history. I merely received the letters and returned what they wanted to see, right on the appropriate letterhead."

"I'll be damned," said Ionata.

I left that one alone.

"There weren't many applicants for the job," Silas continued. "This is far away from anywhere, isolated out on an island in the Gulf of Mexico. It was perfect for me and I got the job."

"You were extremely fortunate," I said. "You were hiding out with little chance of discovery. You were earning a nice salary. You were building a nest-egg to add to the stolen California funds. In a couple of years you could slowly build another new identity and, when you would be ready, pack the cash and the new papers and disappear."

His eyes slowed shrewdly. "Exactly. Also important is that I'd be spiting the society which branded me different." He unfolded from himself a bit more.

And that explained, I thought, the infrequent absences from here. He was working on another—or more than one—false identities. He had the time to build them carefully.

"Henry B. somehow discovered your hand in the till," I said.

"The holding company," Silas said cheerfully, "it was their fault. Some bean-counter got a new computer program into which they input all the historical data they had. Thus they could show on one page what business the Inn had done in the past, what it should be doing now, and projected future revenues. From there it took little for the governor to discover what I'd done and how." Silas paused. "But he never knew about the Unique Dinner Club."

"So," said John Ionata with a deep finality, "he confronted you with the information, you struck him with the tennis racquet, he fell through the railing and died."

"Not at all," Silas said enigmatically.

"Fuck it, it fits," said Trooper with a grim smile. He began toying with his weapon again and furtively watching Silas. I don't think Silas was aware of this.

"Explain yourself," I said, knowing a bunch of stuff had been left out. Like the Orlo connection, the beating, the fire, and the boat. His story had more holes than a colander.

Silas shrugged. "By that time Henry B. Gonzáles wouldn't have dared to turn me in."

"Say that again?" said Ionata incredulously.

"The governor had no choice in the matter. He knew part of what I was doing and let me continue to do it."

17: TUESDAY, 2:30 P.M.

Trooper's hand was around the butt of his gun menacingly. "What do you mean?" The weapon was vaguely aimed toward Silas in the chair.

"I mean," said Silas, "that Gonzáles did not turn me in."

"You're saying you had something on him." Trooper was boring in.

"I am."

"You slimy bastard." Trooper fingered the trigger guard. He looked around wildly. "All you butt-pumpers. Every one of you sonofabitches has sold Henry B. down the goddamn river." He fixed his gaze back on Silas. "You was blackmailing him."

I glanced at Tapes. One of our on-going disagreements was the proper use of the words "extortion" and "blackmail." I usually argued the case for extortion, and Tapes for blackmail. Silas was still unfolding himself. "Not necessarily. I merely traded with him. I wouldn't make public what I knew and he would reciprocate. It simply cost him a bit of money; and that before taxes." He fingered a deep scar on his neck. "He didn't know about the Unique Dinner Club. Gonzáles' concern was the skimming. It was obvious we both were looking for a way out."

Vern nodded understandingly.

"How long has this been going on?" I asked.

"Two months."

To me, this gave Silas motive to kill Gonzáles.

Trooper scratched his mussed hair with the front sight of the weapon. "Henry B. was legit. I mean, he didn't have no—any—secrets. That I know of."

"You sure as hell do," Silas shot out at him.

The muzzle of the weapon rose slowly to target Silas. "Tell me."

"I'm the manager here. You're with him all the time. But here, I know who comes and goes. I know whose wives and daughters Gonzáles slept with, and other women. He'd direct me to prepare one of his sailboats or *HBG'S GATOR GAL* for an afternoon with a lady. I paid attention. Infrequently, he even had me to procure him a couple of hookers at a time." Silas sighed. "The man was indefatigable."

"He could get all the women he wanted," said Vern. "Why'd he need whores?"

Silas twisted his head toward Vern. "The local women with whom he had affairs were all respectable and thought they were the only one in his life. Sometimes Gonzáles wanted more than one woman at a time."

I thought of Mary Lynn and wished for a bucket of Tums.

"So what?" said Trooper. "It's manly."

"I kept a list of times and dates and names," Silas said with a slick grin.

"So what?" said Trooper.

"So what? Husbands might want to know. And—"

"Political enemies," Vern added. "Like Angie Maple could have brought down the governor with that kind of info. In today's realpolitik, you've got to be pretty straight. And even if you can weather the ensuing storm, the numbers," I assumed he meant the constant polls, "work against you. They fall so much easier than they ever rise."

"Exactly," said Silas. "Henry B. was prodigious in his sexual appetites. He couldn't afford exposure."

"Politics just aren't fair," I said, not trying to keep the sarcasm out of my voice.

"Blackmailer," said Trooper.

Silas took a deep breath and stood. He stepped toward the

bed. "You, you officious brute. You know more about his affairs than anybody else. That's what I meant when I said you knew about his secrets."

Trooper looked a bit flustered. "Who cares where Henry B. dipped his wick? It wasn't none of my business."

Silas stepped closer. "Surely, you've protected him. Surely, you've helped a woman or two find a back way into his bedrooms all over the state."

Trooper was nonplussed. "Well, he was my friend." The weapon was back between his legs, tugging down the sheet. "I didn't turn against him, though. It was my job to protect him, not sell him out."

"You did whatever your friend needed done," I said softly.

"Yessir, I did."

Silas took another step toward Trooper. "So. I was just saving my own ass. I wasn't necessarily blackmailing the governor. I'd already made another two hundred and fifty thousand skimming off the hotel and the dining room and the Unique Dinner Club. I was merely withholding some information I happened to have from people who might want to know it and use it." He smiled happily. "Can you imagine what Angie Maple would do with documentation like that? She'd have a copy to every news organization in the state, to every organization with any kind of feminine bent, much less the active feminists." He looked at Ionata. "What would that kind of thing have done to Gonzáles' governorship?"

Ionata shook his head. "If it were documented and one or two of the women confirmed it, it would've ruined Henry B.'s political career. I suspect if all the women learned of each other, several would come forward out of spite. The prostitutes, if found, could be convinced, legally or financially, to cooperate."

"Traitor," said Trooper.

Silas stopped against the foot of the bed. "Gonzáles was always so arrogant. He just issued orders. He hated gays and my respect for him turned sour. I could understand his demeanor, for he'd always been rich and powerful and governors expect to be obeyed. But he made such disparaging remarks about gays."

"Could he have suspected you were gay?" I asked.

Silas shrugged. "It was Orange County all over again. The pressure built and built—"

"Then you killed him," said Trooper viciously.

"No, no, a thousand times I say no." Silas stepped back and dropped his head. His voice turned to a whisper. "I might have fled then, taken the money and disappeared again. But he said one thing that made me stay, that made me want to milk him for all I could, the one thing that kept me here suffering the increased danger of being discovered and jailed for what I'd done at the Inn." The two months. He looked at Pinky.

"Oh, no," said Pinky, folding his hands right below his bow tie.

"Oh, yes," said Silas, now moving toward Pinky. "He even spoke ill of you; he said he'd found he had 'a faggot' on his staff and was looking for the proper opportunity to 'dump the queer.'"

Trooper's gun rose quickly and swiveled to bear on Pinky.

"You killed Henry B.," Trooper accused.

"No. I would never do that." Pinky's hands remained steepled. "Bread of deceit is sweet to a man; but afterwards his mouth shall be filled with gravel." Well, the Proverb was part right: soon Gonzáles would be taking a dirt nap.

Silas stopped in front of Pinky. "It is entirely possible that somehow Gonzáles learned of our affair and drew his conclusions from that point."

Trooper was grinning. "That woulda been great." His gun was forgotten and drooping in his hand.

I cleared my throat. "We're finding out a lot of information, but not answering some basic questions. Silas, did you or did you not start the fire in the generator shed."

He backed away from Pinky. "I did."

"Why?" asked Pinky.

"To create confusion."

"Why?" asked Pinky again.

Silas made a face, the pock marks on his neck appearing like a spotted carpet being rolled out. "You're going to have a murder investigation. Everything is going to come to light. They'll find that I, me, disabled the switchboard in case the phone system made it through the storm. The cellular phone sites on the mainland are usually the first to go and luckily that occurred. Not to mention, many dead cells way out here."

"I'm beginning to see," Pinky said, dropping his steepled hands. "That's why you destroyed the records in your office. Destroying evidence."

"Buying time," said Silas. "And with all that, I'd become a prime suspect, regardless of what John Ionata was doing with these Texans."

I looked at Ionata. Tapes was staring at him, too. Ionata's eyes were fixed on the floor.

"Poor judgment, John," I said.

Ionata kind of shrugged, but said nothing, not even "I'm sorry."

However, my mind was working on a different level. Tapes might have guessed. I glanced at Vern Bernstein who was uncharacteristically quiet and I could tell from his eyes he was thinking.

Silas hadn't needed to fire the building.

"You could've killed people," Ionata said.

"That's arson," said Trooper. "And attempted murder."

Silas shook his head. "In a rainstorm like this? Had the inside of the kitchen, the only place possible, began burning, the internal sprinklers would have doused the flames immediately."

Vern was slick, he might have figured it out, but I doubted it.

That half-hearted attempt to burn the Inn down was just that, a diversion. We could have all escaped, even new mother and child, in plenty of time.

Silas had proved himself so far as very practical, very clever. His secret about the quarter million and the other quarter million from skimming from the Inn and selling protected meat was out. People knew about the money, and he'd foreseen that possibility.

The fire was a diversion to those of us in the know—and perhaps Orlo, too. Who would burn down the Inn if he had a half million dollars, and new fake ID, concealed there? No one. Therefore, we were supposed to think that he'd concealed the money elsewhere or buy the Nassau story. Thus, it followed that the money and the ID were in fact here, right now, in the Inn. But where did *HBG'S GATOR GAL* fit in?

I didn't want anybody else to deduce what I'd just deduced, so I changed the subject. "When you got beat up in the kitchen, it was Orlo, wasn't it?"

Smith's shoulders sank. "It was."

"Why?" I suspected Silas had miscalculated.

"It was a mistake I made," he said. "I went into the kitchen and Orlo was there. I told him that since the governor was dead, then I'd have to stop buying illegal meat from him." Silas seemed to wince in memory. "Orlo did not like that a bit." Silas shook his head. "When I went in there, he was already quite angry. I mean when I walked in, he was slamming his forearm into the door of the big refrigerator. There are enormous dents in the metal." He shivered.

I recalled Mary Lynn dragging me out of there and me baiting Orlo. So I'd contributed to Orlo beating up Silas. I thought of me and Tapes out in the storm fighting the fire and didn't feel so bad for Silas. Also, Orlo didn't know all the background we'd just learned, and thus Orlo had no idea that Silas must escape from here before the law began its murder investigation.

"Silas," I said, "I'll bet that you convinced Orlo he'd better be gone when the law arrives."

Silas grinned sheepishly. "I did."

"That'll likely turn out to be a better diversion for you than any you've come up with until now."

Silas nodded and, oddly, his Adam's apple did not move. "I did that. It stopped the beating—though I was already hurt." His hand went to his eye. "At first opportunity, Orlo and his cohorts will skip town."

"You're not concerned Orlo is the killer?" I asked, curious.

Silas shrugged. "Gonzáles is already dead and he didn't like gays. Tough."

"Let me rephrase that," I said. "You know Orlo more than anyone here. Do you think he murdered the governor?"

Silas stood still. "I've thought a great deal about it. I just don't know. It is entirely possible. Maybe Orlo was up there rifling Henry B.'s suite and came out the door and Gonzáles surprised him. Or any number of similar scenarios."

I said, "However, your judgment is that Orlo is more than capable of killing someone."

"Most definitely."

"Where'd you come upon Orlo? I mean you don't just put an ad in the paper for someone to hunt and butcher endangered species." It was a question I wanted to know the answer to almost as much as who killed the governor and what happed to Amelia Earhart. Tapes gave me a nod showing that was uppermost on his mind.

"A member," said Silas, "of the Unique Dinner Club. An elderly gentlemen, a charter member who started the whole thing. He said he'd arrange for a hunter to provide what he called 'unique' meat for special meals. I saw the opportunities and agreed."

"Who?" demanded John Ionata.

"The name would mean nothing to you. But the man died a year ago. He's long gone, his condo down here," Silas pointed with a crooked hand and two fingers, "has been sold and a family winters there now."

"You're telling us," said Vern, "that there is no way to trace Orlo?"

"I am."

"Do you even know his last name?" asked Ionata.

"I do not. He and his friends do not usually overnight here. However, the storm caught them as it did everyone else." Silas paused. "I'm not entirely stupid," a fact which I was beginning to appreciate how much, "so I've checked. He does not come often, and much of the time his vehicles are different."

I thought it important to know as much about Orlo as possible. He'd mentioned Bangkok and R and R. Likely he was in the "Mystic Far East" with some of the rest of us. So, too, were thousands of others. It probably meant only that he had combat experience. "What do you know about his two buddies, Axe and Pigtail?"

"Nothing. They're very quiet and Orlo does the talking, the negotiating. We've come to an accommodation. The county name on his license tags are always different, so I've never bothered to write them down figuring he's stolen them for the deliveries. They've even come by boat on an occasion or two."

Again, Silas was showing his cleverness—and propensity for documentation. While he'd said he failed to write down the tag numbers, he probably had kept a list and was saving *that* list to use against Orlo—even though the tags were, as Silas had guessed, probably stolen or altered. But a stolen tag could be traced. Suppose they were all stolen from the same county? A small possibility, but one Silas would think of.

My mind was still whirling with all the possibilities. It occurred to me that not everything Silas had told us was true. This maze was becoming a swamp to wade through.

"I don't suppose," I said, "you kept the list you referred to earlier? All the women and the hookers?"

He shook his head. "I did not. As soon as I understood Henry B. was gone forever, I realized that list could be used as evidence against me," and a ton of other people, I thought, "in a court of law. I burned it." He glanced at John Ionata. "Keeping in mind of course, that this conversation is off the record and none of what I say will be held against me."

"I never said that." Ionata was shaking his shaggy head.

"You as much said it," Silas accused.

"You rather implied something similar, John," I pointed out. I didn't care one way or the other, but I didn't think Silas killed the governor and we'd needed his help—and still might need his help some more. I had to quickly bust this session up before someone wanted to know who, by Smith's memory, was on the list. And from what Vern said, Mary Lynn Messenger was on it a lot. I mean, I really didn't want to know how often she visited the governor secretly. My stomach reacted again, acid boiling up.

I'd about decided Mary Lynn was her own person and it was none of my business with whom she'd had affairs; but my jealous gut fought that, telling me a woman who'd fallen for Henry B.'s slick line wasn't good enough to pursue. Damn. Things ain't so easy once you grow up a bit. Oscar Wilde had once said, "In this world there are only two tragedies. One is not getting what one wants, and the other is getting it."

Pinky was talking, but I noticed Tapes not paying attention. He was sliding toward the other side of the door frame and stretching his head around to peek around the door frame. He was so tall, it was right below the transom.

I stepped over there quietly, ready for anything. Tapes would call the shots.

He turned from the doorway. "Thought I heard something."

"You mean like someone eavesdropping?" I asked.

"Like someone shifting position, or fabric rubbing against the wall."

"Does it matter?" said Ionata.

"It does," I said.

"I could've been wrong," Tapes said.

"It really, really, matters," Silas said.

Trooper waved a hand. "Hell, half the population of the Inn is here already."

"It could have been Angie," I said.

"That doesn't scare me," said Silas.

"Orlo or his two stooges," I said, watching the manager.

Silas Smith blanched and I knew that's what he'd been worrying about. Now Orlo had maybe a half a million reasons to stick around a wreak havoc. And only me and Tapes to stop him.

"Oh, sweet Jesus," said Silas Smith. Somebody had just

signed his death warrant.

Tapes realized that, too. "Probably it was nobody."

Silas shook his head. "I insist you place me under arrest. I will stay here in this room with Trooper."

Sure he would. Until the weather relented.

18: TUESDAY, 4:35 P.M.

"I feel like Wile E. Coyote," I said, as Tapes and I walked along the corridor to our room. "No matter what we've done, what we've found out, we still don't know who croaked the governor."

"Road Runner," Tapes said, automatically triggering an argument over which was more the American philosophy.

"The coyote symbolizes everyman's life against the forces at work in the world," I pointed out. "You keep trying, doing all the things that should work, and they don't. Life's like that, you know. Bust your ass and where does it get you?"

"The only thing," Tapes said slowly, "that Wile E. hasn't tried to do, tried to be, is *the* Road Runner. He's been other road runners in disguise, but not *the*. That's where he's erred. The Road Runner is symbolic of what we all wish to be, of how insulated and protected and immune to life's pitfalls we all want to be. The Road Runner goes through life as we all want to go through life: without incident, without stubbing our toes."

"Stubbing our toes? Jeez, Tapes, you're waxing metaphoric."

Tapes followed me through the door to our room. "At least I ain't full of corny homilies."

I was tired. But something was bothering me, eating at the back of my mind and keeping it working overtime.

Instead of falling asleep, I showered and found my last clean clothes I didn't know I had: a pair of cutoff jeans and a garnet and gold Florida State sleeveless sweat shirt. While not sartorial splendor, they were functional. As soon as the electricity came back, I was going to do some laundry. Though I did have some spare clothes outside in the pickup, my boots were wet so I'd changed back to damp Nikes.

Tapes was lying down and starting to fall asleep. His feet rested at the very end of the bed and overhung the mattress a bit, lodged against the brass rails. "Road Runner, he runs down the road all day."

"Wile E. is a schemer."

There was a gas lantern on the dresser hissing and flickering.

"Just like you."

"My point."

"Spinning his heels."

"I'm going to check on the kid," I announced.

Tapes propped an eyelid open. "Don't start anything you can't finish."

"What the hell does that mean?" Was he talking about getting into it with Orlo? Or talking to Mary Lynn Messenger, which in fact was what I kind of had in mind, should the situation arise.

"Whatever you think it means."

"What I think, Tapes, is that the entire world was born a smart ass; most people overcome it when they're young, some when they're old; others never overcome it whether they try to or not. You are one of the latter."

"A homilie to put me to sleep."

"Think of it as Shortcut's Salient Point." I paused. "To finish up, the Road Runner doesn't even have a name that I know of. He's just a generic prop for Wile E. to bat his head against."

Tapes was asleep when I shut the door. I went toward Sandra Dee Kowalski's room. I'd been so tired that I hadn't cared what happened to Silas. He was Ionata and Trooper's problem now. They'd given him run of the Inn, but not to leave. Sure, right in the middle of the storm.

Now I was restless, tired but unable to rest. What I needed was a couple of hours of weight lifting or racquetball. The exercise would get my blood flowing and clean out the impurities which were keeping me awake. I needed to breathe hard and work muscle groups and my cardio-pulmonary system. It would occur sooner than I thought, very much to my displeasure.

And I was rather exasperated with trying to determine who killed Henry B. Gonzáles. It was a draining mental effort. We'd learned a bunch from Silas Smith, and a bunch about many of the others stuck in the Inn. But not enough to find the killer. Additionally, I hadn't decided what to do about *HBG'S GATOR GAL*, Silas, and all his money. If I was on the lam, as Silas had been, I sure as hell wouldn't stick my money in a safe deposit box so far away and in a different country. I'd want it where I could snatch it and run. A quarter to a half million in cash would certainly help in a getaway.

I knocked and the door swung open.

Angie Maple said, "Well?"

"How's the kid?"

"Fine."

I tried to peek over her shoulder but she held the door close. "How's Sandy?"

"Sandra Dee is fine and resting."

"Can I see them?"

"No."

"How about Mary Lynn. I'd like to talk to her."

"She's not here."

"Where is she?"

"I don't know."

"Well, did she leave to sleep or eat or something?"

"I don't know."

I turned to walk away. "Always nice talking to you, Mrs. Maple."

"Mizz," and the door closed behind me.

I should have taunted her that I knew enough dirt about the current administration to fill Tallahassee with Republicans, but I didn't feel like being childish right now.

My mind was still scratching at something and I wished I could put my mental finger upon it.

Now I wasn't even certain that I wanted to talk to Mary Lynn.

Since Vern Bernstein had let it out that she had been the governor's Gasparilla Island Reelection Campaign Chairperson, I'd been in a snit because she hadn't told me herself. I could understand it was her own business with whom she had affairs. But the political post is public knowledge. I guess I expected too much, I'd thought she and I were close enough not to hide important things like that. On the other hand, I hadn't really expounded at length about my past—but my past had little bearing on both finding the killer and the internal social dynamic here at the Inn. The latter was important to understand so that I could keep an idea of who had what motivation.

Still restless, I walked up the stairs to the empty second floor, went past the elevator down a murky corridor so I couldn't be seen from the stairway.

Li Shou, a therapeutic exercise from ancient China. Li Shou, meaning something like "hand-swinging" and taught to me by a young Chinese lady in Hong Kong.

First you rub your hands together, hard and fast, and then stroke your face as if washing it, always in the same direction. Relax seriously and massage your face downward thirty or forty times. I did so. It helps me dissociate my mind and relax.

Then I performed the second half of Li Shou. Eyes half-closed. Raised my hands to tummy level in front and let them swing back and forth no higher than my waist with a rhythm.

Concentrating on toes and fingers, my body began to relax. After five or six hundred, I began to feel a buzz going through my fingers and toes. This biofeedback made me feel mellow. Not as good as two hours of racquetball, but a necessary substitute sometimes. And cleared my mind. I did one thousand swings, by guesstimate, not actual count.

I started downstairs, heading for the lounge to look for Mary Lynn, thinking I'd sort of accidentally encounter her and maybe kind of apologize for my behavior at Sandy's room earlier. I tried to ignore Vern's allegation that Mary Lynn had had or was having an ongoing affair with the governor. What's past was past and anyway not really my business. However, pangs of jealousy shot through me like Amazon headhunters had dipped their arrows in it. I just didn't want to think that Mary Lynn could have fallen for a handsome, slick-talking, powerful and rich man who was governor of the fourth largest state in population and still on his way up the career ladder.

At the ground floor, it hit me, of course. I knew it would. My mind had continued to work on a subliminal plane. Li Shou had cleared and prepared it. But it was too late, I just knew it. I turned and jogged the real short distance down the corridor to Mary Lynn's room.

Orlo.

In Trooper's room, he'd been telling me something. But I'd listened to his words and sentences, what he'd said—not what he was telling me.

About what he'd done to a woman. A blind woman in Bangkok.

Orlo had been stymied and rebuffed by me and Tapes since almost the beginning.

I'd insulted him in the kitchen *with Mary Lynn* present and immediately thereafter he had beat up Silas Smith. From watching Mary Lynn and me kiss and embrace in the kitchen he knew at a minimum what she meant to me. Also, she'd witnessed me and Tapes take the three out when they stomped Trooper. Orlo hated me with a passion only fanatics can achieve.

He had reason, in his mind, to get at me through Mary Lynn. Maybe he thought he was José Gaspar.

My heart was in my throat when I slid to a stop in front of her door. If Orlo had indeed been eavesdropping at one twelve a bit ago, maybe he had hidden in Mary Lynn's room to wait for her.

I didn't know whether to storm in or knock. No matter what you think about in the time of crisis, conventions of civilization stay your hand for critical moments.

Agonizing over the choice, I heard a moan and a crash. The crash had nothing to do with the storm.

Swiftly, I tested the door.

Locked.

I thought about running to my truck where, in a hidden compartment I'd built in the dash, I had a .38 stashed. Behind an innocuous box of Kleenex. But I doubted there was time.

I kicked at the doorframe next to the lock and handle with all my strength and the old door shattered around the lock.

"Thee are late," Orlo said as I caromed into him.

I hit him with two quick jabs before he physically picked me up and threw me against a wall.

With my left hand and foot, I braced myself against the wall just like when I run too hard to make a difficult racquetball shot and have to run up a wall. It merely softened the collision and I sort of bounced off and into the side of a dresser. An overnight bag crashed on the other side. I spun to face Orlo and he was merely watching me. I spared one eye to look for Mary Lynn.

She was sitting against a closed bathroom door as if she'd been flung against it, slammed into it, and had slid down to a sitting position with her legs stretched out awkwardly in front of her. Her chamois leather blouse was ripped. A trickle of blood seeped from her lower lip.

Anger boiled over in me and I crouched.

Orlo apparently read my face. "I have placed my hands upon her, but I have not yet violated her. Thee should never befoul thy bait before using it." He was standing there, supremely confident.

I feinted right and went in left and he didn't buy it and somehow I found myself flying again, glancing off the side of the bed and hit the floor and rolled, just in time because a pair of hunting boots slammed into the floor beside me. I continued the roll, remembering to breathe, a harsh sour thing. I grabbed the leg of the night stand and flipped it in his way and the lamp and cord became tangled and bought me time to make it to my feet.

Orlo kicked the obstruction out of his way and moved inexorably toward me. I spun as if to sprint away, kept spinning like I was lunging for a backhand-save shot, but kicked out with my Nike and missed his crotch but nailed his thigh well. The kick actually appeared to bother him. But he wasn't breathing as deeply and harshly as I was. My adrenaline rush had gone into overdrive and I was gasping more because my body thought it had to than it actually needed.

He grabbed at my leg but I was quicker, my one possible advantage, and kept spinning away from Mary Lynn and came back at Orlo with the edge of my left hand aiming for his neck or anything vulnerable I could find up there.

It bounced ineffectively off his raised shoulder.

Getting dizzy from spinning, I stepped aside from a response blow and backed away quickly.

"Mary Lynn," I gasped.

She must've still been stunned, but her eyes were following the action. If I remembered correctly, the only occupied adjoining room was Angie Maple's and she was with Sandra Dee Kowalski. And Tapes was fast asleep down the hall.

Orlo had me boxed in a corner now. He faked a kick and snaked a fist at me. I blocked his stroke with my upper left arm and the blow hurt like I'd been shot.

Orlo knew he had me. He stood there enjoying his superiority, a bit of drool leaking out of the corner of his mouth.

"This is a felony," I said between breaths, trying to buy time so that I could recover or think of something to extricate us, whichever came first.

He shrugged, watching me like a rattler playing with a field mouse.

"I will not kill thee," he said, not breathing very hard. "I want thee to watch whilst I use the woman."

"Hard time, Orlo. You can say you and I had a fight, but you can't lie about rape."

He shrugged again. "We will be far gone. By then my semen will be far gone from her. And it is well known that thee and her have had carnal relations. Even if I remained here, there would be no proof."

"Me and her, Orlo, our sworn statements."

"Thee will not be able to speak." He looked at her, not fearing me a bit. "And the woman will not want to ever think about me again. She will not speak. She will not allow thee to speak of it."

The chill I'd experienced in one twelve when he'd told of the blind Burmese woman in Thailand returned. I knew what he said was true. Mary Lynn would live the rest of her life in terror, a terrible unspeakable rape bottled up within her, unable to speak of it.

I missed my opportunity because I too looked at Mary Lynn. Her eyes were focused on Orlo and she was feeling worse than I'd felt now and earlier. She knew for certain what Orlo had said was going to come about. She, too, was mesmerized by Orlo and his words. She was hiccupping rapidly.

I faked right, then left, and did the only thing he did not expect: a frontal attack. Fingers splayed, I jammed for his eyes, pushing off from the wall with my left hand. All humans will automatically protect their eyes. I slammed into him, my right knee pumping into his groin one, two, three times in the space of time it took him to react.

He twisted and gave ground and I continued after him, jammed up against him. Being shorter, I was able smash the top of my head from underneath into his chin, jawline, and neck.

Intelligently, he fell. He'd been backpedaling and I went over with him, landing on Mary Lynn's right leg and she cried out but I had no time for her as I was lashing out with both clenched hands into Orlo's face, aiming for the only thing of strategic value, his eyes. I forced one hand open as he turned his head and fingered into his left eye but the turn kept the strike from gutting his eye because the finger rolled past his closed eye and jammed into the side of the socket.

He jerked his head back and looked death at me with his right eye. I expected his breath to be harsh and foul, but it wasn't. It was a bit metallic, coming from deep in his lungs. I slammed my head into his jaw again hoping for a glass jaw, but I was disappointed. It did get me a headache.

Kneeing him in the groin again cost me for he was able to flip me and wind up on top, pinning me. He outweighed me by eighty pounds easily.

Taking his time, he grinned down at me, the message being that this was it. "Pray, thee," he said, slapping me once to show his domination.

Then I saw a shapely ankle and a pointed-toe shoe as it struck Orlo in the right eye.

Off balance, Mary Lynn fell back against the wall and slid down to the floor once more. And hiccupped.

But it helped.

Orlo reacted by jerking his head and torso backwards, giving me the opportunity to snatch his head with my lower legs.

The tens of thousands of leg lifts came in handy, those and the leverage. Slowly, I toppled him off me. We were both on the floor, an alien tangle of two bodies, when he realized he could turn his head and bite my bare leg.

Quickly, I released my leg hold on his head, propped myself up, and pounded his kidney with my elbow as rapidly and with as much power as I could manage.

Both his eyes were puffing up from Mary Lynn's and my blows, but his eyeballs seemed to bulge out now past the puffiness.

Renewing my effort, I twisted my elbow when I struck.

We were still entwined, but he was struggling to escape, which allowed me to continue the pounding. If Orlo lived, I hoped he'd be pissing blood for a year.

Finally, he knocked me aside with a forearm blow that would have killed a cow, but I rolled with it, recalling Silas Smith's words about the dented refrigerator in the kitchen.

Being quicker, I was on my feet first.

His kidney must have been seriously injured for he slipped getting up and had to drop his left arm to block his fall.

Which gave me an opening and I kicked that arm out from under him and, as he went down, nailed him directly on the left ear.

He turned snow-white, but rolled with the kick away from me up against the far wall next to the head of the bed. A good ear shot will disorient and unbalance an opponent.

His eyes darted toward Mary Lynn but before he could act to grab her as a shield, I snatched a drawer from the chest of drawers and threw it at him.

He had to raise a forearm to protect himself.

Swifter than gossip, I began pulling out drawers and flinging them at him.

"Mary Lynn," I hissed. "Get out."

I threw the third drawer with more finesse, just like a Frisbee and that one must really have damaged him, for a look of incredible pain flashed across his face.

It seemed as if Mary Lynn was moving in quicksand, but she actually moved quicker than I thought she could.

Her hand slid up the wall, grasped the bathroom door handle, and pulled herself up.

I overhanded the fourth drawer and the leading edge struck the third drawer with which Orlo was now protecting himself.

Mary Lynn swung the bathroom door open maybe fourteen inches and slid inside.

The snick of the lock was satisfying.

I only wished she could have escaped into the corridor and gone to Tapes for help.

The sixth drawer was the last and I followed that with a framed sailboat print, just like the one in Sandra Dee Kowalski's room.

The frame crunched and twisted and clipped Orlo's knee, a grunt of pain helped my morale tremendously. The son of a bitch had been indestructible.

He kicked out at the tumble of drawers around him and they scattered at me like buckshot.

As I danced aside, he slid partially under the bed in a maneuver I did not understand.

Until he surged upward, the bed on top of him. He moved so quickly that the mattress stayed in the frame, only a pillow tumbling away.

There was nothing I could do as he rushed me. I dodged aside but the chest of drawers kept me from moving any farther and the entire bed, mattress first, slammed against me and pinned me against the wall.

I turned my head so that I could breathe.

The bed banged against me for a few moments, then stopped as Orlo realized he was expending energy and not accomplishing much.

I pushed against the bed, but I couldn't move it. Orlo was too strong and his weight and the bed's weight were too much for me—unless I managed to turn and prop my feet against the wall and push with my back to the mattress. However, I dropped that idea because I'd come out totally vulnerable.

For a minute, it was a Mexican standoff. Pinning me, he was at as much a disadvantage as I was, for he could not release his hold and get at me.

"Birthday?" His terrible voice penetrated the bed and flowed around it as it filled the entire room with its presence. "Thy neck will be aching in the next hours."

I didn't respond, my mind captivated again, but trying to work on any idea to extricate Mary Lynn and myself alive from this situation. I'd pretty well held my own.

"Thy abilities surprise me; thy tactics sufficiently out of the ordinary."

Tentatively, I pushed against the bed: no good.

"About thy neck? It will ache from so much looking over thy shoulder. Thee knows the rest."

I did. Mary Lynn. I could not leave her alone for one second until Orlo was dead or accounted for.

"Thee could have allowed the cop to kill me, but thee interfered. Only I know what thee were up to."

I pushed again and the bed toppled and there was no Orlo. The door was still swinging.

Orlo wasn't that stupid. He knew that he had to kill me or I would kill him. That given the opportunity, I'd get others to help hunt him down in the hotel. We both understood that if he lived, I would be dead and Mary Lynn would be a shell around a terrorized basket case.

I moved toward the door to see where he'd gone and—

"Oh, shit," I said aloud, realizing my mistake.

The bed surged off the floor and Orlo was there coming around beside it, a knife handle in his hand.

A blade snickered out and clicked in place.

I didn't wait. I thought longingly of the open door in front of me, then thought twice again about it.

I lunged for the door and he fell for it.

He jumped toward me, knife slicing through the thick air dense with dust.

But I was quicker, even after the exertion so far. I grabbed the door and slammed it open.

The move caught Orlo by surprise. It knocked his knife arm aside and slashed into his shoulder.

He hit the floor and rolled, as I had earlier, into me, upsetting me. But I did a flip dodging the goddamn knife and he ended up partway into the corridor.

He climbed to his feet as I regained my balance.

He charged at me as I slammed the door in his face.

Only it didn't slam. It pinned his arm. He was on the outside and I was on the inside. But he was bigger and began smashing his shoulder against the door to push it open. However, his arm was pinned and he couldn't get the leverage or the room to step back and hit the door with his entire weight.

Meanwhile I did my best to grind the edge of the door through his skin into bone, which wasn't happening.

The hand with the knife in it waggled like an obscene cobra searching out a victim.

I breathed dust and my own fear and saw the bathroom door opening and renewed my efforts to amputate his arm.

Mary Lynn had heard nothing and must have assumed it was over. She should've stayed in the bathroom, for Orlo could well have triumphed.

But it took her one glance to see what was happening and she hurried over to the door and lent her shoulder to the effort. She moved back and placed her hands against the door and pushed. She was hiccupping, but that didn't stop her.

Orlo grunted. His hand spasmed and I chopped at his wrist with my hand.

His hand opened and the knife fell to the floor and the door surged against us.

I thought we were goners then.

But we held. The door slammed against us again and again. Each time the hand withdrew a couple of inches. It had to be leaving skin. But slowly the arm disappeared until one final forearm blow against the door bounced it open sufficiently and Orlo's hand slid out.

With both of us pushing against it, the door smashed against the frame.

For a minute we held it there, breathing and looking at each other. The terror had faded from her eyes and a trembling determination replaced it.

The door was no longer moving against us and I bent to pick up Orlo's knife. I glanced through the broken wood at the lock and saw nothing in the dim light of the corridor.

"Back in the bathroom, quick like a bunny," I said.

"Nope," she said, letting up off the door and standing aside. She picked up a battery lantern to use as a weapon. Her hiccups were gone.

Slowly, I edged the door open.

Nothing.

On my knee, I peeked around the door jam.

Nothing. The corridor was empty.

Orlo was long gone.

Except the memory of him was still there in the room, a powerful physical thing.

I was just now getting my breath back.

"Come on," I said, taking Mary Lynn's hand.

I held the knife ready in my other hand.

Several pains I didn't know I had assaulted me as we hurried down the corridor.

Just for safety's sake, I paused and listened at our door.

Nothing.

I didn't want to go slamming into the room, because if Orlo wasn't there, Tapes would react so quick he might not be able to stop. It just wasn't a good situation.

I tapped on the door. "Tapes?" I remembered Mary Lynn's door not being locked and thinking about it earlier. I should have done something, but it escaped my attention for some reason. I was apprehensive about our room, too, since I hadn't bothered to lock the door.

There came a soft sound inside, and Tapes' voice said, "Shorts?"

He was on his feet and ready. He knew I wouldn't have knocked, unless there was something dead wrong.

"Yeah, it's me and Mary Lynn. We're coming in."

"All right."

We'd been partners so long that we knew how each other thought and could act accordingly.

We went in.

Tapes was in jeans without a shirt and had his Buck knife out. His hair was unkempt from sleeping—not that he'd slept very long.

"Looks like you had a disagreement with somebody." He inspected me. "Orlo? One of his people?" He turned up the lantern. "Looks worse in the light."

"Mary Lynn will explain," I said. "I'll be right back."

"The gun?" Tapes was jumping to the right conclusions.

"Yep." I pulled the door shut behind me. I would have liked to comfort the trembling Mary Lynn, but I had no time.

I went down the corridor, swift and silent, zigzagging, knife out, like I was running through a jungle.

At the door at the end of the hallway, the one through which we'd entered and heard the scream starting all this, I hesitated, then shrugged and slipped through. A gust of wind grabbed the door and tried to wrench it from my control. With my back, I pressed the door closed.

The GT was still nestled alongside the building and adjacent to a big gardenia and a plumeria, most limbs of which had snapped off at odd places, for the plumeria branches are more brittle than you'd expect.

I circled the truck warily, not trusting anything now. It still had the Texas tags, so Orlo could guess it was mine.

Nothing appeared out of place.

I opened the door after studying the surroundings to insure no Orlos jumped out of the bushes. Not for a moment did I think I was being paranoid.

Popping the cover off the compartment I'd built into the GT's dash, I pulled out the designer box of Kleenex. Why I'd used a designer box where you can't see it, I don't know. Then I pulled the little hidden tab and the back of the tissue compartment folded down. Clamps held the .38 and I snapped it free. There was a box of fifty rounds of ammunition that I took also. I doubted that I'd have time to reload, but the Boy Scout motto intervened.

Closing everything, I locked the truck this time.

Before I went back inside, I thought I heard a motor, but I could have been wrong. It wasn't any more dangerous than rush hour traffic in Houston, but it was stupid to be out and about.

Soon, I returned to the room, knocked softly and, when Tapes answered, went inside.

There was a half-full glass of straight Jim Beam on the dresser next to the lantern.

Tapes pointed at the bathroom. "She gave me a condensed version and just stepped in there."

I took a towel and wiped down the .38. Tapes could read between the lines, and there wasn't much I could add.

He ran his hand through his now kempt hair. "How good is Orlo?"

I didn't care whose drink it was, so I took a big slug. "If I hadn't been quicker and done the unexpected, I'd be dead and—" I couldn't finish, so I took another shot of the liquor. It burned all the way down but when it hit bottom, some of the muscles in my back relaxed and I realized how tense I'd been. American bourbon beats the hell out of Chinese Li Shou.

"Mary Lynn told me. That man is poison." He eyed the pistol on the dresser. "You going looking for him?"

"I am."

"What're you going to do when you find him?"

Mary Lynn came out of the bathroom looking considerably fresher. She heard Tapes ask the question and she stopped to listen to my answer.

I thought about it for a moment. "I was going to kill him. I still think I might try to kill him. There is no doubt he will kill me—and likely you, too. Mary Lynn is under a threat worse than death—"

"That's your opinion, buster," she said, but her eyes belied her words. She was still afraid. "Um, Billy, Tapes made that drink for me."

I sipped again, refilled it, and handed it to her. I didn't need any more alcohol in my system. I needed to be sharp.

She took the glass, sipped a bit herself, and sat the glass down. She fixed her bunny eyes on me and picked up my left hand. "Thank you, Billy Birthday. You'll never know how terrified I was."

I was terrified for her—and scared to death for myself, now that the action was over and I had time to think about it. It had wiped out any jealousy or resentment I'd build up concerning Henry B.

Tapes pulled on a shirt reading "FUCK AUTHORITY." He didn't ever wear that in public, so I thought he was sending a message to John Ionata. Then he saw Mary Lynn's look and pulled it off. He dug in his duffel and donned a tee shirt with a picture of Elmer Fudd on the front, with an automatic rifle, crossed bandoliers, and wearing a twisted red cloth as a head-band. The caption below Elmer read, "WAMBO."

"He doesn't ordinarily switch messages even if a woman asks," I said.

"Don't change on account of me," said Mary Lynn. She glanced down at our hands, still connected.

19: TUESDAY, 6:55 PM.

"I'm so hungry I could eat Spam," I said.

"Don't start," said Tapes.

"Ugh," I said. "I'd never be that hungry."

"Baked? With mustard and a few cloves? Food of the gods," he said.

"Which ones? Gods of salt and chemical additives?"

"Fried in butter," he said licking his lips, "then drenched in mustard and on bread lavished with mayonnaise."

Mary Lynn's head was turning back and forth.

"Cholesterol city," I said.

Tapes picked up the Smith & Wesson, careful not to point it in our direction. "Six rounds, three guys."

"Get Orlo with the first four," I said. If it came to shooting, there'd be no time for reloading.

"You are just going to go out and kill a person?" asked Mary Lynn, taking her hand from mine.

The movement made me wince because I still had a sliver of wood in it from the busted door. "Maybe three of them, if that's what it takes."

I pulled the big splinter out and didn't draw too much blood.

Tapes popped the cylinder aside to check the load, and snapped it back in. He'd carry the pistol because of my hand. "It is possible that if they cooperate, we will decommission them."

"Translated," I said, "that means if we get the drop on them, we'll tie 'em up for the authorities when they finally get here. Attempted rape and attempted murder for starters."

We went to Trooper's room.

"You what?" he demanded.

"Just kind of want to borrow your weapon," I said after explaining.

John Ionata was there. "That's taking the law into your own hands."

"So be it," I said. "The son of a bitch tried to kill me, John. He was using Mary Lynn as bait. He'd started to assault her. He wanted me to watch him, though. He wanted me to see her grovel for mercy. He wanted me to see him use her."

"You say."

"I do. And he told me he'd be back. Next time he won't underestimate me. He'll be better prepared, probably armed and with his two buddies."

"I still can't believe—"

I ignored him. "Trooper? What's the answer?"

Trooper struggled out of bed. He was wearing a tee shirt and boxer shorts. He was still bruised in the face and the arms that I could see. "Gimme my fuckin' pants. I'll go along."

I didn't know if that was what I wanted, but it might work out. I helped him into his official light brown FHP trousers, with the stripe down the leg, and we went out.

John Ionata invited himself along.

Trooper walked better once he got going.

"Here's the drill," I told him. "We'll do a comprehensive search starting downstairs, one wing at a time, and work our way up. Tapes and I will do the entering, you're too immobile. You back us up. John and Mary Lynn will stay near the center stairway while we go about our business. That way you can tell us if the three move while we're searching a wing."

We did the business wing first, the reception area, the offices. We took a skeleton key from the reception desk and opened each door, and Tapes or I would spin in low, pistol waving around like an Italian western flick and then go on to the next room. If there was no light on in the room or office, one of us would carry a flashlight.

Nothing.

"Tapes? I just remembered. When I went to the GT, I heard a motor. Do you reckon?"

After a second, he said, "I do. Let me check." He slipped out the front doors and Trooper and I went to join Ionata and Mary Lynn. Trooper and I searched the lounge and bar wing opposite the kitchen wing while waiting for Tapes. Of course, we didn't find Orlo or his friends.

Tapes caught up with us as we started to search the kitchen wing. "Van's gone. I looked around as much as I could and didn't see it near the Inn."

"Damn. We aren't going to find them. Almost certainly, Orlo had known what would happen and grabbed his comrades and took off." I shook my head in disgust. But I couldn't think of anything we could have done to prevent their escape. We'd moved as quickly as we could.

But we couldn't take the one chance in a hundred that I was wrong.

We finished the ground floor, bothering only a couple people, specifically Angie Maple.

"I don't like it," she said.

"Complain to the lieutenant governor," I told her. "It was his idea."

"Men waving guns snooping in my closet and bathroom."

"It's a macho thing we have to do once or twice a month to keep our touch."

Sandra Dee Kowalski and daughter were doing fine.

All the rooms on the second floor were empty. Trooper had to climb the stairs slowly.

The third floor was almost the same.

Henry B.'s suite was empty. It took up most of the north wing, and had a balconies and windows and all so that he could see both the Gulf of Mexico and Charlotte Harbor. Nice digs.

Silas Smith's suite was next.

The door was unlocked and it was possible that Orlo had hunted Silas, so we went in careful. Mentally, I kicked myself for not thinking of Silas first: besides me and Mary Lynn, he was the obvious target.

Tapes and I both went in, with Trooper following almost immediately.

The door slammed open and I went in bent over and spinning. Tapes jumped in aside and away from the door.

Silas and Pinky were sitting on the sofa talking.

Both mouths fell open and silent.

Since we already knew the layout, it took up only a moment to search the suite.

Nothing.

I gave Pinky and Silas a quick explanation and we moved on. Two more wings left.

More nothing.

We went back to Silas Smith's suite.

"What I thought," I said, "is we watch a bit. We're high enough here and the visibility is decent enough to see people or vehicles moving around the Inn."

"It's dark and sometimes rain squalls hit," said Ionata.

"Each wing overlooks the entrance below. It shouldn't be difficult," I said, "especially if the weather clears up even a little."

"We can help," Pinky said.

"You and Silas take this wing. Check outside periodically and holler if you see something moving. You'll have to watch the entire kitchen entrance. Tapes can do the south wing and John Ionata the west wing. I'll do the east wing."

"I can contribute," Trooper said.

"Me, too," said Mary Lynn. "You aren't going to leave me alone."

"No way, hon." I smiled at her. "You can help me in the east wing. I need some shuteye in the worst way. Trooper, you can spell John Ionata in the west. Pinky, maybe you can find Vern Bernstein to help Tapes." Fortunately, each end suite had windows overlooking the grounds, giving 180 degrees visibility to the next wings, depending on the brightness of day and lashing rain.

"How long you reckon, Shortcut?" asked Tapes.

"Until the storm dissipates a bit or when we all get some sleep. Maybe 'til morning." I checked my watch. "Midnight now." I was flat out exhausted.

"I can get some food from the kitchen," said Silas.

"I don't want any steaks or eggs," I said.

Mary Lynn looked at me curiously.

"I'll explain when we get to our post."

Ionata and Trooper thought my comment very funny.

"See if there's any Spam," Tapes said hopefully.

Of course the east wing was empty and the prime suite at the end of the wing had no permanent residents. I doubt if I fooled anybody with my machinations; however, I accomplished my purpose as Mary Lynn and I wound up alone together.

Waiting for Silas to bring us a snack, I unabashedly took a cold shower. Fortunately, the executive VIP suite had complimentary toothbrushes, shaving gear, and so on, all of which I put to use. The bad part was putting back on my cutoffs and armless FSU sweatshirt. But I felt a great deal better. From the encounter with Orlo, I had aches and pains.

The suite had a big open room, with the primary view out the east windows. There was a balcony on the south side of the room. But not one on the north side, for obviously the planners didn't need the occupants spying on the back courtyard and the kitchen wing. One of the two bedrooms faced to the south.

We dragged a rattan sofa over to the big windows. We sat and watched the lights of Charlotte Harbor and the mainland. Then a heavy cell of rain hit and we couldn't see anything, much less movement on the ground below. It wasn't all that important. The main thing was that Mary Lynn and I were not located where Orlo would look for us.

Silas brought us pineapple and cream cheese sandwiches explaining, "It'll go bad in the fridge," as if he really cared, peanut butter sandwiches, thank God, and some lukecold diet Cokes.

"I'd feel better if you asked Angie Maple to stay with Sandra Dee," Mary Lynn said.

Silas nodded. "I will."

We sat on the sofa and looked out the window, down on the grounds stretching out toward the golf course and the east side of the island.

I'd turned off the battery lamp so we could see better.

After a moment, Mary Lynn said, "Well?"

"Well, what?"

"You told me you'd explain why you made a point of not wanting steak or eggs."

In the feeble light of the room, I looked at the pineapple and cream cheese sandwich and put it down, suddenly not real hungry. "How committed an environmentalist are you?"

She swallowed a bite. "Well, I'm no eco-freak. But I care. I contribute. I'm Earth-friendly. If I find a pelican with a broken wing on the beach, I'll get it to a veterinarian. I don't believe in testing makeup in rabbits' eyes, but then I do eat hamburgers and fried chicken. I give money to the right eco-groups, not the fanatics. It's one of the things Angie and I have in common. Are you a tree-hugger? And what has this to do with beans?"

"I pick up plastic six-pack rings on the beach," I said. "That's about the extent of it."

"Well, spill it, will you? The suspense isn't spellbinding, but I am rather curious."

"Look here, Mary Lynn. I shouldn't have said anything."

"Stop stalling."

Damn, I really shouldn't have made that flippant remark. "No Timoleon I, for I will not abstain from sustenance after being reviled." I wondered how to say it. "The steak and eggs I had the other night?"

"The stuff you burned and sizzled and lathered with peanut butter?" She put her peanut butter sandwich back on the dish.

"Right. Well, come to find out, the steak was manatee and the eggs were turtle, probably endangered loggerhead."

She was silent and pushed her plate away. "A gentleman

would have found a way not to tell me."

"I'm not a very good liar," I lied.

"I bet. Um. Ugh. I helped you eat it."

"Yep."

"It was the Jim Beam," she said. "I was a bit tipsy." She looked at her plate. "I thought the odd taste was because you put peanut butter on burnt meat." She chugalugged some Coke. "Okay, so you told me. I'm not all that hungry any longer."

"Me, neither."

We were silent for a moment, my eyes searching out the window and around the grounds below.

"There are some things about that time that I *will* remember more fondly," she said, voice soft and throaty at the same time. She was watching me closely.

"Me, too."

"I'm not certain that at first I believed you and Tapes were touring Florida to visit all the lighthouses." Her tone softened. "But I believe it now."

"Tapes thinks windmills are best. They're pretty, he says. Pretty! And functional and work-oriented, since most windmills are constantly doing a mechanical job. Whereas, I claim lighthouses are more aesthetic, and while they don't always produce, they do provide an occasional civilized service. Also, they face the biggest threat from nature unchained day and night year after year. Not to mention most lighthouses, ninety-nine percent of 'em anyway, are located amidst splendid scenery or sit there alone in some bleak background o'er which they dominate—"

"I thought you didn't like poetry."

"Sometimes I get wound up and become lyrical." I smiled happily. "Committing poetry ought to be one of the top ten sins."

"I said before that I wanted to get to know the real you." Her voice was back to normal. "I think I'm finding it. You put out fires, you fight mean and terrible men, you deliver babies, you quote Plutarch—"

"I read Plutarch. There's so much of it that it sort of bubbles out—"

"You're very self-deprecating—"

"And becoming self-conscious, aw shucks," I said.

"You certainly do not hide your reading habits," she said.

I shook my head. "I follow the DEAR and USSR principles of reading. Drop Everything And Read, and Uninterrupted Sustained Silent Reading."

Another vicious rain cell burst over the Inn, but I didn't think it would last long.

"So what about you, Sister Mary Lynn?"

"Since you ask, I was on the restoration committee to rehab the Old Port Boca Grande Lighthouse."

"I knew it! I knew there was some subliminal metaphysical connection between us." I beamed. I'd learned part of that earlier in terms of BIPS, the Barrier Island, *etc.*

"Angela Maple was Chairwoman of the committee." Mary Lynn smiled.

"Well, cut me off at the pass," I said.

"I was wondering about that."

I'm pretty dense at times, but it didn't take me long to figure that one out.

After a minute, I came up for air. "You can rehabilitate me any old time."

"Mmmmm," she said.

We leaned back together, arms entwined and watched the rain pelt the big window.

"I suppose you'd like to know about Henry B.?" she said, making things so much easier for me.

"I've decided it isn't really any of my business," I lied. I wanted to know as bad as some want to know if FDR knew about Pearl Harbor before December 7. I'd reconciled my jealousy, or so I thought.

"Do you care about me?" she asked, surprising me.

"Um, ah, hell yes. I thought that was clear."

"Then," she said, "it stands to reason you want to know about my relationship with the governor."

"Some would draw that conclusion," I said diplomatically.

She fixed me with her blue eye. I knew it in the gloom because it was the left one. "You were quite angry about my job as Gasparilla Island Reelection Campaign Chair for Henry B."

"I do, and I apologize for my indiscretion." I tried to make my voice sound rueful. From the softening around her eyes, I was at least partially successful. "I wasn't exactly myself."

She took a deep breath. "From what you told me Silas confessed, you're aware that Henry B. had slept with every woman over twelve in the nearest counties."

"It seemed like it." Vern had referred to Mary Lynn's divorce and had hinted that Henry B. was likely responsible. He'd also said Gonzáles had once given her money and kissed her goodbye, publicly, here at the JG Inn.

"Well, I—"

"Like I said, Mary Lynn, it's none of my business. The governor was handsome, rich, powerful, and had a bright national future. Hell, I even found him very personable." I remembered talking about the weather and "rapidly dissipating."

"Silas called me twice, on pretexts, to meet secretly with the governor." Mary Lynn crossed her arms.

So Mary Lynn was on Smith's list.

I didn't know what to say.

"Silas at times was Henry B.'s, ah, conduit, shall we say?" Mary Lynn was rather uncomfortable. "I don't choose to use the word 'procurer.'"

It could be that Mary Lynn was trying to purge her own conscience by telling me. "Go on." I didn't think I wanted to hear what she was going to tell me.

"I was married at the time," she said, letting her breath out audibly. "You have to understand. My husband, well, if I could have, I would have worked to support him, so that he could fish all day and all year and not have to work. He loved to fish; it's why he lives here. He has a gentle side to him, too. Most of the time he fished, he fished CPR. See, you aren't the only one with acronyms. Catch, Photo, and Release." She hiccupped softly once. Memories, at times, are deadly. She looked straight at me.

"I was a great deal more naive in my life than I am now. The divorce has opened my eyes. I grew up a lot in those ten years." She paused and looked down at her lap. "I took my marriage vows seriously—and, apparently, I was the only one." She was angry now, breathing quickly and shallowly.

"It's okay," I said.

"No, it wasn't okay. Most people don't believe me. How could someone who ran out on her vows to the Lord—poverty, chastity, obedience, charity, the whole bunch—observe her marital vows when everyone knows her husband is running around on her?"

"I believe you."

She gave me a perfunctory smile. "You would, you're the kind who wouldn't see the contradiction."

I did see the contradiction, however, I could understand the forces pulling on a young woman, urging her to quit the nunnery and join life's mainstream.

"Daddy was a coal miner and mother was long suffering. I was supposed to escape." Her face fell a bit. "I remember Daddy always covered with a fine black powder."

"How old were you when you joined?"

"Fourteen." She shook her head.

"In a nunnery?"

She shook her head again, auburn pony tail dancing. "I wasn't cloistered. The Sisters of St. Francis. Our Mother Home was up in Allegheny County."

"Pennsylvania."

"Right."

"I was good at geography bees," I said, trying to lighten the atmosphere in here.

She ignored me and continued. "I almost quit once when I was a postulant, but I didn't. I should have. When I did quit, I had to fill out an application for the Pope to give me dispensation...."

Since she was silent, I asked a question I'd always wondered about. "Is it hard to quit? Being a nun, I mean? Do they hassle you?"

She shook her head once, quickly. "No. If you don't want to continue your vows and do the job any longer, they certainly don't want you."

She turned down the corners of her mouth and I could see the split on the left side, lower lip where Orlo had struck her. I reached over and caressed it lightly with my pointy finger.

"But it was very difficult for me to quit, personally," she said. "I'd devoted my life to it, to the Lord and His good works. I took my vows seriously. It's been ten years, and I recently talked to a Sister, a friend who'd been in my group as we went through the stages. She was the only one left of our original group."

"That should reinforce your decision."

She shrugged this time. "Not really. You always wonder. Especially since I messed up my life by picking the wrong man."

She hesitated and I saw the anger building some more. "A mistake I will not repeat." She paused. "My friend was the only one who elected to change her name to one which was a saint. Mary got me by, and they let me get away with Mary Lynn, even though nobody ever heard of any Saint Lynns."

"How'd you wind up down here on Gasparilla Island? It's rather out of the way."

"I went to college up there; it's Catholic territory. The college was Catholic and the order got a break on the tuition. I lived in a convent on campus. Most sisters opted for teaching or nursing; I chose social work and that's what my degree was in." Her voice turned to a whisper. "Now I'm a counselor who should have counseled herself."

I'd figured something like that. Mary Lynn had shown too many signs, concern for others, to almost a professional level.

She leaned against the back of the sofa. "Until recently, Florida was considered missionary territory. That's how I came here."

"And met your husband?"

"Right. He swept me off my feet. He was a carpenter and very very handsome and well built." Mary Lynn leaned toward me now. "But he wasn't as well built as you are." She ran her hand over my upper arm and over my shoulder under the muscle shirt.

I didn't know what to say.

"He was ten years older than I was and oh, so worldly."

Her words were slow and sad. "I was young and naive and easily swayed."

What would Plutarch say?

"It lasted almost ten years until he found somebody ten years younger than I am."

"Plutarch would say, 'Do not play the number ten in the lottery.'"

That earned me a smile and a light kiss. Both her hands roamed under my sweatshirt through the shoulder holes. I licked the crack in her lower left lip.

"The two times Henry B. called upon me, I was married." She withdrew her hands and sat back again.

I was no Aristides the Locrian who told Dionysius, "I had rather see the virgin in her grave than in the palace of a tyrant."

"His ostensible purpose was to give me some money for a project we'd been working on. But he ended up chasing me around the room." She shook her head angrily. "He'd heard about my marital problems." She fixed me with an intense gaze. "What do you call a woman who doesn't have an asshole?"

Again, I was surprised. I thought she was speaking anatomically. I was wrong. "What?"

"Single." Mary Lynn giggled, and then hiccupped.

"I'm supposed to be the cutup," I said with false anger. It occurred to me that Mary Lynn Messenger had been hurt more than she was showing. I thought about her saying she'd have gladly worked so her husband could go fishing every day. "What project?"

She rubbed her forearms as if to lower the raised-hair thereupon. "That's the thing, one of the things, which infuriate me so."

This was going roundabout. I still didn't know if she'd

succumbed to Henry B.'s charm. And, even though it was absolutely none of my business, I did want to know. I wondered how long Silas Smith's list was. "What infuriates you?"

"Everybody speaks ill of Henry B."

I looked out the window and sighed. Rain pelted the glass. I was still fatigued and the adrenaline was wearing off. Would I ever get any sleep?

"You mean like Ionata and Smith and Vern?"

"Exactly. So, too, does Angie Maple."

"Not Trooper."

"No, never Trooper," she said. "Me, neither."

"Oh," I said. Most of the time you can't ever pinpoint the pit of your stomach. Right then I could. It was the place where I get sick to.

"Gasparilla Island is going modern," said Mary Lynn. "Construction of expensive condos is the island's main industry now. At one time it was fishing, then tourism, now retirement condos and homes. Not thousands, mind you, but plenty enough."

What the hell was she talking about now?

"You're wondering why I'm meandering?"

"Nah," I said, "I don't believe in rushing into anything."

She eyed me. "It didn't seem that way earlier...."

"Well, urn, about Gasparilla Island?"

"Oh, right. With all the expensive property here, there's become an underclass. Mostly fishermen and their families who've lived here forever. When the fish aren't biting or it's not tarpon season, some of the fishermen have a hard time making ends meet. Their families go hungry on this island of plenty. The county keeps reassessing the property. A little cottage is now taxed very highly. See, no one would buy the little cottage or the property right in the middle of other little cottages and fishing homes on stilts, but still the homeowners have to pay higher taxes on the higher assessments. And it really hurts—am I boring you?"

"I'm having about as much fun as you can with your clothes

on."

She gave me a quick flash of even teeth. "So they can't sell their property and most don't want to, for they'd have to move onto the mainland." Mary Lynn looked up, her eyes shining. "Henry B. knew about it. I lived here, my husband doing well, being a subcontractor on most of the condo developments. But we were part of the fishing village life. Henry B. would ask me about the people, 'my people,' he called them; a rather feudal-istic attitude. But his has been the prominent family here for years and years." She paused to breathe.

I put my hand on her knee and rubbed in a circular motion.

"I'd tell him who was having a hard time that month and he'd give me a handful of one hundred dollar bills to give out."

"He trusted you because you had been a nun and were a social worker."

"Exactly," said Mary Lynn. "I was the only one on the island who knew what was going on with the long-term and finan-cially-hurting residents." She shrugged again. "And perhaps the only one he could trust to give out the money without taking a bit myself."

"So you really were an angel of mercy?"

She nodded emphatically. "I was doing what I thought I wanted to do when I joined the Franciscans."

"Makes sense to me." I still wanted to know if she'd slept with the governor. The thing about it all was that I knew goddamnit I was being petty and selfish, but goddamnit again I liked her and I was becoming jealous of a dead guy I liked myself. I almost hated myself for being so. But I damn well could understand Aristides.

"I think," she went on, "that most of them knew where the money was coming from. They're a proud people and accepting the money was difficult for most of them, so they were glad they didn't have to acknowledge the source of the money."

"Did Henry B.'s accountant use you as a reference?"

She looked puzzled for a moment. "You mean for tax purposes?"

"I do."

"Nope."

I sighed. "That and the weather and 'rapidly dissipating' all add up. I hate to admit it, but I liked Henry B. also." I frowned. "Except for when he tried to seduce you."

"Henry B. was a lot of things to a lot of people," said Mary Lynn, not taking my bait. "I thought he was grand, a charitable lord of his land with an inordinate sexual drive. I always attributed his prejudices to too much testosterone."

She sort of collapsed against me and began hiccupping.

I stroked her hair and my palm quivered like a magnet seeking north.

Gradually, her bout subsided. "He was quite powerfully insistent, when he wanted me to go to bed with him. The fact that I liked him, naively I suppose, made it more difficult to resist his charms. I didn't want to get involved with him as I knew many other women had. But he was terribly, um, unrelenting and overwhelming, if you know what I mean."

I think I did, bitterly so. Us mere mortals wish we had some of that charisma and sex appeal.

"I think it was my religious training," she said into my neck, "that made my inner struggle easier. I knew self-denial. And my marriage was falling apart then; I was not happy with the male race."

"Sex," I said.

"Whatever," she said. "The second time he tried to seduce me, I think, was because of his failure the first time. That was at the hotel, in his room. I raised hell with him."

"I bet you did." I was feeling better.

"I told him, '"Goddamnit, Hank'—he hated to be called Hank—'if you touch me again, I'm going to scream and cry rape.' 'They'll never believe you,' he told me. 'I'm an ex-nun, and enough people will believe me to cause you political problems.' I was so angry that he backed right off." Her whole body was relaxing against me, the tension draining through the retelling.

I wondered if secretly Mary Lynn wasn't just a bit glad Henry

B. was dead.

She hiccupped. "But he got even with me." She sighed. "When he couldn't get me into bed, he escorted me downstairs and to the lobby. He told me goodbye and grabbed me and kissed me before I could duck away. I turned to leave and as I walked toward the door, he snapped his fingers and said, 'Wait, I forgot this.' Well, as you can guess, the bastard got me good. He pulled out a stack of hundred dollar bills, stuck them in my hand, and it took me a few seconds to realize what he'd done to me. In that few seconds, he turned and walked quickly down the hall."

"Right in front of witnesses?"

"Exactly, the son of a bitch got me. Silas, a desk clerk, a couple who were old time residents of the island and were at the hotel for dinner, two tourists, and a bus boy." Showing what gossip can do, the story had made it to Vern Bernstein.

"And you couldn't very well explain the money was for poor Gasparilla Islanders because that was your big secret and you didn't want to spoil it for them."

She nodded, her nose swiping my neck. "It would have embarrassed them, humiliated them. I thought about saying aloud something like, 'I'll have my husband build that for you right away, Governor.' But it would have sounded lame by the time I thought about it and said it."

The bottom of the pit of my stomach was no longer my physiological focal point. I actually felt good, though tired to death. "Now you know how politicians work. Ole Henry B. was right Machiavellian." While the late governor pissed me off because he hit on Mary Lynn and embarrassed her, I still had to admire the sheer gall of the man.

It suddenly occurred to me that now Mary Lynn Messenger had a downright good reason to kill Henry B. "Henry B. made you seem like a paid hooker," I said. "And you're on Silas Smith's list. And Gonzáles tried to seduce you. Motive. And you had the opportunity. Why, my dear, I do believe you're a prime suspect in his recent unceremonious and uncalled-for demise."

Her tongue was playing with my earlobe. "Do you really

think so?" Her whisper melted my ear.

"Umm...," I said intelligently. "If you keep *that* up, I am going to die."

Her hands were roaming under the FLORIDA STATE symbol on my sweatshirt. "Your muscles aren't big and knotty and bulgy."

"After I work out, I swim a mile or so. It seems to help. On top of that, ten to twelve hours of racquetball a week keeps me loose." Tapes says I ought to turn professional; but you have to be mid-twenties or younger for that extra step and quickness.

"You were as strong as Orlo when you came to save me."

"Not quite, but my intentions were pure." I was exhausted. I think I expended a ton of psychic energy worrying about Mary Lynn and Orlo and the mental struggle I'd had over the relationship between Mary Lynn and Henry B. I felt drained myself. The relief acting like a one-way check valve pouring my energy out.

Her hands were soft as kitten-fur.

Somehow, I was head and shoulders in her lap, looking up at her looking down at me. I pulled her down and kissed the split in her lip. Her eyes were boring into me.

My hands began roaming and the damn fancy knocker on the door banged resoundingly.

I groaned.

"What is it with you?" said Mary Lynn.

"This place must be full of snakes the way we appear to be snake bit," I opined. I tugged at her, ignoring the knock.

"Whoever it is knows we're here," she said.

"And all that follows." I groaned again and struggled to my feet. I straightened my shirt and made my way to the door in the dark. "Yes?"

"Birthday? It's Ionata."

I pulled open the door and a flashlight beam lanced into the room.

Ionata stepped inside, moving sideways to get around me.

"Come on in, John."

"Thanks." His flashlight beam found Mary Lynn standing at the window and lingered on her for a moment. He walked to her and I followed. He glanced out the window and flicked his light off.

I stopped beside Mary Lynn.

"I came to apologize," Ionata said.

"Fine. It's accepted."

"For hastily accusing you of murder."

"I appreciate your thoughts, John. Maybe you can go apologize to Tapes now."

"I went to see him first and he suggested I visit you now."

"He did?" The son of a bitch. Tapes sometimes pulls my chain to remind me I'm not in charge of the entire world.

"It occurred to me," said Ionata, "that while you had the opportunity, you probably had no motive. Pinky finally said he thought you both came from the other corridor, once he thought about it, and most probably did not arrive by the stairs."

"Good for Pinky." Though Pinky might have had his back toward the stairs. Was Pinky trying to cover for me and Tapes?

"Most of the people here had the opportunity," Mary Lynn said pointedly to John Ionata. "And the motive."

He turned to look at her in the dark. "Oh?"

"You, for instance," Mary Lynn continued.

"Oh?" he said again with more inflection.

"Yep. You. Henry B. told me that you had an insatiable drive to become governor." Mary Lynn was giving no quarter.

Ionata was silent for a moment and so, too, was I, for Mary Lynn was doing well. Go get him, Mary Lynn. The lieutenant governor sighed. "I've a vision for Florida, one that I can and have articulated. I want to work for the people, do the right thing, and not advance my own career." Now we were cutting to the chase. "The current and late governor was more interested in image, in window-dressing; he paid little attention to issues of substance. Tax reform, funding hospitals to treat the indigent, insurance reform, many others."

"John," Mary Lynn said, "you're giving a speech."

A flash of teeth, a grin. "I've given that talk so often my wife wakes me up and says I'm giving it in my sleep."

"It rather confirms your hunger for the governor's chair," said Mary Lynn.

"I'm an old Florida cracker," he went on. "I'm not supposed to have political ambitions. I don't really, not national aspirations. I simply want to be governor of Florida. I've paid my dues and earned my chance." He shook his head, beard rasping on his shirt. "Did you know Henry B. used 'cracker' in a derogatory manner? He said it like 'poor white trash.' You could never tell about Gonzáles, his prejudices wove a web about him." Ionata's voice was bitter.

But he continued. "I consider being a cracker a part of my heritage I'm proud of. I challenge any who think it racist, associating the term with anti-black attitudes. Now, I...."

"Where were you when the governor was killed?" Mary Lynn was relentless and bent on keeping him on the subject.

"I was in my room, yes, that was it. I was shaving." He adjusted his wire-rim glasses.

"Can you prove it?" she asked.

I was getting more tired every second. I doubted we'd get anything out of Ionata. I was wrong.

"Why should I have to prove it?"

"Because you've more motive, haven't you?"

Ionata sagged. "You mean...?"

"Sarah." Mary Lynn crossed her arms. "You've been busy hanging everyone for the crime for much less reason than you possess."

My exhaustion folded back a bunch. "Who's Sarah?"

Ionata sighed again. "My daughter. Mary Lynn has heard the rumors."

"And?" I prompted.

"That Sarah had an affair with Gonzáles," said Ionata.

"And you did not like that?" I asked.

"It cut me to the quick," he said, "and, I suspect, Gonzáles knew I knew and took advantage of it. He would ask after

Sarah's health and wellbeing, but I would not let him get to me. I'd smile and said she was fine. At times he would be quite condescending to me."

"It would be safe to say you were not sorry to see him dead," said Mary Lynn.

"Very safe." Ionata's voice was smug.

The image I'd had of him being Poppa Smurf disappeared. He was a man of convictions and concerns, just like the rest of us. At times he'd been petty, other times just trying to get along and do what he thought was right.

Unable to fight it any longer, I yawned. Then I yawned again and again until both Ionata and Mary Lynn were watching me. "Excuse me. I've been awake since the Cetaceous."

Ionata shook himself. "I intrude. Forgive me. He never looked up. He walked out, led by his flashlight beam. The door closed behind him.

I stepped next to Mary Lynn. "Thanks." I threaded my right arm through her left and yawned again. "Do you reckon he did it?"

She shrugged and her pony tail bobbed against the lighter outline of the sliding glass door. She yawned, too. "It's catching. Do you think he did it?"

I pulled her close. "I've thought about it. From what he showed here tonight, I think he could have done it. That is, he has the inner whatever-it-takes to kill an enemy. The question is, how much of an enemy did Ionata consider Henry B.?" I brushed her cheek with my lips.

"Um, where were we?"

"On the couch being interrupted." I ran my hands around her back.

She led me back to the sleeper and sat down. Soon, my head was again in her lap.

"One thing?" she said. "John truly loves his daughter. However, she's disappointed him often. She's rather a wild woman."

My left arm was under the chamois leather massaging the

hot skin of her shoulders and back.

"Sarah is a free spirit, a real hippie of the old kind, she's a hardcore environmentalist, and especially she is anti-establishment."

"Which makes it strange that she had an affair with Henry B.," I said.

Mary Lynn's hands reciprocated on my chest and stomach. "I know, but it's true, it was no secret except perhaps to John."

I kissed her stomach and it quivered and made me feel good.

Her hands kept running softly over my abdomen, my chest, my shoulders. I was glad I had an inny belly button. I was also glad I was wearing the loose sweatshirt.

I turned my head into her stomach again.

We'd been talking for an hour or two. I was exhausted, so tired, so comfortable....

And I fell asleep.

20: WEDNESDAY, 6:20 A.M.

"Billy," Mary Lynn's voice was an unnecessary whisper. "I see something."

She shook my shoulders.

My eyes popped open and looked up at her. Concern etched her eyes.

I felt the smooth leather of her Prairie shorts under my cheek; more, I felt the warmth under the soft garment.

Groaning, I swung off the couch and stood. I stretched and checked my watch. Not yet half past six. We'd slept several hours.

She stood next to me, bent over, and touched her toes. "I fell asleep, too," she confessed.

I gargled with warm and flat diet Coke. I couldn't see the sun but it was light outside, windy but no rain right now.

She pointed. "There it is again."

A dark shape skulked. Right below us and near the base of this wing.

"Again," said Mary Lynn, voice now excited.

The shape moved at an odd angle, skirting a hedge. A low shape. It went past my GT, past the big plumeria and disappeared when it merged with the gardenia tree.

Then I saw but a flash of movement.

"We're in dire jeopardy," I said. "It's just a dog trying to find its way home or beg a meal." I stretched and looked at Mary Lynn. This tender feeling kind of oozed through me and I wanted to ruffle her hair, but some women are strange about that. I traced her jawline instead. "I'll go down and check it out. Maybe it's Deacon. And I've duffel in the truck with a set of clean jeans and a shirt." Momma had taught me to roll clothes tightly and stuff them in a duffel bag so they'd come out unwrinkled. It takes practice.

I was on the second floor landing when I realized Mary Lynn was following me. "I'll be right back."

She touched the back of my neck. "You are not going to leave me alone with Orlo loose and about."

I shrugged. I wasn't worried. I had the .38 stuffed into the waistband of my cutoffs. Regardless of what you see on the big or small screens, that ain't easy. And an accidental shot does severe damage to your manhood. Revolvers are safest because the cylinder has to rotate to fire. But still, the damn metal stabs into your tummy, so I moved the weapon to the small of my back.

It wasn't raining when I stuck my head out the ground floor door of the east wing. My truck looked okay. "Stay here." I slipped out the door, the revolver in my hand, my palm and fingers around the cylinder and trigger guard. Not very John Wayne, but it's the way I carry a gun. Wind blew my hair.

To my chagrin, Mary Lynn stepped outside and leaned against the door. She wanted to make sure I was all right, I guess.

I reconnoitered the area. Nothing. A quick look around the gardenia down the east wing. Nothing. There was a big tree limb down and I didn't check the kitchen courtyard; Pinky and Silas should have been watching from above. One of the reasons I felt relatively safe.

A hedge had been crushed in two places by a fallen tree and I gave it a perfunctory glance, sort of waving the gun that way tracking my line of sight.

The only thing I can say is that camouflage works.

I stopped at the truck, put the .38 in the bed next to the big tool box which stretched across the entire back of the truck. Opening the handle, I got my Ektelon Xpre racquetball racquet in my right hand to move it off the duffel bag. I've more expensive racquets but this is the one I'd taken on the trip, and I can't even say "Xpre." Back then, it was an awesome racquetball racquet. I went to put the Xpre down when Mary Lynn screamed.

It was wordless and terror filled.

I jerked my head up to see Orlo and Pigtail rushing me from the crushed hedge. Their camo had fooled me, or they'd hidden in a pocket I hadn't been able to see from my vantage point.

With my left hand, I snatched for the revolver. Being ambidextrous, it was no problem. I swung, cocking the revolver with my thumb and a tremendous shock hit my arm.

Deacon must have been flying, because he struck my arm at light speed, chomped down on my left forearm and I shouted involuntarily.

I swung around and slung the dog away from me, but he held on momentarily, his teeth gouging furrows down my arm. They clamped on my wrist and I tried to trigger the revolver but the force of his bite kept the muscles from working until I smashed him into the right front wheel well of the truck and his grip loosened and I triggered off a shot and his mouth opened and closed swiftly, chomping down on my hand and fingers, and he bounced off the truck and ripped the goddamn .38 right out of my hand as if he'd planned it that way but he was dead even as his mouth locked onto the revolver for the .38 slug had gone through his mouth and out the back of his head just below the skull and above the red bandanna collar.

My left hand was sending me messages I didn't need.

An inhuman scream came from behind me and I remembered what was going on. I swiveled, the short racquet still in my right hand, just in time to dodge a slashing blade which clanged dully off the wide-view passenger-side mirror.

Orlo and a machete. A damn machete. No gun, but a machete. Not a sword, but as close as you can get.

I ducked under his back stroke parallel to the ground. Good thing I wasn't too tall, else he'd have cut me down to this size.

Still swiveling and bent over, I lashed out at him with a backhand stroke of my own. The edge of the racquet barely brushed his abdomen.

I spun out of the way. "Inside!" I screamed at Mary Lynn.

But my glance told me we'd both been too slow. Pigtail had her by the arm and was swinging her around. Orlo was coming at me again and I couldn't spare time, but I did see Pigtail slam Mary Lynn into the wall next to the door.

Dodging a clumsy overhand slice was easy. Orlo was too big for his own alacrity. His hair was mussed and his face furious. His eyes were still puffy.

Axe. The other one. Dancing off a bit, I scanned the area for him. Nothing. Pigtail had Mary Lynn up against the wall of the hotel and was holding her immobile and watching Orlo and me over his shoulder. If I failed here, Mary Lynn would suffer at their hands.

I deflected a blow with the handle and almost lost my right thumb. But I was able to slide the blade of the machete off the Xpre and clip his elbow in the follow through. Faking, I pushed away from the truck with my left foot and smashed his left side with a satisfying slice of the leading edge of the racquet.

Getting into stride, I kicked at his knee and slammed the racquet into his side again. After what Tapes and I'd both done to his kidney earlier, this might have a cumulative effect.

Then I faked for his kidney and when he went to protect himself, I backhanded for his neck and hit his solid shoulder instead.

Whereupon he stabbed the point of the blade at me pirate-like and I had to knock it aside with my bad left arm, feeling metal cut into my already lacerated forearm and causing Orlo to grin in a grim, satisfying way.

A gust of wind blew a lick of hair off his forehead and I aimed at that place and the racquet cracked where it struck, but it did draw a spurt of blood. He backed off quickly, dazed for a second. He knew how to fight, did Orlo.

I pursued, not wanting to give up my advantage. Another quick two strokes to his kidney and the top of the racquet was clearly broken and a couple of strings of gut flopped loosely. My $74.99 plus tax Ektelon tapered Xpre.

He backpedaled along the side wall of the hotel and I feinted at his legs, hoping to stop him before he got to Pigtail and Mary Lynn. Pigtail might not realize her tactical value to them, but Orlo certainly did.

He reacted and I faked for his kidney again, allowing me to return in the follow through stroke for his lower legs. The blow staggered him and tore off the top of the graphite and fiberglass racquet.

I was doing everything I could to stall, for I verily hoped someone above had witnessed the fight and told Tapes and Tapes would be running down the stairs by now and heading this way, doubtless with Trooper's gun. Unless Pinky and Silas hadn't been paying attention.

With the wind and the .38 shot being muffled by Deacon's mouth and body, I doubted anyone inside would have heard the shot.

I whipped the Xpre toward Orlo's face, an arc of fiberglass, graphite and cat gut lashing out ahead of the body of the racquet.

But he was quick. His machete went up, deflecting the strike, and severing the cat gut and piece of loose fiberglass rim. I had half a racquet left, a weapon ten inches shorter.

My breathing was coming quick now, fear impelling it more than need.

He was going to reach the two against the hotel's wall and I had to do something so I feinted to my left, and ran up the wall a few feet on my right just like in a championship game and did a full body flip, gymnasts must have a term for it, and swung for Orlo's head when I was upside down and spinning through the air. The shattered end of a piece of fiberglass sliced through his right temple, right eyebrow, and on across his upper cheek and then I was busy landing and pushing off with my injured left arm and hand and lunging for Pigtail and Mary Lynn.

But I didn't have enough momentum, so I just followed the path of the inertia and rolled, sucking in my gut to avoid the swinging machete. I kicked ineffectively at Orlo's legs but kept rolling.

Right into Pigtail and Mary Lynn. The busted racquet busted some more but it was worth it to see the look of incredible pain on Pigtail's face as it slammed into his manhood. His scream was a piercing screech. But, I'll give him this, he was a tough son of a bitch for he kept his feet.

He let loose of Mary Lynn and she fell on me and I grabbed her to toss her away from the action so she could run when Orlo's big boot kicked the hell out of my arm and I had to keep rolling to dodge that goddamn machete which seemed to have me locked into its radar. I pushed Mary Lynn the other way.

I saw the look in his eyes and threw the remains of my goddamn $74.99 Xpre at Orlo and he merely batted it away with the flat of his machete.

Orlo stood there commanding the situation.

I scrambled to my feet and lunged for the dead Deacon and my .38.

"Hold!" commanded Orlo.

A glance, and I held.

Where the hell was Tapes?

"The truck," Orlo told Pigtail.

Pigtail hustled off, limping and holding his crotch.

"Oh, shit," I said aloud.

Orlo loomed over Mary Lynn with the machete poised above her, like the sword of Damocles or some goddamn thing, ready to chop her into pieces for the pressure cooker. Orlo's whole body seemed to swell up and his muscles tensed.

"Orlo!" I screamed, for the machete seemed to have a life of its own and maybe he couldn't control himself.

He shook his head as if to clear it but the machete began moving. Blood dripped from the cut on his head, slung away by eddies of wind.

"Orlo! I saved your life!" My voice was a million decibels higher than was possible. I must have sounded like a cricket.

His arms and the machete still frozen above him, he looked

at me. "Thee did not save my life. Thee kept thy tall friend alive; and thee prevented thyself from earning a life sentence for killing a Florida cop."

He knew. Orlo knew I'd moved to keep Tapes alive and if Trooper had shot Orlo and accidentally killed Tapes I'd have had to kill Trooper. Orlo knew. He'd followed the dynamic undercurrents in 112. Somewhere underneath we were a lot more alike than I wanted to admit.

Carefully to show I was relaxed, I put my left foot up on the bole of a downed palm. Underneath it flopped a common cattle egret, its white feathers stained with blood, its right wing trapped and broken under the bole. Also, the bole gave me purchase if I needed to shove against something to fling myself at Orlo.

Would he kill Mary Lynn?

It was possible. I tried to regain my breathing, but my heart was racing too fast. I knew it wouldn't work, but I'd have to jump between the machete and Mary Lynn.

Mary Lynn hiccupped rapidly. Her leather blouse was askew. The corners of her mouth were drawn back and she stared up at the looming Orlo above her.

I saw it in his eyes. He'd kill Mary Lynn. Just to see my face as he did it. The enmity which had grown and flamed between us was going to fuel the fires in Orlo to kill Mary Lynn.

"She never did anything to you, Orlo. Let her go. She's no threat to you."

"Ye'd have me believe that?"

"Billy! Go—" Mary Lynn gasped between hiccups.

Orlo reached his foot out and stepped on her chest and pushed and I couldn't do a goddamn thing about it. He had her lined up for the coup de grace, like some ancient buccaneer executioner swollen within his camouflage outfit.

Orlo grinned, the machete above him swinging back a little gaining power for the stroke.

I tensed to fling myself, then thought of something.

"Orlo. A half a million dollars."

He paused and looked at me.

"Five hundred thousand," I said. "A king's ransom."

"Money of the innkeeper, I estimate. Ye know where it is?"

"I do," I lied.

"Tell me."

"Give me Mary Lynn."

"No."

What the hell was I to do next? Stall. Wait for Tapes. He should be here by now. Unless Pinky and Silas had missed this. I could only hope somebody would look out eventually. But no one could see us up against the hotel wall.

"Let her go."

"No." The machete never waivered.

"A half a million, Orlo. That's reason enough. I'll buy her from you. Right now." I heard an engine.

"The woman must mean much to thee." Orlo was looking at the almost headless Deacon. Orlo breathed deeply and relaxed. The machete came down as if on its own accord. Tears came unbidden from his eyes.

The engine was louder.

"I did not want a dog which would not fight," said Orlo. "Deacon, he was a fighting son of a bitch."

I said nothing. I didn't want to upset the delicate balance we'd reached.

"He was good. I trained him in the Tennessee mountains and he performed better than any old hound." Orlo's face softened an incredible thing to witness.

The engine whined and I heard the transmission change gears.

Mary Lynn was trying to edge herself slightly away from Orlo, but his foot still pinned her and she wasn't having much success.

"Deacon, the beast, he could climb a tree. Has thee ever seen a dog climb a tree?"

"I have not," I said. "Five hundred grand will buy you a lot of dogs."

"If thee fails to produce the money, I will use thy woman until her eyeballs bleed and she can no longer speak from terror and from begging." He swiveled his eyes down to Mary Lynn and I felt a stab of horror. "That could occur anyway."

"No money, then, Orlo. Not a fucking cent."

He shrugged. "Thee already put the price upon her head; so be it upon thy head to so provide."

Still trying to stall, I said, "You knew about the money?"

His eyes swung back to Deacon. "I listened to part of what the innkeeper spoke." He cocked an eye at me. "It did cause me to make certain plans." He grunted. "But I knew not about the cash. Thy tall friend almost discovered me." He touched his camo jacket. "Silent in the swamps I am, as I was in the jungles of Asia. Smith said he put the money in a bank in Nassau."

"He said that, Orlo." I had to fight to keep my eyes on him and not look around for help.

"And thee knows different?"

"You're aware of the fire in the generator shed?"

"I am."

"Silas set the fire. He knew it would not burn the hotel down. That was impossible in all the rain and the way the thing is structured."

"And what does that mean?" Orlo let the machete swing, pointy end down above Mary Lynn's neck like an Ed Poe story.

"He's a very clever man. He figured with the murder investigation that he'd be found out—as we did find him out. So he set the fire ahead of time thinking, correctly so, that no one would expect him to torch the hotel which contained his half a million in cash."

Orlo nodded. "Thee has thought well. It is not in the boat?"

"No. Not with the storm. He'd be taking too much chance that the boat would sink or be holed at its mooring. No, I'm certain he'd want the cash where he could grab it and run."

The engine approached.

"Give me Mary Lynn."

Wind sluiced water off the roof and onto my face. I wiped it clean.

The engine was as loud as it was going to get. A dark blue van pulled up on the grass alongside Orlo.

Pigtail gingerly climbed out leaving the motor running.

"Bring Deacon and the revolver," Orlo directed.

Pigtail limped around to the rear and opened the back doors.

I couldn't do anything, even knowing what was coming. I gritted an inch off all my teeth.

Pigtail picked up my revolver, wiped the barrel on wet grass, and stuck it in his hip pocket. I hoped he'd shoot himself in the ass.

He then lifted Deacon in both hands. Pigtail staggered to the van. That damn dog was heavy, even without a bunch of skull and brains. Pigtail tried to set Deacon down softly, but the dog fell and Pigtail pushed him all the way in and to the side. I caught a glimpse of the coolers along the interior of the big van.

Pigtail backed away wiping blood off his hands.

"Preserve him," Orlo said.

For a moment Pigtail stared at Orlo, then shrugged and climbed into the van. He snagged the lid of a big cooler with a wire attached on the wall above. He turned and bent and lifted Deacon and placed him into the cooler. He shut the cooler.

"That last held," said Orlo conversationally, "bear meat, we taken the animal from Tate's Hell Swamp up in Franklin County. Thee reckon they eat strange at this inn?"

"To hell with them," I said succinctly, meaning it for they had caused this mess. Gladly would I have forgone the opportunity to have ever met Mary Lynn Messenger so that this would never have happened and she would not be in jeopardy for her life, her sanity, her very soul.

"Cover the man," Orlo told Pigtail and I wondered if Pigtail even had a name, "for he will kill thee given the chance."

Pigtail said nothing. I'd caused him much pain this time and in the incident in the saloon earlier. From the look of him, he would take any opportunity to kill me. He did take my .38 out, cock the hammer, extend his arm, and line the muzzle up with my head. His arm would tire in a few minutes.

Orlo swiftly reached down and lifted Mary Lynn roughly by the arm.

She hiccupped as he pushed her into the rear of the van and climbed in himself.

Orlo kicked a splayed gator hide out the door.

"It'll be all right," I said inanely.

She didn't answer, but her eyes were wild, flashing about like a lighthouse lantern gone crazy.

And there was absolutely nothing I could do. I had to trust the lure of five hundred thousand dollars to protect her.

If I made any kind of move right now, I'd be dead and so, eventually, would she.

"Thee have the money ready," said Orlo after he climbed into the van himself. He faced me, standing there twitching the machete in Mary Lynn's face. "Soon, verily I say, soon." To Pigtail, he spoke softly. "Give me the gun and drive."

Pigtail handed Orlo the .38 and went around to the front and got into the driver's seat.

They were going to escape. Silas and Pinky hadn't been paying attention.

Orlo grinned at me. His thumb held the hammer and he pulled the trigger all the way back. All he had to do was to release the hammer. An amateur would do that, it being more accurate and less movement to trigger off a shot than to release the hammer and move the aim.

Orlo wasn't going to shoot me now. He wanted that half a million dollars.

Pigtail gunned the engine.

"Do thee think about me and thy woman," Orlo said, his voice level and not menacing. But that made me chill even worse without the melodramatics.

"Orlo?" I made my own voice matter-of-fact. "If you do harm her, I will someday learn who you are or who you were before I killed you. I will go to Tennessee and locate your mother, your wife, your daughter, your sister, your grandfather, your children, and I will kill five of them. You have been reading me well and you know what I say is true."

Ignoring his widened eyes and the still aimed .38, I took my foot off the bole of the palm, bent my knees and lifted the huge trunk off the egret. I pushed the tree aside and it thumped thickly and splashed water when it struck the ground.

Bending again, I picked up the egret.

The van was accelerating slowly, but Orlo was staring at me with fascination. His knee was holding Mary Lynn against the wall of the van. Mary Lynn was watching me, too, with wide eyes.

The egret flopped around in my hands and pecked at my already lacerated left arm. The good wing beat against my leg.

I bent the egret's neck and wrung it like I'd learned to do with chickens when I was young in West Texas.

Negligently, I tore the head off and tossed the bird aside, residual energy causing it to shiver and quiver.

It was pretty far to see eyes by now, but I think I finally made an impression on Orlo.

I meant the threat then, but I do not think I could kill somebody's mother in revenge. The thing that bothered me most had been the surprise and recoil on Mary Lynn's face as I spoke. If Orlo started on her soon, then she'd quickly forget my symbolic killing of the egret.

The van swung west and out onto the litter-strewn road and sped off.

Knowing I didn't have them on me, I searched my pockets for my keys. Nope. I'd changed clothes too often and not needed the keys.

I started running to follow the van and saw Trooper, Pinky, Ionata, Vern, and Silas come out the side door. Where was Tapes?

Even as I ran, I knew it wouldn't work. The van cut south behind and past the historic railroad depot. It was now The Loose Caboose sandwich and ice cream restaurant and tourist shops. The van disappeared, heading south on Park Avenue.

I slowed. This wasn't thinking right. I would never catch them, find them, and determine which way they were going. I just didn't have the time.

Mary Lynn was gone as if she had never existed.

21: WEDNESDAY, 7:05 A.M.

A gust of wind swept by and splattered me with rain. My guts were cold enough to skate on.

I was standing on a hump where long dead railroad tracks had once thrived and sliced across Fifth Avenue.

The van was gone.

I didn't know what to do next. Get the others and sweep the island looking for the van? That would take too long.

A spate of rain hit me and was gone immediately, but its chill remained.

I turned and jogged back toward the hotel. If my appraisal of Orlo was correct, very shortly Mary Lynn Messenger was going to wish she were dead.

"Shortcut!"

I stopped and looked around. From the north side of the hotel grounds Tapes emerged through shadows dragging someone behind him.

Jogging toward him, I said, "Where in hell have you been?"

Tapes thrust Axe out in front of him.

"I saw him sneaking around this side of the hotel and went after him."

"Oh."

We both stopped.

Axe tried to run off, but Tapes grabbed him by the camo collar and dragged him back.

"I had to chase him a bit and that makes me mad enough to kick a hog barefoot," Tapes said. It would, because Tapes is only afraid of two things in this entire world: a good woman and being set afoot. His disdain for running exceeds mine and only his long legs give him the advantage.

"That's why you didn't come to my aid," I accused.

"Explain," he demanded.

I did so.

"Shit," he said, still holding Axe. "We got to do something."

"And damn soon."

Tapes lifted Axe off his feet and shook the man. "Where are they?"

"I don't know."

"They obviously abandoned you," Tapes said.

Axe didn't answer. He was a bit taller than me with curly hair hanging over his ears and a young man's sparse three day growth. His teeth were stained brown.

"Axe," I said, "you heard me tell Tapes what happened. You know they have Mary Lynn Messenger. What will they do with her?"

He sort of shrugged and grimaced at the same time, but he didn't answer.

"Let me explain it to you in a different fashion," I said. "Mary Lynn is very special to me. We have you prisoner. If they touch her, I will kill you. Do you understand me?" I was up against him and shouting in his face.

He merely turned his head and licked drool from the corner of his mouth. Tapes swung his left arm up behind him and jammed the hand nearly to the back of his neck.

Axe groaned and sweat broke through his hairline, but he did not answer.

"Tell us where they're hiding," said Tapes, "or I will break your arm."

"Yessir, you will," said Axe.

Tapes twisted and I could hear the snap. Tapes released the fellow's arm and stepped back.

Surprise and pain raced across Axe's face. He bowed his head to look at his left arm hanging at an obscene angle. "Damn if he didn't keep his word." Axe's voice was full of wonder.

"Where were you all hiding?" I asked.

Axe shrugged and pain creased his face again. He moved his right hand over and held his left arm down against his side.

"Loyalty is good, but it's going to get you accessory to a bunch of felonies including maybe murder." I reached out and tugged on his broken arm.

He sank to his knees in agony, grabbing his arm tighter against him and ripping it from my grip.

"Families, you know? I known Orlo since I was a kid." Axe drooled from the corner of his mouth again. "Orlo, he took me with him. I used to sing in my daddy's choir and nobody liked me and I'd sit for days on the ridge up there until Wednesday night or Sunday morning and I'd sing, you know? I'd sing to the birds and the trees and the wind." Axe's voice didn't sound like a singer's voice, but maybe that was the problem. "There was an old barn and a white, white silo in them hills of Tennessee. We had us a dirt road with some clay in it to make it slippery in the rain. They'd say I was 'tetched, you know? But I'd sing and sing, 'Amen,' 'What a Friend We Have in Jesus,' and my favorite, it was 'The Old Rugged Cross' and nobody liked me; and Orlo, I went away from there with him." The kid looked up at me. "Can't you see?"

"I can," I said and meant it. "Shit, Tapes, what we gonna do?"

"Let's go," he said decisively. He snatched Axe up and hurried off.

Axe's legs occasionally spun, missing the ground, Tapes was holding him so high.

We hurried along the side of the hotel, skirting the south side and entrance.

I knew Tapes had something in mind, but what it was, I had no idea.

"Goddamn, Tapes. They got Mary Lynn. Time's flying."

"Take it easy, Shorts. You're panicking."

"Fuckin' A, I'm panicking. Jesus, you know what they'll do to her?"

"It ain't been that long."

"It's been hours."

"A couple minutes. Trust me. I got an idea." He was really confident.

We came upon John Ionata, Pinky, Silas, Vern, and Trooper.

Pinky was carrying a bottle of no star brandy, but I ignored him as he sipped and wobbled.

I explained quickly. "Our only chance," I finished, "is to give Orlo the money Silas has."

Silas turned green. "I told you, the money's not here."

I reached up and grabbed Silas by the hair and jerked his face down. I rubbed my left forearm all across his face.

He coughed and spluttered.

When he stood upright again, his face and head were streaked with my blood.

"I will say this once, Silas." I was addressing all of them. "You come up with the money and it will go easy for you. Otherwise I might personally kill you. Got it?" I squeezed the back of his neck and his eyes bulged out.

"Stop that," Pinky said.

"Convince him to cooperate," I said.

"Silas? Please? For me? The Lord will help you if you let Him."

Smith wiped blood from his lips and his nose crinkled. Some of the pockmarks in his neck had blood in them.

"Trooper," I said, "you do this for us, okay?"

"If he don't cooperate," Trooper said grabbing Silas by the shoulder, "I'll stomp his faggotty ass."

"We'll search for the money," Vern said to assure us of his cooperation.

"You might look," I said slowly and fixed my eyes on Silas, "in the freezers and coolers first."

Silas Smith's eyes bulged even farther out.

"You know something?" Trooper asked.

"I do now," I said. I told them of my guesswork concerning the generator fire and how clever Silas had been throughout this ordeal, and in his previous planning. He could be an adherent of the 7-P Principle. Smith's face was noncommittal, but his eyes showed no remorse about Mary Lynn. Walk-in coolers are safe from fire, I thought. "He's got bear meat, manatee meat, God knows what all hidden in one of the walk-ins. It stands to reason that's where he keeps the money."

From the panic and immediate suffering that hit the manager, I knew it was true.

Tapes had started off a moment before. "Shortcut," he said over his shoulder, "move that tree." He pointed.

A small pine tree lay across Fifth Avenue.

I ran over and lugged the damn thing off the road, sufficient for a vehicle to pass, all the while wondering what Tapes had in mind.

Then I ran to catch up.

Tapes and Axe were at my GT, the green of the truck scratched and pitted from the storm.

Tapes was tossing stuff out of the tool box.

I grabbed the shirt I had been going to put on and wrapped it around my oozing left arm. Blood began to stain the Lone Star Beer logo.

Tapes handed me the heavy rope we kept in the truck for towing. "Tie one end to that palm tree," he said pointing.

It didn't take me long to understand what he was up to. I ran over to the tree and shinnied up about ten feet and tied a knot which would suffice.

The truck roared. Tapes keeps a key. It came to a stop under the tree and I dropped into the bed of the truck.

"Hurry," I said.

Tapes had the sliding glass panel open. "We got plenty of time. Just do it right."

Axe was lying in the bed of the truck where Tapes had thrown him. He held his broken left arm in his right over his abdomen and his eyes tracked me.

I rummaged around in the tool box and came up with a short piece of rope. I tied Axe's feet and wrapped his torso and two arms in rope trying to be gentle, why, I'll never know. I dragged him to a sitting position with his back against the tool box. I went and dropped the tailgate. Then I took the end of the rope I'd tied to the palm tree and made a quick slip knot.

I slipped the noose over Axe's head and around his neck. I tightened the noose. "Ready," I told Tapes through the open window.

He gunned the engine and backed up.

As we went backwards, Axe's eyes got bigger and bigger. It was dawning on him.

I sat above him on the toolbox, my legs holding him in position. "Tapes, he's got calibrated eyeballs. But I don't know how wet the brakes got. He might can stop in time, just in time, if you say the word. But will the truck actually stop?" I shrugged. "Beats me."

Axe turned his head and looked up awkwardly at me. "Please?"

"What I think is Tapes will do a dry run, seeing how fast he can get the truck before the tree. He's got calibrated eyeballs and can figger it pretty close."

The truck stopped and Tapes gunned the engine and the big 396 engine made the GT fairly leap forward. In just a second, Tapes slammed on the brakes and the GT skidded to a stop right where we'd begun.

"Not as exact as you'd ordinarily do," I said to Tapes conversationally. "I guess old Axe is gonna have to tell me to tell you to stop a little earlier."

Tapes backed up until the rope was stretched taut over the cab and Axe's head was tilted back and his neck stretched a bit. He sort of sat up a lot higher than you'd think he be capable of doing.

The truck sat there and I looked through the opening in the rear window and on through the windshield. I saw the men standing beside the hotel watching us with awe. I stood and waved them on to do their job but nobody cooperated.

Tapes stuck his head through the window. "Hey, Axe. Listen.

The rope is one hundred and fifty feet long. I'll get up over thirty, but if you want me to stop, you better tell Shortcut before then."

"You'd do this to me?" Axe was drooling, the spittle tracing a path through the stubble down his outstretched neck.

"I don't really want to, Axe, someone young like you," Tapes said. "But we got to save that lady, understand?"

"Yessir, I understand."

"You know that I am a man of my word?"

Axe tried to nod and couldn't. He swallowed. "You tole me you'd break my arm and you did."

Tapes tipped his head in acknowledgment. "I tell you right now, Axe. I will accelerate Shortcut's truck until you tell him to tell me to stop. Then you talk. Got that?"

"I do." More spittle.

"Ready to talk?" I asked. "See, when you're facing rearward, you can see the ground running away from you. Just like time."

"Nossir, I do not wish to speak."

"Your loyalty to Orlo is going to get you killed."

"Amen," he began singing, his voice terribly off key. "Amen, amen, amen."

"Hit it, Tapes," I said with a finality I didn't feel.

The truck surged.

One of the men near the hotel shouted for us to stop, probably the right Christian and now drunk Pinky.

Tapes went from first to second.

"Amen, amen, amen," shouted Axe, not really singing.

The truck's engine sounded naked, reverbing off the hotel.

"Amen, amen, amen."

"You got maybe five seconds," I said.

"Nearer my God to thee," he shouted.

"Four."

"Amen, amen."

"Three."

Silence.

"Two."

"Sweet Jesus."

"Now or never."

Wind was whipping through my hair and the landscape seemed to jet past us.

"Stop!ThelighthouseohJesus!"

"Tapes!"

But he'd heard and was standing on the binders and jammed it into first gear and the torque of the gear saved Axe's life.

We slid to a stop and I smelled rubber burning off the tires and wet cement.

I wondered if Tapes would have stopped in time without Axe giving in. I decided maybe I didn't want to know.

I reached over and grasped the rope and pulled it tight. There had been maybe two feet of slack left.

"My sweet Lord," said Axe.

"You cut it pretty close," I told him. "Now spill it."

He didn't answer right away. But he'd already said it was the lighthouse.

I jerked the rope.

He squeaked. "Orlo, he sent me to take care of the manager, Mr. Smith."

"To do what?"

"I was 'posed to keep him from running out on us since the storm is going away." His voice lowered. "I was to take care of Mr. Smith and wait for Orlo." Orlo hadn't necessarily abandoned Axe.

"He wanted you to break Smith's leg or something?"

Axe squenched up his eyes. "Gee, I never thought of that."

"What did you do?"

"Well, Orlo, he told us about the boat and said that Mr. Smith would use it to escape." Axe licked drool. "Orlo, he'd sent me out to the boathouse before to check it out since he didn't get to check it out himself following Mr. Silas and all." He meant the time Tapes and I'd seen him sneaking out of the hotel after we'd followed Orlo following Silas.

"What did you do?" I repeated.

"Me? I took that pump, you know the one hitched up to the barrel of gas?"

"In the boathouse."

"Yessir. I pumped all the rest of the gas into the engine compartment and the bilges."

"You did *what*?"

"I pumped all the rest of the—"

"Jesus, Tapes, he's booby-trapped the goddamn boat."

"No skin off my back," said Tapes.

"That's why I thought he had me scout the boat before," said Axe helpfully.

I groaned. We had enough trouble as it was. "The lighthouse, Tapes."

"You might want to remove the rope," he pointed out.

"Oops. Oh, yeah."

"Thank you, Mr. Tapes," said Axe.

I pulled the loop wide and tore it off Axe's head and tossed it to the roadway.

Tapes was accelerating.

"Which lighthouse?" I asked. It wouldn't be the Rear Range Lighthouse, which is merely a metal tower. It would be the Old Port Boca Grande Lighthouse. Orlo would convince himself of the parallels between himself and José Gaspar. It was inevitable, now that I thought about it.

"The one way down at the point," Axe said. "Boy, you all sure got funny names."

That from a guy named Axe.

"I can guess why he chose that lighthouse," I said. "Because nobody would suspect you'd be hiding in the most dangerous place on the island during a storm."

"Yessir."

"And if you broke into a house or condo or something, somebody might escape and get help."

"Yessir."

"And anywhere else, it might be hard to hide that distinctive van."

"Yessir."

"And in a building built to withstand terrible weather."

"Yessir."

"That figgers," I said.

"Yessir. You think just like Orlo, you do."

My gut churned, but I had the same thought earlier myself.

We cut over on 1st Street and then due south on Gulf Boulevard. Gulf ran two miles, maybe a bit less, to the southern tip of the island, which separates Charlotte Harbor from the Gulf of Mexico. On the south side of Boca Grande Pass sits La Costa Island and North Captiva, then Captiva and Sanibel Islands. These cartographers in Florida are crazy. They named some islands, some keys, and they're all the same. "Captiva" came from the old "Cautiva," or female prisoner, named by José Gaspar because that's where he kept most of the women he kidnapped.

It seemed a longer drive than the reverse drive from the lighthouse with the late governor. But it wasn't. The storm had subsided a great deal. The main problem Tapes faced was the standing water on the roadway. Rain occasionally swept over us.

He drove like the devil, swinging on and off Gulf Boulevard, running on the shoulder, on dunes, and when he couldn't avoid it, through deep water.

"Faster!" I shouted through the opening.

He didn't respond, keeping his attention on his driving.

A rain squall hit us and he had to slow down. It damn near blew me off the Trukbox.

So I slid down beside Axe who was bouncing around like popped corn off a red hot pan. The tailgate flapped and banged and Axe was staring at the open end of the truck like he was going to die. He'd slipped a couple of feet that way. I grabbed his camo collar and dragged him up beside me.

"If you're lying, Axe, it'll be the last lie you ever told." I didn't think he was lying, but you can never tell. Anybody who knows all those religious songs can't be *that* trustworthy. And if he was, then we'd be too far away too long and Mary Lynn was dog meat. I chilled some more thinking: Orlo and Pigtail both.

22: WEDNESDAY, 8:15 A.M.

Tapes drove like a madman the entire two miles and I kept hollering for him to hurry up. The road was mostly covered with sea water, but driving over sand dunes and along the sometimes higher bike path that ran adjacent to Gulf Boulevard, Tapes was able to get us to the southern tip of Gasparilla Island.

He was thinking quickly. Instead of driving to the lighthouse itself, he swung the pickup over in front of the Florida Power and Light storage and pumping facility. There were four great green tanks all sitting within a safety revetment. The revetment was full of Gulf water, the drainage not yet able to keep up with the demand.

FPL offloads tankers at Port Boca Grande just east of the lighthouse. Someone had told me that the four tanks hold about a half a million barrels of oil.

Tapes splashed up in front of the entrance shack to the facility, the one containing boilers to generate steam which flows through coils in the bottom of the giant tanks, so the oil is warm enough to flow easily.

From all indications, the shack was abandoned, but I could see steam venting a bit until the wind rapidly dissipated it.

I jumped out of the truck into ankle deep water as Tapes climbed out of the cab.

"You got the gun, right?" he said.

"Ah, Tapes. I kind of left that part out," I said holding up my left arm for sympathy. "They kind of got it."

"Great. How are we going to take on a couple of armed men

and save your woman?"

"She's not my woman, and I'll think of something. Lenin said ideas are much more fatal things than guns." I thought of something, and dug into the Trukbox and came up with an awl and an ice pick. Tapes had his Buck knife. "Let's go." As an afterthought, I stuck a couple of big handled screw drivers in my pocket.

"You've thought of something," Tapes said. "Or are you going to get Lenin to stop the bullets for us?"

"A fleeting yet frightening possibility has occurred to me."

Wind and rain whistled around the great tanks.

"Hey! What about me?" called Axe.

I ran back and tied him better than the brief job I'd done and attached the rope to the rear bumper so he couldn't hop away.

Tapes unclipped a fifty foot retractable from his belt and tossed it into the cab, which told me his estimate was the situation was going to become messy.

We trotted through water around the cyclone fencing which enclosed the tank farm.

Running through the wind and rain, I thought about Silas and his list of Henry B.'s assignations. It had been on my mind a lot in the last few hours.

While the wind was blowing like hell, I thought the storm was in fact abating.

It wasn't more than three hundred yards, but against a forty to fifty mile an hour wind, it was tough going.

The lighthouse sits on a little point which juts out into Boca Grande pass. Beach and dunes line the Pass and Gulf sides. A stretch of huge rocks extends along the beach and into the Gulf, placed there obviously to prevent beach erosion.

You usually reach the lighthouse by parking either at it or in a larger parking lot on the other side of a small grove of trees. Since I didn't want to be discovered I led us to the clump of palms and pine, all of which were bent over in the wind and had seen better days. The storm had lasted a long time. We skirted a big dune line through sea oats and scrub. The dunes were twice as high as Tapes, so it provided a shadowy background which would make it more difficult for someone to spot us. At one point the dune line was cut from the wind and waves, and water had poured in almost like Dutch lowlands when the dike is breached. But no water was flowing in now; perhaps the tide was out.

Orlo's dark blue van was sitting opposite the dune line in the access road running along the tank farm fence. I guess that was as close as they could get by driving. I might should've taken an extra couple of minutes to run across the parking lot and disabled their van, but I didn't want to take the time. I kept envisioning Orlo and Pigtail ravaging Mary Lynn. Well, you don't learn nothing the second time you're kicked by a mule.

At least it proved Axe had been right and this is where Orlo was riding out the storm. I had to admire the creativity and courage it took.

We came upon the lighthouse from this direction, the least likely to be watched and the one with the worst window view, thus making it more difficult to spot our approach.

I scaled the six-foot cyclone fence surrounding the lighthouse and Tapes vaulted it, using his hands like a gymnast on a side horse.

We scurried under the lighthouse, knee deep in water.

The lighthouse sits on twelve, maybe fourteen screw-piles, big cast iron posts with upper support arms. We hunkered behind one and I spoke into Tapes' ear. "We need to find a way in."

He moved his mouth to my ear. "They've got to be armed, they're hunters. First thing they see us, she's a hostage and we're at their mercy."

I nodded. There were three stairways up into the lighthouse. One from the back and two in the front meeting at the wide wraparound porch like an upside down V. The front was facing the Gulf and the pass and the least likely for the Orlo or Pigtail to be watching.

From what I could see, the lighthouse had weathered the

storm well. Just to the east was a building in which normally resided the park officer who maintains the lighthouse and the site. It had originally been the assistant lightkeeper's residence. That building had not fared as well which was probably why Orlo had not chosen it.

I pointed to the front double stairs.

"I knew it," said Tapes.

The wind was strong enough and the sea crashing upon the dunes so that we couldn't hear anybody walking on the wood floor right above our heads. It wasn't going to be easy.

I led off, wondering how long it had been since Orlo had left the hotel. Our driving time might have been faster than theirs. The difference was our running around, briefing the others at the hotel, and convincing Axe to talk; maybe ten minutes, maybe more. A lot can happen in ten minutes.

We slipped up the stairs. This level of the lighthouse was just like a big old Southern style house with the wraparound porch. I went to the left and Tapes the right, cautiously peering in windows. With all the pounding of the surf and the wind, there wasn't much call for extra silence.

From my vantage point I could see into the room with the racks and tables of brochures and display cases. Through an intervening door, I could see into the park ranger's office. The lights were on, probably a generator.

Nothing.

I turned around and tiptoed unnecessarily to find Tapes. He intercepted me near the stairs.

We spoke into each others' ear, Tapes, of course, leaning down.

"Nothing," I said.

"The guy with the pigtail, what's his name?"

"Beats me."

"He's pacing around."

I walked over and looked through the window again. There he was, Pigtail. He was walking purposefully, shotgun in the crook of his arm, going from room to room.

I went back to Tapes. We were standing right in front of the door so Pigtail couldn't see us.

"Where could Orlo and Mary Lynn be?" I asked. Were they in the van? Had I made a mistake by not checking the van?

Tapes shrugged.

I thought and thought swiftly. "Up the stairs on one of the landings?" There was one landing closed to the outside and within the roof structure of the building. That landing had no windows or outside access.

I thought of Orlo and his likening himself to the pirate, José Gaspar.

"Uh, oh," I said, realization swarming over me like a hive of yellow jackets and just as deadly.

Tapes cocked an eye.

Motioning for him to stay put, I scrambled down the stairs and out away from the building. We'd approached from the other direction, more north westerly. I stopped near the gate in the fence facing the south beach and turned.

"Uh, oh," I said aloud.

The gate in the fence banged open and closed.

Right at the top of the lighthouse. The glassed-in room where the fourth magnitude Fresnel lense sat atop a metal pole.

A distinctive upper profile of a woman. Her head turned briefly and the pony tail became outlined. She was facing the southwest, explaining why we hadn't seen her on our approach. And since only her head was moving, more than likely she was tied to the lamppost itself.

It's a four-sided metal room, with big full windows rising from about waist height to ceiling level. Sort of like a giant outdoor lamp in your yard. Being daylight, the photo-sensor had automatically shut off the lamp.

But where was Orlo?

He might be on the stairs going up or down, in the bathroom, or God knows where else.

He could also be below waist level in the lens chamber with Mary Lynn.

Likely Mary Lynn was bait and Orlo was hiding, waiting. The egret incident had convinced him, showed him how committed I was. He knew I'd figure out where they went—we thought alike—and find him and Mary Lynn.

Ignoring all else, I ran back up the stairs. The banging gate should have caught my attention. But I let my panic and sense of urgency overrule my brain.

Briefing Tapes quickly, I said, "She appears to be up there alone."

"If Orlo's with her," Tapes bent over to my ear, "and he's worried we've followed him here, he'll have the trap door locked."

"I didn't need to hear that." There was only one answer, especially with Pigtail standing guard downstairs armed with a shotgun and Orlo maybe lying in ambush. You don't argue with a shotgun, no matter the incompetence of the shooter. "Give me a hand up."

We stepped out from the porch and onto the top of the stairs. Tapes cupped his hands, I grabbed his shoulders, and up I went, flipping myself onto the sloping roof. I kneed myself up carefully so that the thump would not alert Pigtail and/or Orlo.

Wind slapped at me and knocked me off balance. I lay down on my belly and stuck the awl into the roof softly to provide me a purchase. With my other hand, I reached down.

Tapes grabbed my hand and I swung him onto the lip of the roof. He went down on his stomach, too, and wormed up the slope. I handed him the two screw drivers and we began working our way up the incline of the asphalt shingle roof, like climbers on an ice-cap: insert tool and pull up, wiggle-walking hand by hand. The wind was blowing like hell and occasional rain pelted us. I tasted salt flung off the crest of waves.

Now having a better vantage point, I turned my head to survey the area.

"Damn," I said and nudged Tapes. He looked where I pointed.

The tide must have really been out.

Orlo stood out on one of the huge rocks comprising the

miniature jetty.

That was why the gate had been open and slamming in the wind.

In his upheld hands was a dark bundle.

"Jesus," Tapes said. "It's Deacon wrapped in chains."

Tapes has the best eyesight around.

José Gaspar had allegedly wrapped himself in chains and jumped into the Gulf, committing suicide and thereby avoiding capture.

In my mind's eye, I could see spray and rain dripping off the Rottweiler and turning red from the congealed blood, pouring off the dog onto Orlo. The red bandanna collar would be flopping in the wind.

A blink and Orlo threw the dog into the sea.

Tapes and I continued to watch with fascination, though it takes longer in the telling than in the happening.

I had been right, just off with the timing. Orlo'd first taken care of his dog, then he planned to have his way with Mary Lynn, and then behead her with his machete for me to find. He just hadn't thought we'd find him as fast as we did.

Orlo turned, jumped to another rock and then onto the beach.

Whereupon he looked up and saw us.

Just as I was deciding to skinny back down the roof and jump on him as he came up the stairs, he pulled a revolver out of his pants and aimed it at us.

The crack of the shot was oddly muffled in the intense wind.

Both Tapes and I redoubled our efforts to crawl upwards on our bellies.

I felt like a fly on a white ceiling. "Split up," I shouted as the crack of another shot came and I imagined the slug plowing into the place I'd just vacated. Maybe it wasn't imagination.

Dangerous winds, climbing up a high-pitched roof, and a madman shooting at us. I'd always wanted to exit life and run out of money at the same time. Well, I still had money in the bank and the situation wasn't all that auspicious for continuing to live.

No longer having to worry about discovery, we increased our speed. I fairly flew, slamming the awl in with my right hand and the icepick with my left and dragging myself up the high pitched roof, scrabbling with my feet like a GI on an obstacle course.

Tapes obviously had the same idea. He was squirreling to the right, me to the left, aiming to surmount the roof and scramble behind the upper structure projecting above the roof level.

I was on the Gulf side and scraped my gut I was in such a hurry. The wind blew like North Dakota and knocked me off balance for a moment.

I was able to see Orlo running through the open gate and dancing below, aiming the revolver. He'd chosen me instead of Tapes. He raised his arm, extended it and the gun tracked me. So I rolled up and sideways, flipping myself by using the awl and icepick.

The bullet "thunked" into the upper structure, the part above the attic level of the house and right below the light chamber. Tapes stepped around from the other side and threw one of his screwdrivers at Orlo.

Orlo jumped aside, giving me enough time to scramble behind the structure and rise to my feet. Which wasn't all that easy because the roof was still steeply sloped and I couldn't find much of a handhold and the wind was trying to shove me off.

Each side of the upper structure had windows. Unfortunately, these were shuttered. But the shutters offered some small handhold. Gingerly, I scooted around the other side and looked down in time to see Orlo fire again, do a double take, and run for the stairs. Obviously, he was going inside with the intention of climbing up the inside of the building.

I edged my way back around the other side worried about Orlo's double take.

Tapes was on his knees and a dark stain was coming from his leg. He'd grabbed the leg as a reflex action and when I came around the corner, a great gust of wind toppled him over.

The gust made me stumble to my feet, causing me to lose

my hold upon the shutter. I slammed the ice pick into the roof and surged forward, stretching my other hand. The awl tumbled down the roof like an errant tumbleweed.

I did grasp Tapes' now outstretched hand.

"You okay?" I said.

"Just my leg."

I tried to pull him up and was partially successful.

His ear to the roof, he said, "Listen."

I put my head down and heard a series of thumps.

Orlo running up the stairs.

"Oh, shit," I said.

The wind became stronger. If I were to release Tapes, he'd blow right off the roof.

He knew it, too. And Orlo was going to beat us to Mary Lynn.

The moment stretched into an eternity as I debated internally.

In his eyes, I saw Tapes decide a split second before he did it.

Tapes nodded at me, and released his grip on my hand.

The sudden loss of weight caused me to recoil a bit.

Tapes rolled across the roof, angling sideways and downward, unable to stop himself. Even as he spread-eagled himself, he slid down the wet, slippery surface.

The last I saw of him was his right hand grabbing for a hold on the lip of the roof and the fall jerking his hand loose and he was gone.

No stairs on the east side of the building and a sixteen, maybe twenty foot drop. Son of a bitch.

No time left.

Mary Lynn in the lighthouse above me.

But.

Around the entire lantern room above was a Catwalk.

It loomed over me, like an unreachable balcony, but was really a catwalk with an inviting waist-high railing.

The problem was that the balcony over my head extended out over the roof where I was standing. The overhang here was perhaps six feet up, seven when I stepped farther out and therefore down the slope of the roof so that it would be above my head.

One jump is all I had, for if I missed, I'd hit, slip, and fire down the roof like a human avalanche.

Icepick to my mouth, step out and down, await for a split second the wind which seemed to be a million miles an hour, crouch, no time left, leap up, the jump of my life.

I made it to the lip of the balcony and in a blink my other hand was on the railing and I was pulling myself up like my life depended on it, which it did. Trying to ignore the pain in my left arm, I levered myself over the railing and onto the balcony. I dropped down to the access panel in the side of the metal housing and dove into the lantern room dripping water and eyes searching for Orlo and Mary Lynn.

Being right at her feet, I noticed her first as I scrambled to my feet.

"Billy, oh dear Lord!"

She was indeed tied to the lamppost. Her face was pale and hair mussed. Her chamois leather prairie shorts and blouse were twisted and wrinkled beneath the bindings.

I lunged for the trap door in the floor on the other side of the light post with the intention of slamming and locking it. Orlo would play hell shooting through a thick metal plate.

The explosion came close to my face and I recoiled automatically and the goddamn slug hit the cone of the metal ceiling above and ricocheted about the room with several metallic thunks.

Mary Lynn gasped when it struck her.

How many shots had Orlo fired? Had he reloaded? Was it my .38? If so, he was out of ammo had he not reloaded. I hoped the latter was the case and he had no .38 shells.

The ladder jerked as a heavy body pounded up it.

Nothing I could do.

Like hell.

Icepick in hand, I lunged at Orlo's head as it came above the floor level through the trap door.

He ducked, I missed, he pointed my gun at me and pulled the trigger and I didn't have time to go to the bathroom in my pants before the revolver clicked on the empty chamber and I slashed at his head again, barely scraping it near the hairline where I'd sliced him open with my Xpre.

Awkwardly, he threw the revolver and hit me on the cheek as I rose back to my knees.

I scrambled to my feet so I could kick his head in as he climbed the final few rungs but the son of a bitch produced his machete like Houdini and it clanged off a support column of the lamppost and he was up, quicker than a chicken on a June bug.

The only positive to me was the room wasn't large enough for big wide swings. On the other hand, I had nowhere to run and Mary Lynn was tied there at his mercy.

I backed against her. She was trembling. But she was not hiccupping.

"You hit?" I asked.

She shuddered. "Grazed my cheek." Her head was near the photo-sensor. This affair had developed a tougher Mary Lynn Messenger. "I've never even been shot at before."

"Ex-nun stops bullet with head," I said with more joviality than I felt.

Orlo topped the ladder and stepped into the small room with us. Only the lamp and its post were between us. He edged slowly around to face me.

I brandished the icepick and he laughed and flashed the machete at me.

"Does thee know what José Gaspar done to the woman who spurned him?"

I did but I didn't say it; and Mary Lynn lived here and had to know all the legends.

"I—he—beheaded the woman, they say her name was Josefa and she was a princess, hijadalga," he said using the Spanish word for noblewoman, "of Spain. Gaspar interred the hijadalga in the sand here."

"Gaspar also committed suicide," I said, trying to control my breathing because Orlo was raising the hairs on the nape of my neck again and scaring the bejesus out of me. "Wrap yourself in chains and follow Deacon into the Gulf."

"Ah, Deacon, a fine beast he was." Orlo's eyes narrowed at me and the machete twitched. It looked small in his ham of a hand. "Thee has thwarted me too often. It too shall pass, even as I now speak."

"Kill me and let Mary Lynn go," I said, trying to stall but knowing it was to no avail. All I could see was the tunnel at the end of the light.

Where was Pigtail?

And was Tapes still alive?

"But thee knows that is not acceptable—" The cut I'd made along his head from his hairline through his eyebrow was a mere slit, cleansed by the rain. However, it leaked blood.

"Why did you kill the governor?" I asked quickly to keep him talking while I tried to think of a way out.

He blinked and his face became quizzical.

"I did not."

"But since the first minute you tried to pin the murder on me and Tapes. Your every action was as if you were guilty."

"The altercation with the cop?"

"Among others."

"Nor did my two friends do that killing," he said slowly, eyebrows coming together in thought. "We did not want to become part of the investigation. The law would discover our malfeasance, bear meat, manatee meat, all of the things the innkeeper needed for his special dinner club."

"You've spent time in prison before, haven't you? If you were convicted, you'd catch more hard time."

"Aye, that's a fact. There's also a matter of an outstanding warrant in Tennessee."

"Regardless," I said, "all of your actions since then have pointed the finger of guilt at you." Mary Lynn shifted against my back, trying to loosen her bonds.

Wind and rain pelted the windows of that death-box.

"It is gospel that I wanted thy woman. She attracts me greatly. For was not José Gaspar a man of passion, one who took the beautiful women he wanted against their will? Did he not bend them to his will?"

"You're saying you became out of control and another crime or three on top of the others did not matter."

He nodded slowly. He was tiring, I could tell. Of course, so was I. We'd both been on the go for too long and spent too much mental energy.

"I was José Gaspar," he said in a booming voice and his eyes glowed.

"Yet you did not kill the governor?"

He slapped the post support next to me with the flat of the blade.

"No."

"Can you prove it?"

His face fell. "I have some formal education, sufficient for the government to post me in the jungle. But with my record.... Thee doesn't know it, but at the time Gonzáles died, I was not with my two friends. I was walking Deacon."

"And they'd lie for you, but a lie-detector would find them out and in turn make the evidence more likely to convict you."

"Aye. I would be the prime one they'd think done the deed, I would."

I thought short and deep. "On the other hand," I said so softly he had to lean forward to hear me, "you well could have killed the man."

Orlo seemed surprised. "But, I did not."

"Yeah, sure, Orlo. You've been trying to kill me and Tapes, and do worse to Mary Lynn. You just told us you were going to decapitate her."

Mary Lynn cringed at that but didn't hiccup. She'd overcome some personal obstacle. I didn't want to frighten her—although we were well past that point—but I was probing Orlo to find a weak point.

"It matters not what thee thinks. Thee knows, I see in thy

eyes."

He was going to be charged with kidnapping, attempted rape, attempted murder, more. Me and Mary Lynn were dead, we just hadn't stopped breathing yet. I thought quicker and harder.

But he spoke first. "I been pissin' blood on accounta thee."

From where Tapes and I'd repeatedly struck his kidneys.

He swiped blood from his brow. "Other injuries, I lay at thy feet."

"You're a killer, Orlo. I lay the murder of the governor at your feet." I think I was trying to convince Mary Lynn.

"Thee are extenuating my time; the ploy, it shall not work." He tensed and began to bring the machete up, probably planning a stabbing attack with the point.

"Orlo! Five hundred thousand dollars. One half million."

He hesitated. "Surely? I almost believe thy words."

"Silas was getting the money when we left."

"How did thee know we were here?"

"We followed you."

"No. It was too long before thee arrived."

"I will trade Axe for Mary Lynn's guaranteed safety."

"Axe, he cannot sing for shit."

"He sung for us."

Kaboom, kaboom, echoed up the tower. Double discharge of a shotgun.

Orlo smiled widely. "Thee will not live to bury thy tall friend. I been waiting."

His smile grew.

"Wrong, Orlo." I glanced quickly at the ladder running through the trap door. Orlo didn't take the bait. He smiled wider until the lower part of his face looked like it was all teeth. Blood dripped from his jaw.

But he was anticipating too much.

I snapped my fingers as if to say, "Damn, he didn't fall for that old one," and he liked my theatrics but my hand ended up close to the photo-sensor and I closed my eyes and the damn thing worked like it was advertised and the light sprang on and

I could see it through my eyelids and I hoped it had blinded Orlo but I didn't wait to see, just slapped the machete aside and lunged with my icepick; but because I was shorter and had my eyes closed, I missed his throat but the icepick caught a fold of neck-skin and he twisted and the thing tore out of my hand and by now the lamp had clicked off, the Fresnel lens no longer flooding the chamber with light, and I could see better than he could but it didn't help my left arm as the machete lanced into it.

More damage to the Lone Star Beer logo on the shirt wrapped around that arm.

His vision wasn't hindered; the third magnitude light isn't blinding bright for the Fresnel lens does most of the work—but it had diverted his attention.

He was floundering around, the icepick in the side of his neck flopping around like a head with its chicken cut off. He slashed and swung with the machete but it only bounced off the glass and a support post.

He was trying to kill me and decapitate Mary Lynn at the same time.

"Shorts!" Tapes voice cut through the light chamber and the ladder rattled.

That distracted Orlo and I chopped at his arm trying to dislodge the machete. Tapes and I together could take him, unless Tapes was too injured, which hopefully he wasn't because he'd made it this far.

A sudden thought hit me. "Tapes, don't shoot, you might hit us." Whether or not Tapes had the shotgun, I knew not, but it was worth saying.

I slashed at the machete wielding arm again and Orlo dropped the machete unwillingly.

He faked to my right and scooted around the lamp post counterclockwise and before I could get over there and stop him, he'd dropped to his hands and knees and dived through the access panel out onto the balcony. Then he went over the rail and disappeared from sight.

The last sight I had of him was his eyes staring through the heavy glass at me, fixing me with hatred and fear, the icepick dangling from his neck like an obscene earring.

23: WEDNESDAY, 8:45 A.M.

Tapes cut Mary Lynn loose and she fell into my arms.

"I have never seen such evil." Those were her words, but she was not hysterical and she was in control and she did not hiccup.

"He cared more for Deacon than for Pigtail or Axe," I said, smoothing errant hair away from her cheek so I could check her wound.

"I'm okay," she said, stepping back.

"You can say that again." I traced under the wound. "Not much blood. If you have a scar, it'll be a light one."

Her hand went to her cheek.

"It'll add unique character to your already major attractiveness," I said.

"He have a way with words, or what?" said Tapes as he put his Buck knife away. He looked out the window. "There he goes."

Turning, I saw the van's brake lights briefly and then it accelerated through the parking lot, spraying water as it went.

"Let me see your wound," I said.

His hand went to his upper leg. "It's okay." His handkerchief was tied to the wound with his Scovill sewing tape, the one he always carries in his pocket, the sixty inch reinforced fiberglass tape made in England.

"Do we have to worry about Pigtail?" I asked, turning Tapes around to check the rest of him.

"No. And lemme alone."

"I got to check you, Tapes. You fell a long way down."

"Wasn't much. Water cushioned the fall."

Other than being soaked and covered with sand and muck, he appeared well.

"I guess it ain't as far for you to drop as for the rest of us," I said. Still, it was fifteen or twenty feet.

"Stop mothering me. You know we got to get going."

"We do." I peeked under the handkerchief. "Slug go all the way through?"

"It did."

"Looks clean."

"I'll live. Let's go." He picked up the empty .38. I think we had some extra cartridges in the Trukbox.

I hurried down the ladder and turned to help Mary Lynn.

It wasn't necessary, of course, but her body felt good in my hands.

Tapes swung from the light chamber and his feet brushed the floor.

I went ahead.

Below at the base of the stairway, I stopped.

Pigtail was lying against one wall. From what I could tell, both his forearms were broken, as well as his jaw. He was just regaining consciousness.

It wasn't hard to choreograph. "You suckered him to shooting at you through the door and slammed it on him?"

"Worked fine, Shortcut. Think I screwed up a good gun, though, and my hearing ain't a hundred percent yet."

"We have no time for him," I said.

"He won't go anywhere."

I took Mary Lynn's hand. "Let's go."

"Why are we in a hurry?" asked Mary Lynn.

"Orlo. He knows Silas has the five hundred thousand. He knows I made Silas get the money ready to exchange for you."

She touched her cheek again. The scar, while a bit bloody and a welt, would make her look quite fetching. "Orlo will kill Silas."

I nodded. "That's why we've got to hurry. Orlo has nothing to lose. He knows he's going to be nailed for the murder, never mind his protestations."

"Another thing," Tapes added. "Orlo could be blaming Silas for getting him trapped into this whole mess."

I nodded again. "You reckon Trooper can take Orlo?"

Tapes shrugged. "Both are injured, both are armed. But you can bet that Orlo won't advertise his coming."

Ambush and surprise.

Silas would probably be with Pinky and I liked Pinky. It wouldn't bother Orlo to take either or both out.

I stepped around Pigtail. "We're wasting time."

As we waded through the parking lot, I noticed that the rain squall had passed by and the wind had died down significantly.

"Something else, Tapes."

"The boat?"

"Yep."

"What are you talking about?" Mary Lynn asked. Her hand felt good in mine.

"That's why Axe wasn't with Orlo and Pigtail. What's Pigtail's name anyway?"

Nobody answered.

I went on as we paralleled the fence around the tank farm. "Orlo sent Axe to quote take care of Silas end quote or something similar—to keep Silas from escaping with the money. Axe misread Orlo's instructions and booby-trapped *HBG'S GATOR GAL*. Orlo was there, me and Tapes followed him as he watched Silas prepare the boat. Orlo needs to escape right damn now and the boat is his best bet, the bridge being out and all. Suppose while trying to get Smith's half million cash that Orlo takes one or more hostages? They go onto the boat, he hits the starter switch and instant Fourth of July."

"Oh." She paused. "Oh! Angie. Sandra Dee and her baby!"

"It'd be his tough luck if he took the old bat," I said flippantly.

"Billy!"

"She's too ornery to die. I didn't mean it anyway."

"Sure you did," said Tapes.

"Stay out of this."

When we reached the truck, I untied the rope from the rear fender and tossed it into the bed with Axe. While Tapes and Mary Lynn got in, I slammed the tailgate.

"What's going on?" Axe asked.

"Orlo's running out on you."

"No, *sir.*"

"He is. The only way you're going to get out of this," I said pointing my right pointy finger at him because my left was on the end of my damaged left arm and not working too well, "is to be prepared to formally testify that Orlo wasn't with you when the governor was killed."

He didn't answer.

"Sit up, or your broken arm will trouble you during the trip." I pulled him to a better sitting position against the Trukbox.

I climbed in and started the GT.

Mary Lynn was sitting over the hump. "Let me see your arm."

The Lone Star shirt was soaked in blood and had helped in my fight with Orlo. However, the shirt was in bad shape. "No time." It was difficult to believe that it had lasted through the climb up the outside of the lighthouse. On the other hand, could you expect less of a Texas product? I wished I had a Lone Star beer right then.

I swung the GT in a circle and headed out, blasting a wave behind us. One of the few things I do better than Tapes is drive.

Tapes had found a couple of .38 rounds in the glove compartment and was loading them into the cylinder.

"When this gets over, I'm going to get me a case of beer and sit on the beach and watch sunsets for a week." I pointed to our immediate left.

"Sunrises," Tapes said automatically.

"You're on the wrong coast for that," I replied smugly.

"There's Charlotte Harbor and Charlotte Sound over which the sun can rise," Tapes pointed out.

I downshifted to second, and ran two left wheels over a sand dune to avoid a deep looking pool on the road.

Mary Lynn grabbed my leg to keep from sliding into Tapes' bad leg.

"Not enough water for effect," I said. "The sun would still rise over the mainland, so the view and the emotional effect would be ephemeral."

Tapes groaned his "Why me, Lord?" groan. But he gamefully continued the traditional repartee. "Sunrises get you going in the morning, they foreshadow the rest of the day."

"Sunsets remain and linger. Sunrise, bang it's over and it gets brighter which burns out the after-image. Sunsets are artistic and worthy of long-term contemplation," I responded.

"So's your brain," he said. "They ought to pickle it like Einstein's."

Mary Lynn was turning her head back and forth, following the conversation.

"Sunrises," I continued, "come early in the morning."

"That's a fact, fortunately," he said. "Sunrises, in themselves, reflect the work ethic, portend an honest day's labor."

"For you plebians who need such. Sunsets are esoteric, literary almost—"

"I thought you didn't like 'literary,'" he accused.

"Oh, yeah, I forgot." I pumped the brakes, double-clutched and shifted down to first, ran through a hibiscus hedge and onto the bike path. I followed the bike path until I could safely get back to Gulf Boulevard.

The truck tossed and banged. It was going to need a bunch of body repairs.

"I'll sit with you and drink a beer with you and watch the sun set," Mary Lynn said. She patted my right leg.

"I'd like that."

Occasionally, we could hear Axe in the back. He was singing "How Great Thou Art," and Bev Shea didn't have to worry about losing his job.

Tapes leaned forward and stared at me. "I think Shortcut would like that, too." He was bestowing his blessing, before now withheld.

I didn't know what to say, so I said it anyway. "Alexander thought something Euripides said so significant that he quoted the Greek. 'I wonder not that you have spoke so well/'Tis easy on good subjects to excel.'"

Out of the corner of my eye I saw Mary Lynn color a bit.

Tapes took out a new tin of Copenhagen from the glove compartment, ran his thumbnail along the seam, and popped the lid off. He sniffed at the tobacco and I hit a pothole and dumped Copenhagen all over his lap. "Who the hell is Euripides?" he asked.

"The Greek tragedian," I said. "Just prior to 400 BC."

"Is this a Robert Altman movie and you're both funning me?" asked Mary Lynn.

I whipped east on 5th and blasted past the José Gaspar Inn and headed for the marina.

We were silent as we neared the end of our journey.

I drove down the gravel path to the boathouse. Our way was barred by two golf carts and Orlo's faded blue van.

"Uh, oh," Tapes said, hefting the revolver.

We jumped out and ran around the vehicles, along the path, and came to a screeching halt near the side of the boathouse.

John Ionata and Vern Bernstein were standing together about thirty yards from the building.

Vern was holding Trooper's weapon. The big blue .357 seemed to diminish the political aide.

At the door of the boathouse fought four men, a tableau I will never, ever forget.

Trooper had apparently surprised Orlo and ripped the hunting rifle from his hands not a second before we got there.

"Shoot him," Ionata told Vern.

"I can't," Vern said.

"What's going on?" I asked.

Pinky and Silas were alongside Trooper fighting Orlo, too. I thought Trooper could vanquish Orlo in his injured condition, which would help Trooper because Orlo had been the one to take the mighty Trooper out of action.

Mary Lynn and Tapes stopped beside us.

Ionata spoke quickly. "Trooper and Vern and I came here to use a marine band radio on one of the boats to summon help." He pointed to a cabin cruiser with a caved in side against the dock. "Then Silas and Pinky came."

"Smith had the money," Vern said. "He was making his break and Pinky was trying to dissuade him."

"Then came Orlo," Ionata finished. "And Trooper screamed and jumped him."

With a surge of strength, Orlo pushed Trooper aside and, quicker than you could see it, whipped an icepick from his belt and thrust it into Trooper. Trooper fell back, blood squirting from his chest. Henry B. would have been proud of his longtime friend.

Trooper hit the ground holding my icepick with his hand.

Orlo looked around for a second, and then grabbed Silas by the throat. Orlo's own neck was bleeding.

"Shoot, shoot," Ionata shouted at Vern.

"Too far," Vern said. "Besides, I don't know how."

"Gimme." I snatched the gun from him.

Tapes had his revolver up and was aiming, but Silas was in the way.

Just as Orlo turned enough for Tapes and me to get shots off, Pinky jumped on Orlo's back, the brave little stupid son of a bitch.

"Pinky!" I shouted.

"Pinky's drunk," said Vern with considerable awe.

"Shoot! Shoot! Shoot!" Ionata's shouting was becoming a chorus.

I started moving forward. It was going to be Orlo or me.

No, it wasn't.

Orlo flung Silas aside, reached up and picked Pinky off his back and shoulders like a ragdoll and tossed him aside.

I fired an instant before Tapes, but neither shot struck home because Orlo had bent to retrieve his rifle from the ground.

Tapes and I were running forward now, never an accurate

platform from which to shoot.

We tried anyway and missed, but it kept Orlo from grabbing Pinky and dragging the political aide with him. Orlo must've wanted a hostage, but realized it wouldn't work. Instead, he dived through the door into the boathouse.

I ran for the door, flopping in the brisk breeze.

"Shotcut!" Tapes grabbed me from behind. "He'll pick off anybody goes through that door."

"Jesus, Tapes. The fuel—"

I grabbed Trooper under his arms and Tapes took Silas and Pinky by the collars and we dragged them back toward the others. Trooper's blood ran down my good right hand.

"Take cover," I shouted. "Down!"

"My money, my money," cried Silas.

"Where is it?" Tapes asked.

"I just stowed it on board the *Gator Gal*. Oh, please. Don't let him get away with my money."

"He isn't going anywhere with it," Tapes said. He let go of Smith's arm. The manager stumbled after us.

"Yes he is," I said. "He's going to hell. He should say his prayers." *When the pirate prays, there is great danger.* And there was great danger.

"What's going on," Ionata asked.

"What's the hold up?" I said as we made it around the corner of an adjacent boatshed and propped Trooper against the building.

"Moorings I reckon," Tapes said. He let go of Pinky. "It's taking him a minute to untie the boat."

I stepped back around the corner and cupped my hands. "Orlo! Don't start the boat! Axe rigged it to explode."

I don't know whether he heard me or not, or believed me or not, but I thought I heard a hollow laugh. And to this day, I do not yet know why I tried to warn him.

Whereupon the side walls of the boathouse seemed to suck in and then rush out. The top of the building spewed chunks of sheet metal and erupted in a blinding fireball.

Then the noise hit me and less than a blink later as I was diving back, the force of the explosion washed over me.

I hit gravel and scraped my damn left arm again. My hearing died for a moment and it was deathly quiet.

The explosion seemed to have rolled back the wind and put us in a silent capsule. The boathouse we were behind shuddered and chattered.

I was first on my feet and pulled Mary Lynn up with me. We walked around the corner and saw where the governor's boathouse had been.

Bay water was sloshing against the seawall. Debris and pieces of green bills floated everywhere; it had just finished raining chunks of wood, plastic, money and fiberglass. *GATOR GAL*'s engine was a misshapen mass of metal embedded in the dock.

A flotation seat cushion slid off the roof beside me.

There was no sign of Orlo.

Mary Lynn's hand found my good right one.

I felt her sag against me. "Is he gone?"

"Finally. He went to join José Gaspar." I will always wonder if Orlo knew or suspected *HBG'S GATOR GAL* was rigged to blow and just took that way to suicide.

The ringing in my ears was receding.

Silas was whimpering. "My money, my money."

Stumbling around, Pinky was trying to soothe him.

Trooper was eying the two of them, the two homosexuals whom he'd just saved. I could see the realization come over his face, enough to make him ignore the blood flowing from his chest. He pulled the icepick out and tossed it aside with disdain. He looked at me with another realization, one that I had just saved his life. He had more than enough to keep him thinking for months to come.

I disengaged my hand from Mary Lynn's and walked toward the charred earth and dock where the boathouse had been.

They all sort of followed.

I stepped over twisted corrugated metal and I thought of Orlo. I bent and picked up a handful of sand and dribbled it into the water where the boathouse had been. Orlo had rapidly dissipated.

"I echo Callisthenes the sophist. 'Death seized at last on great Patroclus too/Though he in virtue far exceeded you.'"

24: WEDNESDAY, 9:20 A.M.

"Billy?" Mary Lynn stepped up beside me. "We've got to get Tapes and Trooper inside and work on their wounds."

"All right." I was reluctant to leave. It was over.

Almost.

We loaded the wounded and the hurt into my truck and I drove back to the inn. I parked right at the entrance to the lounge and saloon.

We got Tapes and Trooper onto couches. Axe sat quietly at a table, his broken arm resting on the green felt. I sent Pinky and Silas for medical supplies.

While they were gone, I served as bartender.

I knocked back a shot of Wild Turkey, and took Tapes a gin and tonic in a thirty-two-ounce mug. He smiled his appreciation.

I handed Trooper a Budweiser but he shook his head. "Liquor?" I asked.

"Nothing." He looked at me. "You bailed me out of a tough one there."

"The least I could do for Henry B.'s friend," I said. "I liked him."

Trooper nodded. "You would've gotten along well with him."

"I doubt that," I said. "But I liked him anyway."

"Thanks, Birthday, irregardless of why you did it."

I looked Trooper in the eye. "Maybe I did it because you saved Pinky and Silas."

He looked disgusted. "If anybody finds out I saved two faggy asses, I'll never live it down." He pried the cloth off his wound and looked at it. It was ugly and puckered and crusty with blood on one side and blood seeped slowly from the middle. "Old Pinky, he was doing his goddamndest to keep Smith from running off. Pinky, he was drunk as a dog with a saucer of beer. Smith took the bag of money and tossed it onto the boat and here came Pinky, weaving and stumbling and crying. Pinky was dragging Smith outside when Orlo came and jumped 'em."

"Pinky came through when the chips were down," I said.

Trooper nodded. "You were right about the money, too. It was in the damn cooler, right under some slabs and packages of meat." He shivered. "Jesus, it was next to Henry B.'s body. The goddamn ghoul."

I no longer disliked Trooper a lot. I don't think I could stomach him for long, though. And it settled Silas Smith's fate. I was going to make it my decision.

Pinky and Silas had come back and were listening to us.

Pinky wobbled and glared at Silas and Silas looked ashamed. He knew how much his occasional lover revered the environment and especially the dwindling endangered creatures therein. Now he'd just heard a blanket condemnation of Silas and his activities. But Pinky was strong, for he'd dealt with those same concerns since the episode in Trooper's room where Silas confessed. And Pinky had stood by Silas since then and had tried to do whatever stupid thing he was trying to do at the boathouse. Some sort of misguided sense of righteousness.

Pinky moved over and pushed me aside. "I'll fix Trooper's wound."

"Shit," said Trooper.

"Don't worry, Trooper," said Pinky with an accentuated lisp, "you won't get AIDS from me."

"Shit," said Trooper again.

Mary Lynn and Angie Maple had a first aid kit and were working on Tapes' leg. They'd cut off the blood-soaked leg of his jeans and the wound looked like it would heal easily. The bullet had gone through his leg without hitting any bones or major arteries. And he'd jumped off a lighthouse right after that. Like I say, Tapes is tough as an old cowhide.

But he was holding the two halves of his sewing tape measure he'd used to bind the wound. He looked sourly at the red-stained and sliced up tape.

"What's his problem?" Angie Maple asked.

Vern and Silas were wrapping Axe's broken arm.

Ionata came to help with Trooper.

Pinky looked at Silas. "I was wrong. I should have let you go."

Silas shrugged. "But you didn't. You did what you thought was right, Pink. In doing so, you kept me from killing myself in the explosion."

"It must be God's will," Pinky said. "Mark 13:13. 'He that shall endure unto the end, the same shall be saved.'"

Axe riveted his eyes on Pinky.

I took a deep breath and jumped into the deep end. "John?"

The lieutenant governor looked up at me.

"Pigtail is lying around the old lighthouse waiting for help. He and Axe over there will testify that Orlo was alone at the time of Henry B.'s death. Right Axe?"

"Yessir," Axe nodded, and hummed "Amen" a couple of times.

Pinky eyed Axe.

"Orlo," I continued, "must have been tossing the governor's suite to see what he could steal. He heard a noise and it was Gonzáles at the door. Orlo was big, he shoved Gonzáles away and against the wall. Gonzáles must have started to shout for help or something and Orlo grabbed whatever was at hand: the tennis racquet right there on the wall. Or, more likely, the governor was using the racquet as a weapon and Orlo wrestled it away from him. One slash and Gonzáles falls backward, smashes the railing, and tumbles out and down three floors."

Ionata was sponging blood. "That would explain Orlo's violent reaction when Trooper asked them to identify themselves."

Trooper was stretching his neck to watch them work on his wound. "Where'd he get that fuckin' icepick?"

Mary Lynn and Tapes looked over at me but none of us answered.

Then I said, "It's better than being shot, don't you think?"

"Well—"

I continued. "You're an attorney, John. You can see Orlo likely did it. That's why he had no compunction about rap—, attacking Mary Lynn. Add in kidnapping, false imprisonment, attempted murder of me and Tapes, violating endangered species and spitting on the sidewalk. He knew he would be accused and convicted of killing the governor. Don't forget he beat up Silas pretty badly, too. And after that, he assigned Axe to 'take care of Smith' or something like that. Right Axe?"

"Yessir."

"Did he say why he wanted you to take care of the manager?"

"Nossir."

"See?" I said, hoping I wasn't laying it on too thick.

"At least the bastard's dead," said Trooper. "Saves us a trial and a million goddamn appeals and some goddamn supreme court asshole judge in Tallahassee or appeal's court judge in the Eleventh up in Atlanta from overturning it on a technicality and him getting off with time served," Trooper was convinced Orlo killed the governor.

Tapes was watching me over the heads of Angie Maple and Mary Lynn Messenger. He knew I was up to something.

Angie's eyes were flashing hostility at me. I shot her a knowing grin. I'd solved the murder, sort of, and she hadn't. On top of that, Orlo was one of the few people who weren't politically motivated and would probably ruin her revenge on Gonzáles and his party. To add insult to injury, Ionata was the heir and he hated Henry B., so the political fallout wouldn't touch him—it might even help John to sweep all HBG's people out of office.

Mary Lynn indicated my Rottweiler- and machete-lacerated arm. "Sit down, you're next."

"I'll be all right," I said evasively.

Tapes was watching me closely.

Mary Lynn's hand went to the bullet wound in her cheek, and then she dropped her hand and shrugged. She was considering what'd I'd just said. "I understand."

I looked at her for a short moment. Perhaps she had in fact figured it out and did understand.

"Silas," I said, trying to keep my voice calm, "if you're finished with Axe, maybe you can come with me for a minute? I think we need to check some storm damage to the hotel."

Silas shrugged and stepped toward the door.

It even sounded lame to me and I'd said it. Out of the corner of my eye, I saw Mary Lynn and Tapes watch me leave and I couldn't look at them.

Pinky and Axe were together now, softly singing "We shall gather at the river" not very well in tune. Pinky was drinking from a bottle of four star brandy. I was reminded of something Melville said in *Moby Dick*, that it was better to sleep with a sober cannibal than a drunken Christian.

I led Silas to the kitchen.

The electricity had been restored and I could see the darkened and curled paint from the heat of the generator shed fire. The fire which had first started me thinking in the right direction.

No one was in the kitchen, most people being occupied with tending to the wounded.

Inside the kitchen, I turned to Silas. "I want them."

"What is that?" His eyes were mild and he stroked his scarred neck.

"You know exactly what," I said. "You are the most intelligent and cleverest person in the hotel right goddamn now and you know what I want."

His eyes lighted up a bit. "You've an interesting way of putting things, Birthday."

"You've an interesting way of playing dumb," I accused.

"My act is not as practiced as yours," he said. "It takes one to know one. I am not fooled by that countrified veneer—"

I stepped closer to him and held out my fingers. "Look, Silas, I'm dead tired and I don't want to screw around with you. Here's the deal. You give it to me and I'll let you go."

"Clear and free."

"Done."

"Why?" He was genuinely curious.

My fingers popped out of my fist for each point I made. "One. I like Pinky and he likes you. He wears a bow tie even now that George Will has mostly quit doing that thing. Two. You just lost five hundred thousand dollars. That's penalty enough for a man who cherishes money and what it can do. Three. You're one of the ugliest people I've ever seen." I was being a bit brutal, but I think he saw through it. "You must have had a terrible childhood. And Pinky likes you anyway, the little Christian twerp. Four. You put up with Trooper's homophobia. Five. You've been through enough. Finally, six. I appreciate your penchant for documentation."

"Aye, there's the rub." He was taller and more in control.

"It is," I said. "You documented Orlo's appearances. You obviously well documented the Unique Dinner Club and the skimming you did at the hotel. And what I want."

His Adam's apple bounced a bit. "No recriminations? I have your assurance?"

"Look, Silas. I don't have much assurance to give you—only a bit of time. They know you're with me and trust me to keep an eye on you. You're a wanted criminal and have performed felonies here in Florida. They want you bad."

"Not as bad as the murderer."

Here it was.

I spoke very carefully. "They have Orlo as the killer."

He studied me for a long minute. He had figured it out just as I had; maybe he'd talked to Orlo and accused him of murder and Orlo had beat him up in response. Maybe there was more to the episode when Silas told Orlo in the kitchen that he would no longer be able to buy for the Unique Dinner Club.

"A trade," he said, "plain and simple."

"It is." I dropped my hand and stood back. "Let me point out that there is a great sense of urgency you ought to be concerned about. Time is dying for you. Trooper called in help and the bay is no longer the center of a storm; the law will be here shortly. And the longer lead time you've got, the farther away you can be."

"There *are* other boats at the marina," he said speculatively.

"In fact, you could drive north and steal a boat and head for Placida. It wouldn't take you as long to disappear. The bridge has got to be still out of commission."

"Either or, I'll decide." His voice was a tough as the Rockies. "I've memorized the charts to get me to the Bahamas." He nodded decisively. "I can add two and two. Your list of six reasons you want me to escape should be seven."

I shrugged. It was the most important and deciding factor of them all. "I think, Silas, without number seven, I'd likely do this same thing anyway. Like I said, I think well of Pinky."

"Follow me."

Freezer. Henry B. Gonzáles lying there, not in state. I stopped and looked at him for a minute, pulling back the blanket. Old Henry B. had not as yet rapidly dissipated, though his legacy was fast doing that very thing. The mark of the tennis racquet was the same. Henry B. appeared as if he didn't give a damn what was happening now, even though it was all his fault.

"We've been in and out too frequently," Silas said.

"He won't thaw, the electricity is back on."

In the back of the walk-in, Silas pushed some freezer boxes of chicken aside and took out a similar carton. He pulled the lid off and dropped it. "Let's go." An ordinary brown briefcase.

We went back into the kitchen and he put the briefcase on a counter.

He snapped the latches and opened it. He handed me a sheet of JG Inn stationery. It was a list of names, license numbers, and vehicle descriptions. Documentation of Orlo's visits. It would help convince the state's attorney of Orlo's guilt.

"Nice try," I said. "Now give me what I really want."

He sighed, shrugged, and said, "There's no fooling you. He spun the briefcase around. Right on top was a manila file folder. He handed it to me. "Satisfied?"

I glanced at the contents. Obviously, there were no other copies, but I checked anyway. Under skivvies and socks, was a stack of money. And a wallet containing a totally different set of identification with his picture on the driver's license. "I'm satisfied." I closed the lid on Silas Smith's emergency getaway kit.

"Ten grand," he said.

"Smart man. Your time's running on empty, Silas."

He hefted the briefcase. "I don't know whether to thank you or not."

"Don't bother."

"I won't. Even if they catch me, you are betting that since I no longer possess that evidence, I won't talk."

"I am."

"They won't catch me." He patted the case.

"I hope for your sake they don't,"

He pawed his neck one last time and walked to the kitchen exit. He turned. "Sorry about the generator, I really am."

"Sure."

It was the ostensible attempted arson which had tipped me to the manager's depth and cleverness.

He went through the doors with his shoulders more square than I'd seen them.

I opened the folder again and read.

I put the list of Orlo's visits in it and I closed the folder.

Wearily, folder in hand, I went out of the kitchen down the corridor past the elevator and into the hotel proper to confront the murderer.

25: WEDNESDAY, 10:40 A.M.

I turned left at the staircase where the wings all joined and where this had all begun.

I walked down the corridor, stopped, and knocked softly.

"Yes?" she said.

"It's Shortcut."

"Come in."

Sandra Dee Kowalski was scrubbed, in a clean shift, and sitting in a lounge chair breast-feeding her baby. She appeared tired. Bearing a kid for nine months and then giving birth will do that to you.

Her face lighted up. "I'm so glad to see you."

I closed the door behind me. "You're looking much better, Sandy."

She dimpled. "I like the way you say that. And thank you. Thank you, too, for all you've done."

"You're welcome." My voice felt as flat as Kansas.

She spotted my bloody arm and concern leapt onto her face. "You're hurt!"

"I've been through a lot."

"Here, I can move about. Let me bathe it and I think there's still a first aid kit in the bathroom and—"

"Not now, okay?"

"What's wrong, Billy? Tell me what's been going on, will you? I feel so, so left out. Why are you hurt?" She frowned at the blood again.

I remained standing, looking down at her. Something fleeting skittered through her eyes. Maybe she knew.

"Orlo is dead," I said. "Orlo will be charged with the murder of the governor."

She looked down at her baby and said nothing. She must have been going through hell. Having a baby is bad enough, but especially with a stranger helping and no loved one present to support you. And, most specifically, carrying guilt.

She looked up at me with a firm jaw and steady eyes. "I'm going to name her Billye Lynn."

"All my OB patients fall in love with me." I didn't feel the humor I should have, but it was coming back.

"You were very, very good," she said. "Your wit saved me."

"Your own determination and guts saved you," I said savagely. "You are a lot tougher woman than you'd have people believe."

"I do what I have to."

I opened the folder. Silas Smith's handwriting was meticulous. "Date, time, name, location. Lots of assignations on *HBG'S GATOR GAL*, here at the hotel, on other boats. Now the sailboat, that's the first one, right?" I pointed to the hotel sailboat painting. "That's why you didn't want to use the picture as a focal point. You focused on the cross-patterned tapestry instead."

Her eyes were harder. "What paper is that you're referring to? Did our governor keep records? I thought he merely made notches in his bedposts."

Billye Lynn Kowalski had fallen asleep and Sandra Dee Kowalski pulled the shoulder of her shift up and covered her swollen breast.

I shook my head. "Silas Smith did."

"That son of a bitch."

"He's long gone." I leaned back against the dresser. "Your name appears frequently from nine months ago to present, but mostly in clusters from the nine month point to the six month ago point."

"It would," she said calmly. "However, my name isn't the

only one on that list, of that I am certain."

"It isn't. Mary Lynn is on it several times."

Sandy looked surprised. "Mary Lynn Messenger? She's older than I am. She's mature enough she won't fall for a man because he's attractive. I don't understand." She paused and glanced down at the kid. "Of course, Mary Lynn is so very attractive herself. She'd be a perfect target for Henry."

I explained about the hundred dollar bills for needy families.

"Does his charity supposed to make me feel better? I can tell you what he *did not* do for his own child-to-be." Some of the bitterness was coming out. And I didn't want to hear about Gonzáles ignoring his responsibility.

"You could've gotten an abortion," I said.

"Tell *your* mother that." Her eyes were flint.

Sandra Dee had not yet admitted she killed the governor. Did I want to hear her say the words?

"Nobody's asked you to account for your presence when Gonzáles was killed," I said waving the folder slightly. "I recall you coming from the kitchen wing. Why would you be there? What reason?"

She just watched me.

"There's an elevator. A pregnant woman would take an elevator from the third floor to the first floor." I recalled Pinky's wailing covering the noise of a motor—the elevator motor.

"If it was me, I sure would."

I nodded. "The governor had more or less dripped off in my truck. The water I found in a small puddle wasn't rain from Henry B.'s sweatshirt. It was amniotic fluid." I remembered sticking my finger in it and tasting it as Angie Maple watched me.

The baby was wrapped in a pillow case, an item of which the hotel had plenty.

Sandy rose and went to the bed. She carefully laid the baby on a thick towel. "I've read a thousand pages of Doctor Spock in the last month and still know nothing." She turned to face me. "I was playing word games earlier." She stepped toward me. "I will admit nothing. Why are you here?"

"I wanted to know why."

"Does anybody else know?"

The question I'd feared. I looked her right in the eye and lied. "No." Silas would never tell if he were caught. "It is slightly possible that Mary Lynn might suspect something." Tapes had probably guessed.

"Why?" Sandy's hands were on her hips.

I had to explain about the late Orlo kidnapping Mary Lynn and the lighthouse episode where he'd vehemently denied he'd had anything to do with the demise of the governor. "Orlo had nothing to lose," I finished. "He was going to kill us and knew he'd be nailed for the murder as things stood."

She stepped closer. "It appears I've more to thank you for than I thought." My height, her green eyes were staring straight into my eyes. She moved against me. Her fat breasts rested against my chest. "Is that what you want? Payment?"

She saw the hurt in my eyes. "After I delivered your baby, you can ask that?"

"I'm sorry." Her breath was Aqua Fresh fresh—I'd been in her bathroom. She looked down then back into my eyes. "It's what I've come to expect from men."

I could understand that. Gonzáles had shunned her like a bad relative. "I forgive you. Even though you've caused untold pain."

"Who'll miss Orlo?"

I ducked my head. "Point well taken. How about Henry B.?"

"There will be many empty beds for a while," she said, still pressed up against me. Weary lines ran from her eyes. "You've got a thing for Mary Lynn, haven't you?"

I nodded. "Is it that apparent?"

"You were the last one in the José Gaspar Inn to know it, I reckon."

I thought fleetingly about one Rebecca Ann MacKenzie in Tallahassee.

"Would you tell me what happened?" I asked. I really wanted to know. I wanted to know if all my actions were justified. I had a lot to reconcile, especially misleading justice and falsely accusing someone else—even if it was Orlo—of the murder. I was stage-managing a cover-up.

"No, I will not," she told me and stepped back away from me. "Like Henry B., I attended the University of Florida. I've read most of the Amendments to the Constitution." She was saying she didn't want to confess, especially in case I was wired or someone was somehow listening.

"It's important to me," I said. "Perhaps from your special perspective you can surmise what someone would have gone through, how it happened."

She moved back against me, eyes aflame, nodding. "I can, that. You know me as well as anyone does; hell, you know me from the inside out. I trust you." Her eyes questioned me and I nodded.

"The tennis racquet," I told her, "had one of those terrycloth sleeves to improve the grip. No prints. With Orlo dead and now the prime suspect, there is more than sufficient doubt and you'd never be indicted."

"Half the women and men on the island have used those racquets. Me included."

"Nine-month-pregnant women don't play tennis."

Her hands went to my shoulders and I saw a ghost in her green eyes.

"Go ahead," I said softly.

"A young woman, pregnant and having labor pains. Maybe false labor, I wouldn't know." She breathed in deeply. "One who'd attended a divorce party for her friend. Ugh. One who was about as far down as possible. The end of her rope, rock bottom, more clichés. Drags herself up to the third floor—by the elevator—to confront the father for the last time."

Just as I'd figured.

"It was early. I—the woman—knocked repeatedly. The father never answered, ignoring her she thinks in her distressed state. She hates to be ignored; she's endured it so long. Or perhaps he's in there with another woman. Her anger and resentment build."

I moved my arms around hers until I was holding her and her arms folded up on my shoulders. I massaged her neck.

"That feels good."

"Relax, huh?" I said as she laid her head on my shoulder.

"So she turns and starts walking away when the father bounds up the stairs. There follows a short and acrimonious exchange. The father shoves her aside and she hits the wall—it wasn't intended, she doesn't think, as physical abuse, just an angry response from him...at least she doesn't think so later when she thinks about it." We were nose to nose, sensuous to say the least.

"Take it easy," I said. My eyes were locked onto hers.

"That's what he said. He said he wasn't going to be black-mailed into marriage. I said, 'I don't want to marry you, you son of a bitch.' He said, 'You're blackmailing me for money?' and moved toward me menacingly. 'No,' I said and he kept coming and the racquet was right there by my hand and before I could realize what I was doing I banged him with it, it was just going to be the gut at the center but he deflected it and it hit him wrong, and he staggered backwards, this incredible look on his face and I looked at the racquet and threw it away from me and it bounced off his arm and he flailed and went through the railing and oh, God." She began sobbing and the shoulder of my FSU sweatshirt was getting wet all over again.

I didn't know what to say, an annoying recurrence, so again I said nothing. I let her weep. It'd probably been bottled up within her and she needed the release.

After a while, I said, "Look, Sandy, you did nothing wrong. It was an accident. Even if it does come out, nobody will blame you."

She lifted her tear strained face next to mine. "Oh? Then why didn't I say something immediately, like it was an accident?"

There was that. "You were emotionally unsettled because of what happened and the onset of labor. You couldn't stand the public scrutiny of your life and illegitimate child." Hell, I ought to be a defense attorney. But I'd rather have a sister in a whore-house than be an attorney.

"I was." She blinked to clear her eyes.

"Look at it a different way," I said. "Orlo's gone. Pinky's happy because the destruction of endangered species has halted, or slowed. Ionata's happy, he'll be governor, something he's coveted."

"And Henry?"

I shrugged. "He can't be too happy with the way things turned out. But he was the one who got all of us into this mess to begin with. You run with the big dogs, you got to expect to get some of them big fleas."

She digested that for a minute. "Trooper?"

"Trooper's off the sauce. He's a grown boy. He lost a friend."

"Silas is on the run?"

"Silas will land on his feet anywhere he goes. Don't forget he is sort of a bank robber and quite a white collar criminal." I told her about the money and the explosion. "So not everything that happened as a result is bad."

Sandy disentangled herself from me and went over and looked down at the kid. "Not everything."

"I agree." I missed the warmth of her nearness.

She turned back to me. "When you picked up Henry for the ride, where were you going?"

"A quick morning visit to the lighthouse, then back to the hotel for breakfast and checking out."

"If none of this had happened, you'd be on the road."

"Could be."

"Without Mary Lynn." Sandy seemed a bit smug.

I grinned at her. "Good things did happen." I didn't mention that the storm had nothing to do with the governor's death and that we'd have been stuck here anyway. And I damn sure would have made an attempt to get to know Mary Lynn—and it wouldn't have had to be under fire. But I didn't say any of it. "There is a tradeoff."

"What do you mean?"

"It's going to cost you a ton of money. As soon as you claim a share of Henry B.'s enormous estate as inheritance for Billye Lynn, you become an instant suspect."

She sighed. "I know. I've thought that through—money doesn't seem very important right now."

She was already putting it in perspective.

"You'll make it." I was betting she would.

Sandy sat down next to her infant daughter and caressed the child on the back. "Why?"

"Why what?"

"Why is it that you are going through so many machinations to help me? Again? You could just turn me in. You know all the facts."

I took Silas Smith's list out of the folder and began tearing the sheets into strips and the strips into tiny pieces. "Maybe I did it for Mary Lynn. You're her friend."

"It'd have to be more than that. We're both practically strangers to you."

"Nuh uh," I said with a leering grin.

She blushed. "Well, you know what I mean."

"Maybe it was your name, Sandra Dee, and a gesture to your mom who named you."

She thought about that for a minute. "That's truly nice of you to say."

"Maybe it was because of the way you handled yourself in childbirth."

"I don't believe that." She crossed her arms.

She'd shown concern for my bloody arm when I walked in the door, too. That was indicative of the kind of real person she was, even though she had to have known almost immediately why I was there. And maybe it was because of her sitting here in this room hour after hour waiting for the knock she knew had to come. Then when it came, she asked after my arm, filled with dread at what I was going to do, going to say.

"Maybe it was because of the hardship you endured, a pregnancy without a father, his denial, and all that entailed."

She tilted her head to the side. "You're rather empathetic, aren't you?"

I shrugged, embarrassed. "I don't want to be...."

"You're coming to it, aren't you, Billy?"

"I am, goddamnit. I'm doing it for me. For the oppressed everywhere. Sure. I'm doing it because of all those things I just said. I'm doing it because of the raw and naked intimacy you shared with me during the birth. I'm doing it because I bonded with you, Sandra Dee Kowalski, and your Billye Lynn Kowalski. I did it for those reasons and more. I did it because I knew all the goddamn time you couldn't have killed the man, yet he died. I did all those things so that no one would suspect you *because I knew Henry B. and that's what he would want me to do.*"

"Jesus Christ," she said. She was staring at me in awe. "You've more empathy than all of us put together."

"It doesn't matter." I stormed into the bathroom and dumped the tiny pieces of Silas Smith's list into the toilet and flushed them to hell.

When I came out of the bathroom she barred my way. She purposefully put her hand on my bloody Lone Star Beer shirt-bandage. "You make me look at things differently now." She shook her head. "I don't feel so guilty. You did that to me." Her voice was full of wonder.

"Yeah, sure."

"If you and Mary Lynn, you know? Don't click? You call me right away."

"Immediately. Promise."

"Cross your heart and hope to die?"

"I do," I said. "And stick a pin in my eye and call the FBI."

"I will hold you to it." She speared her left pointy finger into a gob of gooey blood atop the Lone Star logo and put it in her mouth and swallowed the lump.

"Jesus, Sandy." But I felt what she was doing.

"That shows you how serious I am, Billy Shortcut Birthday. I owe you my child and now my sanity."

My empathy told me she needed to be alone.

She lay down next to her baby and simply stared at the child. Which highlighted my other main reason: now she would not ever have to be looking over her shoulder, year after year. I think she was realizing that thing.

I let myself out the door and closed it softly behind me.

Mary Lynn Messenger was standing there. "I've been waiting." She took my right arm. "Let us go and fix your arm."

EPILOGUE: SUNDAY, SUNSET

"Spidey," I said.

"Phantom," Tapes said.

"Spidey," I repeated. "He's a real person. His wife gives him a hard time. He can't make a buck to save his life."

"The Phantom is dark and mysterious," Tapes said, sipping from his Budweiser. "He's got a jungle kingdom."

"Yeah," I shot back, "half in Asia, half in Africa, and half in South America."

The sun was setting and Tapes was sitting in a beach lounge chair on my left and Mary Lynn Messenger was sitting in a lounge chair on my right. The beer cooler was between me and Tapes and we were watching the sun go down over the Gulf of Mexico.

"If you think geography is important," Tapes said.

"I do." I sipped my own Bud. "Not only that, but each of those guys is running around in a full body sock. How do they undress? How do they pee?"

"I thought those clothes were leotards," Tapes said.

"And another thing. If their suits are so tight, how come their sex doesn't show? Are they castrated?"

"Billy!" scolded Mary Lynn but I saw her smile secretly. She was wearing a peach colored Brazilian bikini with a sliding-triangle top and high-cut bottoms. Dynamite. The fading scar on her cheek added an exotic character to her beauty.

"The wall-crawler is a reluctant hero," I went on.

Mary Lynn looked at me with a blue eye and a brown eye.

Men kept walking by and trying not, but failing, to stare at her. I tried not to be jealous. But as Plutarch once said, to deprecate envy is the mark of a disciplined character. Well, hell, I enjoyed being the one sitting next to her.

The top of the sun dipped below the Gulf and I saw the flash of green.

"I feel like singing 'Happy Trails,'" I said.

We drank beer and watched life go by.

"This is boring," Tapes said.

"I nonconcur," I said. "I need the peace and quiet." I grinned. "Plutarch said the mark of a man is to bear prosperity like a gentleman."

Mary Lynn twisted her brown right eye to look at me. "Is life around you always so crazy and interesting?"

"Not nearly," I said.

"Mostly," Tapes said.

"Life is like a cattle range," I said, "you just got to watch where you step."

"Gimme a break," said Tapes.

"You've cured me of my hiccups." Mary Lynn's smile was as big as her heart. But we all knew she'd overcome them herself.

A blonde haired woman in a wet, sheer white one-piece walked by for the third time. She couldn't be more obvious.

Tapes sighed, finished his beer, handed me the can, and rose. He caught up with her and they struck up a conversation. They continued walking down the beach, Tapes limping a bit and milking the bandage on his leg.

"Billy?" Mary Lynn's voice was serious.

"Yes?"

"I heard from Sandra Dee Kowalski today. She's in Portland and she's very happy."

"She deserves it."

"Does she?"

I nodded emphatically. "She really does."

"Will you tell me one day?"

I looked out to sea. "I suspect you've guessed most of it."

"I have."

"Maybe later I'll let you coax it out of me, bit by bit."

"Ummm." Her head tilted back and she leered at me.

"Me, too," I said. I thought, Rebecca Who?

"It's a date."

I remembered something. "Uh, a late date?"

"Okay."

"I got to work."

"The Unique Dinner Club?" she asked.

"Right."

I was now the new manager of the José Gaspar Inn. Tapes was the "superintendent." He was in charge of facilities and grounds including the golf course and marina. I was in charge of everything and everybody. The new governor, John Ionata, had recommended us. And why not? We had to stay around and answer questions from the state's attorney and make depositions and all.

"What are you going to do?"

One of the members of the Unique Supper Club had surreptitiously contacted me and I'd led that great sportsman to believe I was going to continue Smith's tradition.

"Laxative in the chocolate dessert. For the main course, Alpo, I think. Then I'll let 'em see, um, maybe a piece of toilet paper—no, make that a rat's tail I got yesterday, in the bottom of the serving bowl."

"It won't be good for business," she said.

"Business like that I don't need."

Tapes and I each had big, expansive suites on the third floor of the hotel.

Behind us stood the solid Old Port Boca Grande Lighthouse and I felt comfortable.

Mary Lynn leaned over me and took my left arm. "It's healing well." The movement was awkward because she had to lean across my body. Her hair smelled of gardenias.

"That's probably because nobody's tried to chop it off lately, nor have any crazed killer beasts attempted to rip it off." I smelled her hair again and her skin and her sweat and I thought I'd died and gone to Heaven.

She put my arm down and twisted her face to just an inch in front of mine. "You, dear Billy, are a dinosaur in the Ice Age." She brushed my lips with hers.

"Whatever it takes," I said.

In a little while it would be dark enough for the lighthouse beacon to kick on automatically.

AUTHOR'S NOTE

Gasparilla Island and Boca Grande are more attractive than words can describe. There is a Gasparilla Inn, an elegant and wonderful establishment. However, for obvious reasons, I had to design my own hotel, the José Gaspar Inn, and its accompanying facilities, grounds, golf course, and marina.

Gasparilla Island is part of two counties, which makes for awkward wording when addressing political and law enforcement boundaries; therefore, I arbitrarily treated it as one political entity, assigning and removing two sheriff's deputies.

From May through August, Boca Grande Pass is full of tarpon, more than in any location in the world. Schools on top of schools of tarpon roil the water of the pass.

ABOUT THE AUTHOR

JAMES B. JOHNSON has written seven novels: *Trekmaster*, *Habu*, *Mindhopper*, *A World Lost*, *Daystar and Shadow*, *Counterclockwise*, and *When the Pirate Prays*, all of which are being published by The Borgo Press. *Mindhopper* was optioned twice for a movie, and three of his books were translated into French and German. He has also penned numerous short stories and articles. Jim has sold advertising, worked for the Post Office for fifteen years, and spent eleven years in the Air Force. He lives in Sarasota, Florida, with his wife Beverly.

www.ingramcontent.com/pod-product-compliance
Lightning Source LLC
Chambersburg PA
CBHW020609260626
47157CB00003B/924